T4-APT-637

IT'S PERFECTLY TRUE

IT'S PERFECTLY TRUE

AND OTHER STORIES

by Hans Christian Andersen

Translated from the Danish
by Paul Leyssac

ILLUSTRATED BY RICHARD BENNETT

HARCOURT, BRACE & WORLD, INC.
NEW YORK

WITHDRAWN
CENTER SCHOOL LIBRARY

COPYRIGHT, 1938, BY
PAUL LEYSSAC

All rights reserved, including the right to reproduce this book or portions thereof in any form.

0.2.67

PRINTED IN THE UNITED STATES OF AMERICA

FOREWORD

I AM SURE that Mr. Paul Leyssac may at times have felt that it must seem a little impertinent to provide the world with yet another translation of the stories of Hans Andersen. There have been so many, and they have been so poor, some of them! There have been some good ones too, but nothing in English, so far as I know, that is thoroughly satisfactory. In the old days, the translations were pedantic, with rather a goody-goody air about them, and a very recent one by the author of the magnificent *Ghost Stories of an Antiquary* proved that Dr. James was no Dane.

That is the first of Paul Leyssac's qualifications as a new translator. He is a Dane of the Danes, although partly French too. His mother knew Hans Andersen. He was brought up, so to speak, jumping about in the shadow of the long legs of that extraordinary man. Then he is an actor, well known in New York and Paris. Then, if I may speak personally for a moment, he is a most delightful *raconteur*. In fact, I will confess at once that I am a little prejudiced in favor of these translations because I am sure that nobody yet reads (writes, or acts, whatever word you please) the Andersen stories as Leyssac reads them. If anyone wants to know just what these stories really are, let him go and listen to the wireless or watch Leyssac on the television and he will perhaps for the first time understand, because these stories were always meant, I think, to be told first before they were read, and it is exactly that colloquial rhythm that translators have always found so difficult to catch. You ought to hear the voice, not exactly of Andersen himself, but of some old, friendly, and rather sardonic story-teller, who holds you as the Ancient Mariner did the Wedding Guest, with a fierce insistence.

It is just this tone of voice that Leyssac gets so beautifully in these stories. They must be read aloud: don't say to yourself that everyone has read them already. There are a number of stories here—"It's Perfectly True!," "The Butterfly," "The Shirt Collar," "The Darning Needle," "The Jumpers," to name only a few—that are very little known in England, and even the familiar ones, like "The Little Mermaid" and "The Ugly Duckling," take on a new kind of life in this translation. Leyssac understands that Danish mingling of sentiment and irony.

Hans Andersen was not, I would say, exactly a charming person. He was ugly, conceited, sensitive, quick-tempered, and elusive. As the hero of a novel he would annoy many readers. He would seem feckless and ungrateful, and a bit of a muff. And yet he is part of all of us. If you feel the pathetic and humorous and lonely uniqueness of human beings, you must know that only the very unperceptive and heavy-minded are irritated by him; and out of that strange personality he produced these wonderful fairy stories, wonderful because they are filled through and through with that sense of oddity and loneliness that gives human beings so much beauty.

Anyway, for me this translation of the stories is the best, the most living, the most human, that has yet appeared in English.

HUGH WALPOLE

TRANSLATOR'S NOTE

IN DENMARK, Hans Christian Andersen's native land, his stories are read mostly by grown-up people, while the children usually ask to have them read aloud—they hardly ever read them themselves. Outside Denmark, on the other hand, it is the children who read Hans Christian Andersen, and, curiously enough, very seldom their elders. The result has been that the tales seem to have vanished from the bookshelves of grown-ups, and appear to be considered only suitable for the young. This was far from Andersen's intention. His stories were written to be heard; he was always reading them himself, mainly to adult audiences, both in public and in private. He meant them to have the form and the unexpected turns of phrase of the spoken word. The many exclamation marks and dashes in his manuscripts were, as far as one can see, inserted after his readings, and were presumably meant to indicate the places where he wanted dramatic emphasis and suitable pauses. He himself used these to a great extent, as well as gestures and facial expressions.

Many of my older friends and acquaintances, who heard him read in their younger days, have told me of these characteristics.

Hans Christian Andersen created an entirely new literary form in his stories; they make the same vivid impression today as they did when they were first published, and were so severely criticized for their careless construction.

It has been my aim to present a truer and clearer picture of our Danish writer's personality than has so far been given to the public outside Denmark. I have tried to find the equivalent expressions to fit Andersen's colloquial style, which has never been brought out vividly enough in English because the translations—except the four stories done by Mr. Keigwin—are rather pedantic; they lack the everyday simplicity which is so typically "Andersen," and which can hardly be understood except by those who from their childhood have known the Danish language, with its own individual modes of thought.

I am thinking particularly of stories like "The Happy Family," "Numskull Jack," "The Butterfly," and "The Top and the Ball," in which his sense of humor is displayed in the finest irony and the wittiest satire. This light touch has been totally overlooked, just as it used to be in some of the Ibsen and Chekhov plays, where a laugh was never permitted. They were "Nordic" and "Russian," and that was enough to get them a name for being somber, and without a ray of sunshine—a point of view that has fortunately changed.

Perhaps this volume will contribute in some measure towards giving the English-speaking public a brighter impression of Andersen's stories than it has had before, a hope based on the innumerable letters I have received after broadcasting many of the present translations; and I hope that the book will find its way into both library and playroom, and that all readers, of whatever age, will enjoy the stories equally, because they touch the chords of humor and grief, of smiles and tears—in other words, the living human heart itself.

Note. My best thanks are due to Miss Elsie R. Tetley for her devoted help, and to Mr. Jakob H. Helweg for his valuable suggestions.

Copenhagen, August 1937

CONTENTS

CONTENTS

IT'S PERFECTLY TRUE

IT'S PERFECTLY TRUE!

"IT'S a dreadful business," said a hen, and she said it in a part of the town where the incident had not taken place.

"It's a dreadful business to happen in a hen-house. I wouldn't dare to sleep alone tonight. Thank goodness there are so many of us on the perch!"

And then she told her story in such a way that the feathers of the other hens stood on end, and even the rooster's comb drooped. It's perfectly true!

But let's begin at the beginning.

It happened in a hen-house at the other end of the town. The sun went down and the hens flew up. One of them was a white-feathered, short-legged, nice little thing who laid her eggs regularly—a most respectable hen in every way. She settled herself on the perch, preening herself with her beak. One tiny feather fluttered down.

"There's that feather gone!" said the hen. "Well, well, the more I preen myself, the more handsome I shall become, no doubt!"

She said it only in fun, you know. She was the life and soul of that crowd, but otherwise, as we've said, most respectable. Then she fell asleep.

All was dark. There sat the hens, packed closely together. But the white hen's neighbor wasn't asleep; she had heard and not heard, as one must do in this world for the sake of peace and quiet. But she couldn't resist telling it to her neighbor on the other side.

"Did you hear? Well, my dear, I won't mention names, but there's one hen I know who is going to pluck out all her feathers just to make herself look smart. Humph! If I were a rooster I should simply treat her with contempt."

Up above the hens lived Mother Owl, with Father Owl, and all the little Owls. They were a sharp-eared family and they heard every word; they rolled their eyes, and old Mother Owl flapped her wings. "Don't take any notice—you heard what she said, of course. I heard it with my own ears. Upon my word, I don't know what the world is coming to! One of the hens, so utterly lost to all sense of henly decency, is sitting there plucking out her feathers with the rooster looking on the whole time!"

"Little pitchers have long ears," said Father Owl. "Be careful what you are saying!"

"Oh, but I shall have to tell the owl across the road," said Mother Owl. "She is somebody, and well worth associating with, you know." And off she flew.

"Tu-whit, tu-whoo, tu-whit, tu-whoo," they hooted together outside the pigeon-house over the way. "Have you heard the news? Have you heard the news? There is a hen who has pulled out all her feathers just to please the rooster. She is freezing to death, if she isn't dead already, tu-whit, tu-whoo, tu-whit, tu-whoo. . . ."

"Where? Where?" asked the pigeons.

"In the yard opposite; I saw it, so to speak, with my own eyes! It's not at all a nice story to tell, but it's perfectly true!"

"Trrrue, too trrrue—trrrue, too trrrue," cooed the pigeons, and they flew down to tell the story in the chicken-run below. "There's a hen—in fact, some say there are two hens who have plucked out all their feathers to be different from the rest, and to attract the attention of the rooster. A dreadful thing to do, what with the risk of chills and fever; and they caught cold and died, both of them!"

"Cock-a-doodle-doo! Wake up! Wake up!" crowed the rooster, flying up on to the fence. He was still half asleep, but he crowed all the same. "Three hens have died of a broken heart, all for the sake of the rooster; they've plucked out all their feathers, and now they

are dead! It's a dreadful business, but it's no good trying to keep it quiet. Tell anyone you please!"

"We'll tell, we'll tell!" squeaked the bats; and the rooster crowed and the hens clucked, "Tell, tell, tell, tell," and so the story flew from one hen-house to another, until at last it came back to the place where it had really started.

"Five hens"—that's how it was told—"five hens have plucked out all their feathers to show which one has lost the most weight for love of the rooster; then they pecked at one another till they bled, and all five dropped down dead—a shame and a disgrace to their relations, and a serious loss to their owner!"

The hen who had dropped the little loose feather naturally didn't recognize her own story, and as she was a respectable hen, she exclaimed, "I despise such hens! But there are others just as bad! Things like that ought not to be hushed up; I must do what I can to get the story into the papers, then it will soon be known all over the country, and serve the wretches right and their relations too!"

It was put into the papers, all clear in plain print. And it's perfectly true—one little feather can easily become five hens.

THOUSANDS OF YEARS FROM NOW

(Written in 1853)

WELL, thousands of years from now people will come over the ocean on wings of steam through the air! The young inhabitants of America will visit old Europe. They will come to see our monuments, and the great cities that will then be disappearing, just as we nowadays make pilgrimages to the crumbling splendors of Southern Asia.

Thousands of years from now they will come.

The Thames, the Danube, and the Rhine will still be rolling on their course, Mont Blanc will still be standing there with its snow-capped summit, and the Aurora Borealis will shine over the countries of the North, but generation after generation will be dust, ranks of the mighty of today forgotten, like those who already slumber in the burial-mound where the rich corn-merchant, who now owns the land, has put up a bench to enjoy the view over his wide waving cornfields.

"To Europe!" is the cry of the young generation of America, "to the land of our fathers, the glorious land of memory and phantasy—to Europe!"

The airship is arriving; it is overcrowded with travelers, for the crossing is quicker than by sea. The electro-magnetic wire under the ocean has previously cabled the number of passengers in the aerial caravan.

Already Europe is in sight. The coast of Ireland looms up on the horizon, but the passengers are still asleep; they have asked not to be called until they are over England.

Here they set foot on European soil in the "Land of Shakespeare,"

SUN MON TUE WED THU FRI SAT
1 2 3 4 5 6 7

as the literary call it; others call it the "Land of Politics," the "Land of Machinery."

One whole day will be devoted to a visit here, for this bustling generation will spare as much time as that to the famous sights of England and Scotland.

The journey is now continued through the Channel Tunnel to France, the land of Charlemagne and Napoleon. Molière's name comes up, the scholars talk of a classical and a romantic school of remote antiquity; there is great excitement over heroes, poets, and men of learning of whom our age knows nothing, but who are yet to be born in that crater of Europe, Paris.

The air-steamer flies over the country from which Columbus set out, where Cortez was born, and where Calderón wrote dramas in melodious verse. Beautiful black-eyed women still live in the flower-filled valleys, and the poetry of bygone days celebrates the names of the Cid and of the Alhambra.

Then through the air, over the sea to Italy, where once stood ancient "Eternal Rome." It has gone! The Campagna is a wilderness; a solitary bit of wall is pointed out as all that remains of St. Peter's, but it is doubtful whether or not it is authentic.

Next, to Greece, to spend one night in the fashionable hotel at the top of Olympus, so that they can say they have been there. The course is then set for the Bosporus for a few hours' rest, and a visit to the spot on which Byzantium once stood; poor fishermen are now spreading their nets where, according to legend, the gardens of the harem used to be in the days of the Turks.

The travelers fly over the remains of great cities by the mighty Danube, cities unknown to our generation; but here and there, on places rich with memories of events still to come, which Time has not yet brought forth—here and there the air caravan lands and takes off again.

Down below lies Germany, once covered with a perfect network of railways and canals—the country where Luther preached, where Goethe sang, and where Mozart in his time held the scepter of music. Other great names shone there in learning and in art, names already forgotten.

One day is allotted to seeing Germany, and one to seeing the North, the countries of Örsted and Linnaeus, and Norway, the land of the old Vikings and the young Norwegians.

Iceland is visited on the way back; the great Geyser no longer boils, Hecla is extinct, but the mighty, rocky island stands as an everlasting monument to the Sagas, battered by the foaming sea!

"There is a lot to be seen in Europe," says the young American, "and we have seen it in a week, so it is quite feasible, as the great traveler"—he names a contemporary—"tells us in his famous book *How to See Europe in a Week.*"

THE OLD HOUSE

SOMEWHERE in the street there stood a very, very old house. It was almost three hundred years old, as you could read for yourself on the beam, where the date was cut, with tulips and hops all round it; there were also whole verses spelled in the old-fashioned way, and over each window was carved a grinning face. One story jutted out a good way beyond the one below it, and right along the edge of the roof was a leaden gutter, ending in a gargoyle. The rain-water was supposed to run out of the gargoyle's mouth, but ran out of its stomach instead, for there was a hole in the gutter.

All the other houses in the street were very neat and new, with large window-panes and smooth walls. It was quite obvious that they did not want to have anything to do with the Old House; they were evidently thinking, "How long is this ramshackle old thing going to make an exhibition of itself here in our street? The bow-window sticks out so far that nobody can see from our windows what's going on beyond it. The front door-steps are as broad as those of a palace, and as steep as if they led up to a belfry. The iron railings on each side look like the gate of an old family vault, and to cap it all, they have even got brass knobs! It's disgraceful!"

Just opposite stood some more neat new houses, and they thought exactly the same as the others did, but at the window of one of them sat a little boy with fresh rosy cheeks and bright shining eyes. There was no doubt in his mind about preferring the Old House, in sunshine as well as by moonlight. When he looked across at the wall where the plaster had fallen off, he fancied he saw all kinds of curious pictures. He could see exactly what the old street had looked like in the olden days, with steps, bow-windows, and pointed gables; he could see soldiers with halberds, and gutters twisting about in the shape of snakes with dragons' and griffins' heads. That was indeed a house worth looking at!

An old gentleman lived over there; he went about in plush knee-breeches, and wore a coat with big brass buttons, and a wig that you could see was a real wig. Every morning an old servant came to tidy up his rooms and do errands for him; otherwise the old gentleman in the plush breeches was quite alone in the Old House. From time to time he came to one of the windows and looked out; then the little boy nodded to him, and the old gentleman nodded back—that's how they first became acquainted, and then they became friends, though they had never spoken to one another; but what difference did that make?

One day the little boy heard his father and mother say, "The old gentleman opposite is very comfortably off, but he's so frightfully lonely."

The following Sunday the little boy wrapped something up in a piece of paper, and went downstairs. As the servant who did the errands went by, he said to him, "Please will you give the old gentleman this? It's one of my tin soldiers. I've got two, and I want him to have one, because I know he is so frightfully lonely."

The old servant looked quite pleased, nodded his head, and took the tin soldier over to the Old House. Later on he was sent across to ask if the little boy would like to come himself and visit the old gentleman. His parents said he might, so he went over to the Old House.

The brass knobs on the railings shone much brighter than usual; you would think they had been polished up specially in honor of his visit, and it seemed as if the carved trumpeters—there were actually trumpeters carved on the door, standing in a mass of tulips!—well, it seemed as if the trumpeters were blowing with might and main,

puffing their cheeks out like balloons.

Yes, they blew, "Tarantara! the little boy is coming! Tarantara!"—and the door opened. The whole entrance-hall was hung with old portraits, of knights in armor and ladies in silken gowns; the armor rattled, and the silken gowns rustled. Then came a staircase which had many steps up and a few steps down, and then you found yourself on a balcony which certainly was very rickety, having big holes and great cracks everywhere, with grass and plants growing out of them all; for the whole balcony, like the courtyard and the walls, was overgrown with so much greenery that it looked like a garden. However, it was only a balcony. Here stood old flower-pots that had faces on them with donkeys' ears; as for the flowers, they grew all higgledy-piggledy. One of the pots was simply brimming over with carnations, that is to say, with their green shoots, and each one said quite plainly, "The air has caressed me, and the sun has kissed me, and promised me a little flower for Sunday, a little flower for Sunday!"

Then they came into a room where the walls were paneled with pigskin, on which flowers were printed in gold.

"Gilding vanishes fast,
Pigskin forever will last,"

said the walls.

In this room there stood armchairs with ever such high backs, and ever so many carvings, and they even had arms on both sides. "Sit down! Sit down!" they said. "Ooh! I'm creaking all over! I shall probably get rheumatics, like the old cupboard. Rheumatics in the back! Ooh!"

Then the little boy came into the room where the bow-window was, and where the old gentleman was sitting.

"Thank you for the tin soldier, little friend," said the old gentleman, "and thank you for coming to see me."

" 'K-you! 'K-you!" or rather "Ooh! Ooh!" went the old furniture; there was such a lot of it that the pieces almost stood in each other's way to see the little boy.

In the center of the wall hung the portrait of a beautiful lady, looking very happy and very young, but wearing an old-fashioned gown, powdered hair, and stiff spreading skirts. She said neither " 'K-you" nor "Ooh," but looked down at the little boy with her kind eyes, and he immediately asked the old gentleman, "Where did you get her from?"

"From the antique dealer's round the corner," replied the old gentleman. "The shop is full of portraits of people nobody knows or cares about, for they have all passed away. Many years ago I knew this lady, but now she has been dead and gone these fifty years."

Beneath the portrait hung a bouquet of withered flowers under glass; they were probably also fifty years old—at least they looked it; the pendulum of the big clock swung to and fro, and the hands went round; the things in the room were growing older and older, but they did not notice it.

"They say at home that you are so frightfully lonely," said the little boy.

"Oh," answered the old gentleman, "old memories and all they bring with them come and visit me, and now you have come too. I have no reason to complain."

Then he went to a shelf and took down a book full of pictures; there were long processions of people, the most extraordinary-looking coaches that you would never see nowadays, soldiers like the Knave of Clubs, and city guilds with their waving banners. The tailors had on their banner a pair of scissors held up by two lions, and the shoemakers had on theirs, not a boot, but an eagle with two heads, as shoemakers must have everything so arranged that they can say, "That makes a pair!" It *was* a picture-book, and no mistake!

The old gentleman now went into the other room to fetch jam, apples, and nuts. What a treat it was to be in the Old House!

"I can't stand it!" said the tin soldier, who had been put on the chest. "It's so lonely and dull here. When one is accustomed to family life, one can't get used to this kind of existence. I cannot stand it. The whole day is long enough, and the evening is still longer. It isn't at all the same here as it was in your home, where your father and mother were always talking cheerfully, and you and all the rest of the nice children made such a jolly noise. The old gentleman is really too lonely for words! Do you suppose he ever gets a kiss? Do you suppose he ever gets a friendly look or a Christmas tree? All he'll ever get will be a funeral—I can't stand it."

"Don't be so miserable," said the little boy. "I think it's fun to be here; besides, all the old memories and what they bring with them come visiting, don't they?"

"Yes, but I don't see them, and I don't know them," said the tin soldier. "I can't stand it."

"You've got to," said the little boy.

The old gentleman now came back looking very cheerful, and bringing the most delicious jam, apples, and nuts, and the little boy thought no more of the tin soldier.

Happy and delighted, the little boy went home again. Days passed, weeks passed, there was a great deal of nodding going on to the Old House and from the Old House, and at last the little boy went over there again.

The carved trumpeters blew "Tarantara! the little boy is here! Tarantara!" The old pictures rattled their swords and armor, and rustled their silken gowns, the pigskin spoke, and the old chairs had rheumatics in their backs—"Ooh!" It was exactly like the first time, for over there the days and hours followed one another without ever changing.

"I can't stand it," said the tin soldier. "I have cried tin tears! It's really too depressing here. I'd rather go to the wars and lose my arms and legs. That would be a change, anyhow. I can*not* stand it.

Now I know what it means to have visits from one's old memories and all they bring with them. I've had visits from my own, and believe me, that's no pleasure after a while. I nearly jumped down from the chest in the end. I could see you all over there in the new house just as clearly as if you had been here. I was back again at that Sunday morning which I'm sure you must remember. You children all stood in front of the table singing the hymn you sang every morning; you were standing reverently with folded hands, and your father and mother were just as solemn as you; then the door opened and they brought in your little sister Mary, who is not yet two years old, and who always dances when she hears music or singing of any kind. They ought not to have brought her, for she immediately began to dance, but she couldn't get into the rhythm; the notes were held too long, so she stood first on one leg bending her head forward as far as she could, then on the other leg, bending her head forward as far as she could, but it was never long enough. You all kept straight faces, every one of you, though it was rather difficult, but I laughed to myself, and so I fell off the table and got a bruise which is still there, for it was not right of me to laugh. All that and all the other things I have witnessed go round and round in my head; I suppose these are the old memories and all they bring with them! Tell me, do you still sing on Sunday mornings? Tell me something about little Mary. And how is my comrade, the other tin soldier? He's a lucky fellow! I can't stand it!"

"You've been given away," said the little boy. "You've got to stay here, don't you see that?"

The old gentleman then brought out a drawer in which there were all kinds of things, little boxes for coins, pomanders, and old cards much bigger and more elaborately gilded than you ever see nowadays. Then a lot of big drawers were opened, and the spinet was opened—it had a landscape painted inside the lid, but how tinny it sounded when the old gentleman played it!—then he hummed a song.

"How beautifully she used to sing that!" he said, and he nodded to the portrait he had bought at the antique dealer's, and the old gentleman's eyes shone so brightly.

"I want to go and fight! I want to go and fight!" shouted the tin soldier at the top of his voice, and he threw himself down to the floor.

Why, what had become of him? The old gentleman searched, the little boy searched, but he had gone, gone for good.

"I'm sure I shall find him," said the old gentleman. But he never did, as the floor was too full of gaps and holes. The tin soldier had fallen through one of them and there he lay as in an open grave.

So that day passed, and the little boy went home; the week passed, and several more weeks passed. The windows were quite frozen over, and the little boy had to keep breathing on them to make a peephole through which he could look across to the Old House. The snow had drifted into all its scrolls and inscriptions, and smothered the front door steps, as if no one were in the house at all; and in fact there was no one in the house—the old gentleman had died.

That same evening a carriage stopped at the door, and he was carried down to it in his coffin; they were taking him into the country, where his burial place was. That's where he went, but nobody followed him, for all his friends were dead. The little boy blew a kiss to the coffin as it drove off.

A few days later, the Old House was put up for sale, and from his window the little boy watched everything being taken away: the old knights and the old ladies, the flower-pots with the long ears, the old chairs and the old cupboards. Some of the things landed here, and others landed there. The portrait of the lady that had been found at the antique dealer's went back to the antique dealer, and it remained in his shop, as nobody knew her any more, and nobody cared for the old picture.

In the spring the house itself was pulled down, for it was a ramshackle old thing, people said. From the street you could look straight into the room with the pigskin panels which were being torn and ripped, and the creepers from the balcony hung in a tangle round the toppling beams. Then the site was cleared.

"Thank goodness!" said all the neighboring houses.

. . . .

A beautiful house was built with large windows and smooth white walls, but before it, in the place where the Old House had actually stood, a little garden was planted, and Virginia creepers climbed all over the neighbor's wall. There were great iron railings in front of the garden, with an iron gate: it looked so smart that people stopped and looked through. The sparrows clung by scores in the creepers, all chirruping away together, but not about the Old House, for they could not remember that—so many years had gone by that the little boy had grown to be a man, and a clever man too, of whom his parents had every reason to be proud. He had just got married and he and his wife had moved into the house with the garden. He was standing by her side while she planted one of the wild flowers she was so fond of. She planted it with her own hands, and pressed the earth down with her fingers. Ow! what was that? She had pricked herself; something sharp was sticking out of the soft ground.

It was—yes, just fancy!—it was the tin soldier, the very one that had been lost in the old gentleman's room, and had afterwards been tumbled and jostled about amongst the timber and rubbish, and had finally lain hidden in the ground for many years.

The young wife now wiped the soldier, first with a green leaf, and then with her dainty, delicately scented handkerchief; the tin soldier felt just as if he had come out of a long sleep.

"Let me look at him," said the young man; and then he laughed and shook his head. "Well, it couldn't possibly be the same one, but he does so remind me of something connected with a tin soldier that happened to me when I was a little boy." Then he began to tell his wife about the Old House, about the old gentleman, and about the tin soldier he had sent across to him because he was so frightfully lonely, and he told it all so vividly that the young wife's eyes filled with tears at the thought of the Old House and the old gentleman.

"It might be the same tin soldier after all," she said. "I'll keep him and remember all you have told me; but you must show me the old gentleman's grave."

"I don't know where it is," he said. "Nobody knows. All his friends were dead, nobody looked after it, and I was only a small boy at the time."

"How frightfully lonely he must have been," she said.

"Frightfully lonely," said the tin soldier, "but it's wonderful not to be forgotten."

"Wonderful!" shouted something near by, though no one except the tin soldier saw that it was a scrap of the pigskin paneling. It had lost all its gilding and looked just like a clod of wet earth; still it had an opinion of its own, and was not afraid of airing it:

"Gilding vanishes fast,
Pigskin forever will last."

However, the tin soldier had his doubts.

THE BUTTERFLY

THE butterfly wanted a sweetheart; naturally he wanted to pick a nice little one from among the flowers. He looked them over; there they all sat quietly and demurely on their stalks, just as young ladies ought to sit before they are engaged. But there were such a lot to choose from! What a job it would be! The butterfly couldn't face it, so he flew off to the daisy. The French call her Marguerite; they know that she can tell fortunes, and she does so when they pluck off her petals one by one, asking about their sweethearts: "Does she love me? A lot? Passionately? A tiny bit? Not at all?"—or something like that. Everyone asks in his own language. The butterfly also came to enquire; but he did not pluck off her petals; no, he kissed them, one after the other, for he knew that kindness is the best policy.

"Dear Madame Marguerite," he said, "you are the wisest woman among the flowers. You can tell fortunes. Pray tell me, am I to have this one or that one? Which one am I to have? As soon as I know, I can fly straight off to her and propose."

But Marguerite did not answer him. She was offended at being called "Madame," for she was not married, and in that case one is not "Madame." He asked a second time, and he asked a third time, and as he couldn't get a word out of her, he did not feel like asking again, but without more ado he flew off on his courting.

It was early spring; the snowdrops and crocuses covered the ground. "Very nice!" thought the butterfly. "Charming little débutantes, I'm sure, but just a trifle insipid." He, like all young men, was attracted by the older girls. So he flew away to the anem-

ones. They were rather too bitter for his taste; the violets were a little too sentimental, the tulips too showy, the narcissi too middle-class, the lime-tree flowers too small, and besides he would have far too many in-laws. The apple-blossoms, it is true, looked like roses, but they bloomed today and were gone tomorrow at the slightest breath of wind; such a marriage would last too short a time, he thought. The pea-flower pleased him best of all; she was pink and white, dainty and delicate, like one of those domesticated girls, who are good-looking, and yet useful in the kitchen. He was on the point of proposing when, close by, he spied a pod at the end of which hung a withered flower. "Who is that?" asked the butterfly. "It's my sister," replied the pea-flower.

"Oh, so that's what you'll look like later on?" This rather frightened the butterfly, and off he flew.

The honeysuckle-flowers hung over the hedge; there were masses of those girls long in the face, and yellow of complexion. No, he did not care for their type at all—but what type did he like? Ask him yourself.

Spring passed, summer passed, then it was autumn, and he was no nearer.

Flowers now appeared in most gorgeous dresses, but what was the good of that? There was none of the fresh fragrance of youth about them; and it is fragrance that the heart needs as age creeps on. Of course there isn't much of that in dahlias and hollyhocks.

So the butterfly flew down to the mint.

"She has nothing of a blossom, but is all flower herself, perfumed from top to toe with fragrance in every leaf. She's the one I'm going to take."

And in the end he proposed to her.

But the mint stood stiff and silent: at last she said, "Friendship—but nothing more. I am old and you are old; we could very well live for one another, but marry! no, we must on no account make fools of ourselves in our old age."

And so it happened that the butterfly did not find any sweetheart at all. He had been too particular, and that doesn't pay. He remained what is called a bachelor.

It was late autumn, with rainy and gusty weather. The wind sent cold shivers down the backs of the willow trees, so that they creaked all over. This was no weather for being out of doors in summer clothes: it might play you a dirty trick, as they say; but the butterfly was not out of doors—by chance he had found shelter in a room where there was a fire in the stove, and a comfortable summer temperature. He could keep alive there.

"But it isn't enough merely to keep alive," said the butterfly. "To live you must have sunshine, freedom, and a little flower!"

Then he flew against the window-pane, was seen, admired, and stuck on a pin in the curio-box. It was all that could be done for him.

"Well, now I'm perched on a stem just like the flowers," said the butterfly. "It isn't altogether pleasant; I'm sure it must be something like being married, for you're pinned down then, all right!"

And with this thought he consoled himself.

"That seems very poor consolation," said the pot-plants in the room. "But pot-plants," thought the butterfly, "are not quite to be trusted; they've had too much to do with human beings!"

THE LITTLE MERMAID

FAR out at sea the water is as blue as the bluest cornflower petals, and as clear as the clearest crystal, but it is very deep—deeper than any anchor cable can fathom; many church steeples would have to be piled one on top of the other to reach from the very bottom to the surface of the water. Far down in the depths live the sea-folk.

Now, don't imagine for a moment that there is nothing but bare white sand on the bed of the ocean, no, the most fantastic trees and flowers grow there, with such pliable stems and leaves that the slightest motion of the water makes them move just as if they were alive. All kinds of fishes, big and small, flit in and out among the branches, just as birds do in the air up here. At the very lowest depths stands the Palace of the Sea-king; the walls are made of coral, and the long pointed windows of the very clearest amber, but the roof is made of mussel-shells which open and close with the motion of the water. It is a wonderful sight, for every shell contains gleaming pearls—a single one of which would be a perfect ornament for a Queen's crown.

The Sea-king had been a widower for many years, but his old mother kept house for him. She was an intelligent woman, though proud of her noble birth, and that is why she went about with twelve oysters on her tail, while the other high-born ladies were only allowed six. Apart from this she deserved a great deal of praise because she was so fond of her grandchildren, the little Princesses. They were six beautiful girls, but the youngest was the prettiest of them all; her skin was as clear and delicate as a rose petal, her eyes were as blue as the deepest sea, but like all the others, she had no feet, only a fish's tail.

All day long they used to play down in the Palace, in the great galleries, where living flowers grew out of the walls. When the tall amber windows were opened, fishes swam in just as swallows fly into our rooms when we open the windows, but the fishes swam right up to the little Princesses, ate out of their hands, and allowed themselves to be patted.

Outside the Palace there was a large garden with trees of fiery red and deep blue, with fruits glimmering like gold, and flowers like a burning fire, ceaselessly moving their stems and leaves. The ground itself was of the finest sand, but blue as a sulphur-flame. Down there a strange blue mist enveloped everything; you would sooner have thought that you were standing high up in the air, with only the sky above and beneath you, than that you were down in the depths of the ocean. When the surface was dead calm you could just faintly perceive the sun, looking like a crimson flower out of which a flood of light streamed forth.

Each of the small Princesses had her own little plot in the garden, where she could dig and plant as she liked. One of them gave her bed of flowers the shape of a whale, another thought it nicer to have hers like a little mermaid, but the youngest made hers as round as the sun, and used only flowers shining red as the sun itself. She was a strange child, quiet and pensive, and while the other sisters decorated their gardens with all kinds of extraordinary things that they had taken from stranded ships, she would have nothing in hers but a beautiful statue, and the flowers, red as the sun up in that dim distance above them. It was the statue of a handsome boy, in the purest white marble, that had dropped down to the bottom of the sea from a ship which had been wrecked. Beside the statue she planted a rose-red weeping willow which grew splendidly and shaded it with fresh delicate branches hanging right down to the blue sandy bottom, where their shadow showed quite violet, and moved as they moved. It looked as if the tips of the branches and the roots were playing at kissing one another.

Nothing gave the youngest Princess greater pleasure than to hear about the world of human beings up above them; she made her grandmother tell all she knew about ships and towns, people and animals; but what fascinated her beyond words was that the flowers on earth were scented, while those at the bottom of the sea were not, also that the woods were green, and that the fishes you saw among the branches could sing so loudly and sweetly that it was a delight to hear them. It was the little birds that Grandmother called fishes, otherwise the mermaids would not have understood her, for they had never seen a bird.

"As soon as you are fifteen," said their grandmother, "you will all be allowed to rise up above the water and sit on the rocks in the moonlight, watching the big ships sailing by; you will see forests and towns as well."

The following year the eldest sister would have her fifteenth birthday, but as there was just one year between each of them, the youngest had still five whole years to wait before her turn came to rise up from the depths and see what things are like on the earth. Each of them promised the others that she would tell them what she had seen and thought most wonderful on the first day, for their grandmother had not told them nearly enough—there were so many things they wanted to know about. The most curious of them all was the youngest, the very one who had the longest time to wait, and who was so quiet and pensive. Many a night she stood by the open window and looked up through the dark blue sea, where the fishes were lashing the water with fins and tails. She could just perceive the moon and the stars, though their light was very faint, but through the water they looked much bigger than they do to us; and if something like a black cloud passed under them, she knew that it was either a whale swimming above her, or a ship with many people on board. They probably never dreamt that a lovely little mermaid was standing below, stretching up her white hands towards the keel of their ship.

The eldest Princess had now reached her fifteenth birthday, and was allowed to rise above the surface.

When she came back, she had hundreds of things to tell the others, but the most wonderful of all, she said, was to lie in the moonlight on a sandbank in the calm sea, gazing at the huge town close to the shore, where the lights twinkled like hundreds of stars; to listen to the music, and the noise and stir of carriages and people, or to look at the many church towers and spires, and hear the bells ringing. Just because she could not get there, that was the very thing she longed for most of all.

Oh, how eagerly the youngest sister listened; and whenever after this she stood at the open window in the evening looking up through the deep blue sea, she thought of the great town with all its noise and bustle, and seemed to hear the sound of the church bells coming right down to her.

The following year the second sister was allowed to rise up through the waves and swim wherever she liked. She reached the surface just at sunset, and that sight was the most magnificent she had ever seen. The heavens had looked like liquid gold, she said, and the clouds, well, she never tired of describing their beauty! All rosy-red and violet had they sailed over her, but faster than the clouds, like a long white veil flung out towards the sky, a flock of wild swans flew away over the water beyond which the sun was setting. She swam towards it, but it sank, and the rosy tint faded away from sea and cloud.

The year after that, the third sister went up; she was the most daring of them all, so she swam up a broad river which flowed into the ocean. She saw beautiful green hills with vineyards; palaces and farms were faintly visible amongst splendid woods; she heard how sweetly the birds were singing, and the sun was so hot that she was often obliged to dive under the surface and cool her burning face. In a tiny cove she found a whole crowd of little human children, splashing about quite naked; she wanted to play with them, but she gave them a fright and they ran away. Then came a little black animal—it was a dog, but she had never seen one before. It barked at her so furiously that she was frightened and took refuge in the open sea, but she could never forget the beautiful woods, the green hills, and the lovely children who could swim in the water, although they had no fishes' tails.

The fourth sister was not so daring; she remained far out in the stormy ocean, and told her sisters that staying there was the best part of her adventures. You could see for miles and miles around you, and the sky above was like a great glass dome. She had seen ships, but only far, far away; they looked like sea-gulls. The amusing dolphins had turned somersaults, and the gigantic whales had spouted water through their nostrils, giving the effect of hundreds of fountains playing.

Now it was the turn of the fifth sister. Her birthday happened to be in the winter; therefore she saw things which none of the others had seen when they first went up to the surface. The sea was quite green, and large icebergs were floating about; they looked like pearls, she said, but were much bigger than the church towers built by human beings. They appeared in the most wonderful shapes, and sparkled like diamonds. She sat down on one of the largest, and every ship gave it a wide berth when the sailors saw her sitting there with her long hair floating in the wind. Late in the evening the sky became overcast, thunder crashed and lightning stabbed the sky, while the black waves lifted the huge icebergs high up on their crests, so that they glittered in the fierce glare of the light. Sails were furled on all the ships, everyone stood there in fear and trembling, but she sat quietly on her floating iceberg, watching the blue lightning flash in zig-zags down into the shining sea.

The first time each of the sisters rose above the water, she was delighted with all the new and beautiful things she had seen, but as she was now grown up and was allowed to rise to the surface whenever she liked, she lost interest in it; she longed for her home, and after a month had gone by, she said that no place was more delightful than the bottom of the sea—besides, one felt so comfortably at home there.

Many an evening the five sisters would rise up arm in arm. They had beautiful voices, more beautiful than those of any human beings, and when storms threatened to wreck the ships, they would swim in front of them, sing their most seductive songs of the wonders in the depths of the sea, and try to persuade the people on board not to be afraid of coming down to them. But the seafarers could not understand the words; they thought it was the storm they heard. Nor did they ever see the promised splendors, for when the ship sank, they were drowned, and only reached the Palace of the Sea-king as dead bodies.

At night, when the sisters rose up through the water arm in arm like this, the youngest remained behind quite alone gazing after them, and she would have wept; but the mermaid has no tears and so she suffers all the more.

"Oh, if I were only fifteen!" she said. "I know I shall love that upper world and the people who live there!"

At last she too reached the age of fifteen.

"Well, now we are getting you off our hands," said her grandmother, the old Dowager-Queen. "Come here, let me dress you up like your sisters!" And she put a wreath of white lilies on her head, but each petal was formed of half a pearl; then the old Queen made eight large oysters fasten themselves to the Princess's tail to show her high rank.

"Oh, how it hurts!" said the little mermaid.

"Well, one must suffer to be beautiful," said her grandmother.

She would gladly have shaken off all this finery and laid aside the heavy wreath. The red flowers in her garden suited her much better, but she did not dare to change anything. "Good-by," she said, and light and shining as any bubble she rose up through the waters.

The sun had just set when her head appeared above the surface, but all the clouds were still tinted with rose and gold, and in the pink-flushed sky the evening star twinkled bright and clear; the air was mild and fresh and the sea dead calm. She saw a big three-masted ship with only a single sail set, for not a breath of wind stirred, and the sailors were sitting on the rigging and on the spars. She heard music and singing on board, and as the darkness was gathering hundreds of many-colored lanterns were lighted; they looked like the flags of all nations waving in the air. The little mermaid swam right up to the port-hole of the cabin, and every time the swell lifted her up, through the clear glass she could see crowds of people in evening dress, but the handsomest of them all was the young Prince with great coal-black eyes. He could hardly be more than sixteen years old; it was his birthday, and that was the reason for the party. The sailors danced on deck, and when the Prince appeared among them hundreds of rockets shot up into the air, turning night to day, and frightening the little mermaid so much that she had to dive under the water; but she soon ventured to put her head up again, and it looked as if all the stars were falling down to her from the sky. Never had she seen such fireworks. Great suns whirled round, gorgeous fire-fishes darted about in the blue air, and everything was reflected in the clear calm sea. It was so light on board ship that one could see every little rope, to say nothing of the people. Oh, how handsome the young Prince was! He shook hands with the sailors, laughing and smiling, while the music rang out in the beauty of the night.

It got quite late, but the little mermaid could not turn her eyes away from the ship and the beautiful Prince. The many-colored lanterns were put out, no more rockets shot up through the air, no more guns were fired, but deep down in the sea there was a dull humming and rumbling. The whole time the water was lifting her up and down so that she could look into the cabin, but the ship started to move, sail after sail opened out in the wind, the waves grew mightier, great clouds gathered, and lightning flashed along the horizon. Oh, there was terrible weather ahead, so the sailors furled the sails. The great ship plowed on, pitching and tossing in the angry sea, the waves rose like enormous black mountains which threatened to crash down upon the mast, but the ship disappeared like a swan in the trough of the waves and was lifted again the next moment to the top of their towering crests. The little mermaid thought that the way the vessel flew along was most amusing, but the sailors did not. The ship creaked and cracked, the thick planks bent under the battering blows of the waves, the mast broke in two like a reed, and the ship rolled over so far to one side that the water rushed into the hold. Then the little mermaid saw that the people were in peril, while she herself had to beware of the beams and pieces of wreckage which were floating about in the sea. At one moment it was pitch-dark and she could see nothing at all; then there came a flash of lightning and it was so bright that she could recognize everybody on board. Each one was doing the best he could for himself. She looked particularly for the young Prince, and when the ship parted asunder, she saw him sink into the deep sea. Her first impulse was to be full of joy because he was coming down to her, but then she remembered that human beings could not live in the water, and that he could only come down to her father's Palace as a dead body. No, die he must not! So she swam in among the drifting beams and planks, quite forgetting that they might crush her; she dived deep into the sea, rose high up again among the waves, and at last reached the young Prince who could hardly keep on swimming in the stormy ocean. His arms and legs were beginning to fail him, his beautiful eyes were closing, he would have died had not the little mermaid come to his rescue. She held his head above the water, and let the waves carry her with him wherever they pleased.

At dawn the storm was over; not a trace of the ship was to be seen. The sun rose red and shining out of the water, and seemed to bring life and color back into the Prince's cheeks, but his eyes remained closed. The mermaid kissed his high noble brow, and stroked back his wet hair. She thought he looked like the marble statue down in her little garden; she kissed him again and wished from the bottom of her heart that he might live.

In front of her she saw the mainland, with high blue mountains on whose summits the snow lay gleaming like a flock of white swans. Down near the shore were glorious green forests, and before them lay a church or a convent—she did not quite know what it was, but at any rate it was a building. Lemon and orange trees grew in the garden, and outside the gate were tall palm trees. There the sea had formed a little cove; the water was without a ripple, but very deep close to the foot of the rock, where the fine white sand had been washed up. Thither she swam with the handsome Prince, and laid him on the sand with his head carefully raised and turned towards the warm rays of the sun.

Then the bells rang out from the great white building, and a group of young girls came through the garden. The little mermaid swam further out and hid behind some large rocks showing above the water, covered her hair and her breast with sea-foam so that no one could catch sight of her little face, and then kept watch to see who would come to the rescue of the poor shipwrecked Prince.

It was not long before one of the young girls arrived; for a moment she seemed quite frightened, then she fetched help, and the mermaid saw the Prince come to, and smile at those who stood round him, but he did not smile at her far out in the sea, for he did not know that she had saved him. She felt very sad, and when he was carried into the great building, she dived sorrowfully down into the depths and returned to her father's Palace.

She had always been quiet and pensive, but now she became much more so. Her sisters asked what she had seen on her first visit to the surface, but she would tell them nothing.

Many an evening and many a morning she rose up to the place where she had left the Prince. She saw how the fruit in the garden ripened and was gathered, she saw how the snow melted on the high mountains, but she never saw the Prince, so she always returned home sadder than before. Her only consolation was to sit in her little garden and throw her arms round the beautiful marble statue which was so like the Prince, but she took no care of her flowers—they grew as in a wilderness, all over the paths, and they wove their long stems and leaves in and out of the branches of the trees, until the whole place was shrouded in darkness.

At last she could endure it no longer, but confided in one of her sisters, and at once all the others knew about it, but nobody else, except for a few more mermaids who just told their most intimate friends. One of them knew who the Prince was; she too had seen the party that had been held in his honor, and knew whence he came and where his kingdom lay.

"Come, little sister," said the other Princesses, and with their arms about each other's shoulders, they rose in a long line up through the water opposite the place where they knew the Prince's Palace stood.

It was built of a kind of pale yellow shining stone, with a great flight of marble steps leading down into the sea. Splendid gilded cupolas were seen above the roof, and in between the pillars surrounding the whole building stood marble statues which looked as

if they were alive. Through the clear glass of the tall windows one looked into magnificent halls, where costly silk curtains and tapestries were hung, and where all the walls were covered with large paintings, which it was a pleasure to see. In the middle of the biggest hall a great fountain was playing, its jets soaring high up towards the glass dome, through which the sun shone down upon the water and upon the beautiful plants growing in the great basin.

Now she knew where he lived, and many an evening and many a night she haunted the place. She swam much closer to land than any of her sisters had dared to do, and she even went up the narrow creek under the splendid marble balcony which cast its long shadow upon the water. Here she would sit and gaze at the young Prince who thought he was quite alone in the bright moonlight.

Often in the evening she saw him sailing to the sound of music in his splendid ship with the waving flags. She peeped through the green reeds, and if the wind caught her long silver-white veil, those who saw it thought it was a swan spreading out its wings.

Many a night, when the torches of the fishing boats were shining through the darkness, she heard the fishermen praising the young Prince, and rejoiced that she had saved his life when he was tossed about half-dead on the waves, and she thought how closely his head had rested on her bosom, and how lovingly she had kissed him, though he knew nothing about it, and could not even dream of her.

She became more and more fond of human beings, and more and more did she long to be among them. Their world seemed to her much larger than her own; they could fly over the sea in ships, and climb high up the lofty mountains, above the clouds; the lands they possessed stretched with their woods and fields farther than her eyes could reach. There was so much she wanted to know, but her sisters could not answer all her questions, so she asked her old grandmother who knew so well that upper world, as she rightly called the countries above the sea.

"If human beings aren't drowned," asked the little mermaid, "can they live forever? Don't they die as we do down here in the depths of the sea?"

"Yes," answered the old lady, "they must die too, and their lifetime is even shorter than ours. We can live to be three hundred years old, but when we cease to exist, we only turn to foam on the water, and have not even a grave down here among our dear ones. We have no immortal soul, we never have another life; we are like the green reed—once it is cut, it never grows again. Human beings, on the contrary, have a soul which lives forever, which lives after the body has turned to dust. It rises up through the limpid air, up to the shining stars! Just as we rise out of the water and see the countries of the earth, so do they rise up to unknown beautiful regions which we shall never see."

"Why were we not granted an immortal soul?" asked the little mermaid in a melancholy voice. "I would gladly give the three hundred years I have to live if I could be a human being for only one single day, and then have some part in that heavenly world!"

"You must not brood over that," said her grandmother. "We have a much happier and a far better life than the people up there."

"So I am fated to die and float like foam upon the sea, and then I shall no longer hear the music of the waves, nor see the beautiful flowers and the red sun. Can I do nothing at all to win an immortal soul?"

"No," answered the old lady, "that could only happen if a human being held you so dear that you were more to him than father and mother; if he loved you with all his heart and soul, and if his right hand were joined to yours by a priest, with the promise to be faithful to you here and in all eternity, then his soul would pass into your body, and you would have a share in the happiness of mankind. He would give you a soul and yet retain his own. But that can never happen. The very thing that is considered beautiful here in the sea—

your fish's tail—is considered ugly on the earth. They have very poor judgment; people must have two clumsy supports which they call 'legs,' in order to be beautiful."

Then the little mermaid sighed, and looked sadly at her fish's tail.

"Come, let's be sprightly!" said the old lady. "Let us leap and jump about during the three hundred years we have to live; that seems a fair enough amount of time. After that we can rest the more merrily in our graves.—Tonight we are giving a Court ball."

Truly it was a magnificent affair such as you never see on earth. The walls and ceiling of the great ballroom were made of thick but transparent glass. In rows on each side stood several hundred gigantic shells, rose-red and grass-green; a blue fire was burning in each—it lit up the entire room, and, shining through the walls, lit up the sea as well. All the innumerable fishes, great and small, could be seen swimming towards the glass walls; some of them had scales gleaming scarlet, while others shone like silver and gold. Down through the middle of the hall there flowed a broad stream on which the mermen and mermaids danced to their own beautiful singing. No voices like theirs are ever heard among the people of the earth. The little mermaid sang more beautifully than anyone else, and they clapped her, and for a moment her heart was filled with joy, for she knew she had the loveliest voice of all, on the earth or in the sea. But soon she began to think once more of the world above her. She could not forget the handsome Prince, nor her sorrow at having no immortal soul like his. So she stole out of her father's Palace, and while everything within was joy and gaiety, she sat sadly outside in her little garden.

Suddenly she heard bugles sounding down through the water, and she thought, "Now he must be sailing up there, he whom I love more than father or mother, he to whom my thoughts are clinging, and in whose hand I would gladly place the happiness of my life. I will risk everything to win him and an immortal soul. While my sisters are dancing in my father's Palace, I will go to the old Sea-witch. She has always terrified me, but perhaps she can advise and help me."

So she left her garden and set out towards the roaring whirlpools, for beyond them lived the witch. The little mermaid had never been that way before. No flowers grew there nor any sea-grasses, only the bare gray sandy bottom stretched as far as the whirlpools swirling round like roaring mill-wheels and sweeping everything within reach down into the fathomless sea. She had to pass right through those crushing whirling waters to enter the territory of the Sea-witch, then for a long way the only road went over a hot bubbling morass—her peat-bog, as the witch called it. Behind it lay her house in the midst of a strange-looking forest. All the trees and bushes were polyps—half animal and half plant. They looked like hundred-headed snakes growing out of the ground. All the branches were long slimy arms with slithery worm-like fingers, moving joint by joint from the root up to the very tip. They twined round anything they could reach, never loosening their grip. Terror-stricken, the little mermaid stopped on the edge of this forest. Her heart beat faster with fear, she almost turned back, but then she thought of the Prince, and of the human soul, and her courage came back. She bound her long flowing hair tightly round her head so that the polyps might not seize her by it, she folded her arms closely across her breast, and darted off as a fish darts through the water, in among the hideous polyps which stretched out their supple arms and fingers to catch her. She saw how each of them clung tightly to something it had caught; its hundreds of little arms held their prey in an iron grip.

People who had perished at sea and sunk deep down to the bottom were visible as white human bones in among the arms of the polyps. They clutched ships' rudders and chests, and skeletons of land animals, and most horrible of all, she even saw a little mermaid whom they had caught and strangled.

She came next to a great slimy clearing in the forest, where big fat water-snakes writhed and rolled, showing their ugly yellowish-white bellies. In the center of the clearing was a house built of the bones of shipwrecked men; there sat the Sea-witch, letting a toad feed out of her mouth exactly as we let a canary eat sugar. She called the hideous fat water-snakes her little chickens, and let them creep and crawl over her great spongy bosom.

"I know what you want," said the Sea-witch. "It is very foolish of you, but all the same you shall have your way, for it will bring trouble upon you, my pretty one. You want to get rid of your fish's tail, and to have two bits of stumps to walk with instead, like the people of the earth, so that the young Prince will fall in love with you, and you will win both him and an immortal soul." Here the witch let out a laugh so loud and so ghastly that the toad and the snakes tumbled down to the ground, where they lay wallowing about.

"You have just come in time," said the witch. "Had you waited until sunrise tomorrow, I could not have helped you for a whole year. I am going to brew a potion for you. Before the sun rises you must swim to land with it, sit down on the shore, and drink it; then your tail will part in two and shrink to what the people of the earth call 'pretty legs,' but it will hurt as if a sharp sword were cutting through you. Everybody who sees you will say that you are the prettiest human being they have ever seen. You are to keep your gliding motion, no dancer will be able to move as gracefully as you, but at every step it will feel as if you were treading on a sharp-edged knife, so sharp that your feet will seem to be bleeding. If you can bear all this, I shall be able to help you."

"I can," said the little mermaid in a quivering voice, and she thought of the Prince, and of winning an immortal soul.

"But remember," said the witch, "once you have taken human

shape, you can never become a mermaid again. You can never plunge down through the water, back to your sisters and to your father's Palace, and if you do not win the love of the Prince, so that for your sake he forgets father and mother and clings to you with heart and soul, and lets the priest join your hands, making you man and wife, then you will not win an immortal soul. On the very morning after he has married someone else, your heart will break and you will become foam on the sea."

"I am willing," said the little mermaid, pale as death.

"But you will also have to pay me," said the witch, "and it is not a trifle that I require. You have the most beautiful voice of anyone down here in the depths of the sea. You think that you will be able to charm the Prince with it, but you must give that voice to me. I want the best thing you possess in exchange for my precious potion. I must drop some of my own blood into it so that the draught may be as sharp as a two-edged sword."

"But if you take my voice," said the little mermaid, "what shall I have left?"

"Your beautiful form," said the witch, "your gliding motion, and your eloquent eyes—they will be enough for you to beguile any human heart. Well, have you lost your courage? Put out your little tongue and I will cut it out and take it as my payment, and you shall have the potent draught in return."

"So be it," said the little mermaid, and the witch put her caldron on the fire to brew the magic draught. "Cleanliness is a good thing," she said, and she scoured out the caldron with the snakes that she had tied up into a knot. Then she made a cut in her breast and let her black blood drip into the caldron. The steam shaped itself into the most terrifying and horrible forms. The witch kept on throwing in different ingredients, and when the mixture was bubbling it sounded like the sobbing of a crocodile. When at last the potion was ready, it looked as clear as the clearest water.

"There you are," said the witch, and she cut out the tongue of the little mermaid, who was now dumb and could neither sing nor speak.

"If the polyps should clutch you when you are on your way back through my forest," said the witch, "just throw one single drop of this draught upon each of them, and their arms and fingers will scatter into a thousand pieces." But there was no need for the little mermaid to do that—the polyps shrank back in terror when they saw the shining potion gleaming in her hand like a twinkling star; thus she passed quickly through the forest, the bog, and the roaring whirlpools.

She could see her father's Palace. The torches had been extinguished in the great ballroom; the people were probably all asleep, but she had not the courage to approach them now that she was dumb and was going to leave them forever. It seemed as if her heart would break with sorrow. She stole into the garden, picked one flower from each of her sisters' flower-beds, blew a thousand kisses towards her home, and rose up through the deep-blue sea.

It was not yet sunrise when she saw the Prince's Palace and went up the stately marble steps. The moon was shining beautifully clear. The little mermaid drank the sharp burning draught, and she felt as if a two-edged sword cut through her delicate body; she swooned with agony and lay as if she were dead. When the sun spread its rays over the sea she awoke and felt a stinging pain, but before her stood the handsome young Prince. He fixed his coal-black eyes upon her, and under his gaze she lowered her lids and saw that her fish's tail had gone, and that she had the prettiest pair of white legs any young girl could desire; but she was naked, so she veiled herself with her long thick hair. The Prince asked who she was and how she had come there, and she looked up at him with her dark blue eyes, so mild and yet so full of sadness, for she could not speak. Then he took her by the hand and led her into the Palace. As the witch had foretold, she seemed at each step to be treading on sharp knives and pointed daggers, but she bore the pain gladly. Led by the Prince, she moved light as a bubble, and he and everyone else marveled at her graceful gliding motion.

They clad her in costly robes of silk and muslin. She was the fairest of all in the Palace, but she was dumb and could neither speak nor sing. Beautiful slave-girls, dressed in silk and gold, came before them and sang for the Prince and his royal parents. One of them sang more delightfully than any of the others, and the Prince clapped his hands and smiled at her, which saddened the little mermaid, for she knew that she herself used to sing far more beautifully; and she thought, "Oh, if he only knew that I gave away my voice forever in order to be with him!"

The slave-girls now danced gracefully and charmingly to the accompaniment of the loveliest music imaginable, and then the little mermaid lifted her pretty white arms, and rising on the tips of her toes, flitted across the floor, dancing as no one had ever danced before. With each of her movements her beauty became more and more evident, and her eyes spoke more deeply to the heart than the song of the slave-girls.

Everyone was enchanted, especially the Prince, who called her his own little foundling; and she danced again and again, though every time her foot touched the ground it seemed as if she were treading on sharp knives. The Prince said that she must always remain with him, and she was allowed to sleep on a velvet cushion outside his door.

He had a page's dress made for her, so that she might accompany him on horseback. They rode through the fragrant woods, where the green boughs brushed her shoulders, and the little birds sang, hidden among the fresh leaves. She climbed the high mountains with the Prince, and though her delicate feet bled so that even the others noticed it, she only laughed, and followed him until they could see the clouds moving far below them like flocks of birds on their way to distant lands.

At night, when the others were asleep in the Prince's Palace, she would go out on to the broad marble steps and cool her burning feet in the cold sea-water, and then she would think of her dear ones in the depths of the sea.

One night her sisters appeared arm in arm, singing mournful songs as they swam along; she beckoned to them and they recognized her and told her how much she had grieved them all. They visited the little mermaid every night after that, and once, in the far, far distance, she saw the old grandmother who had not been above the water for many years, and the Sea-king with his crown upon his head. They stretched out their hands towards her, but did not venture so near the land as her sisters.

Day by day she grew dearer to the Prince. He loved her as one loves a dear good child, but had no thought of making her his Queen, yet his wife she must be, or she could never win an immortal soul, but would become foam on the sea the morning after he wedded another.

"Am I not dearer to you than anyone else?" the little mermaid seemed to ask with her eyes, when he took her in his arms and kissed her fair brow.

"Yes, you are the dearest of all to me," said the Prince, "for you have the kindest heart of all. You are more devoted to me than anyone else, and you look like a young girl whom I once saw, but whom I shall probably never see again. I was on board a ship which was wrecked; the waves carried me ashore near a holy temple where a group of young maidens were serving. The youngest of them found me and saved my life. I saw her but twice. She is the only one in the world I could ever love, but you look so much like her that you almost take the place of her image in my heart. She belongs to that holy temple, and therefore destiny sent you to me.

We will never part."

"Alas, he does not know that I saved his life," thought the little mermaid. "It was I who carried him over the water to the wood where the temple stands. I stayed hidden in the foam to see if anyone would come. I saw the pretty maiden whom he loves better than me." And she gave a deep sigh—for mermaids have no tears. "The maiden belongs to the holy temple, he tells me, she will never come out into the world, so they will never meet again. I am with him, I see him every day. I will cherish him, love him, and give up my life to him."

But soon it was rumored that the Prince was going to marry the beautiful daughter of a neighboring King, and that was why he was fitting out such a splendid ship. They said that the Prince was paying a state visit to the country of the neighboring King, but the real reason was to see the King's daughter. He was to have a great suite with him.

The little mermaid shook her head though and laughed; she knew the Prince's thoughts far better than anyone else.

"I must go away," he had said to her. "I must go and see the beautiful Princess—my parents insist upon it; but they will not compel me to bring her home as my bride. I cannot love her! She is not like the beautiful maiden in the temple, as you are. If I ever had to choose a bride, I would sooner choose you, my dear dumb foundling with the speaking eyes." And he kissed her red lips, played with her long hair, and laid his head on her heart, so that it dreamed of human happiness and an immortal soul.

"I hope you are not afraid of the sea, my poor dumb child," he said, when they stood on the splendid ship which was to carry him to the country of the neighboring King. Then he told her of storm and calm at sea, of strange fishes in the depths of the ocean, and what divers had seen down there, and she smiled at his description, for she knew more than anyone else about the bottom of the sea.

In the moon-clear night, when all were asleep except the helmsman at the wheel, she sat by the rail, and as she gazed down through the clear water, fancied she could see her father's Palace. On the top stood her old grandmother with a silver crown on her head, gazing at the keel of the ship through the fast-flowing current. Then her sisters came up above the water and looked at her with deep sorrow in their eyes, and wrung their white hands. She beckoned to them, smiling, and tried to make them understand that she was well and happy, but when the cabin-boy came towards her, her sisters dived down again, so he felt quite certain that the gleam of white he had seen was nothing but foam on the sea.

Next morning the ship sailed into the harbor of the neighboring King's magnificent city. All the church bells rang, and from the tall towers trumpets were blown, while the soldiers stood to attention with flying colors and glittering bayonets. Each day had its own festivity, balls and parties were given all the time, but the Princess had not yet arrived. People said she was being brought up in a holy temple, where she was learning every royal accomplishment. At last she came.

The little mermaid waited anxiously to see her beauty, and she had to admit that she had never seen a more graceful form. The Princess's skin was fine and delicate, and behind the long dark eyelashes smiled a pair of dark blue eyes, full of devotion.

"It is you! You who saved me when I lay like a corpse on the shore!" said the Prince, and he clasped his blushing bride-to-be in his arms. "Oh, I am more than happy!" he said to the little mermaid. "My dearest wish, the thing I have never dared to hope for, has been granted me. You will rejoice in my happiness, for you are more devoted to me than anyone else." Then the little mermaid kissed his hand, and already her heart seemed to be breaking. The morning after his wedding would bring death to her, and change her to foam on the sea.

All the church bells were ringing; heralds rode about the streets and proclaimed the betrothal. On every altar fragrant oil was burning in costly silver lamps. The priests swung their censers, and bride and bridegroom joined hands and received the Bishop's blessing. The little mermaid, clad in silk and gold, was holding the bride's train, but her ears heard nothing of the festive music, her eyes saw nothing of the holy ceremony; she thought of the last night she had to live, and of all she had lost in this world.

That very evening, bride and bridegroom went on board the ship. Cannon were fired, banners fluttered in the wind, and in the middle of the ship a royal tent of gold and purple was set up, furnished with great sumptuous cushions on which the bridal couple were to sleep in the calm cool night.

The sails swelled out in the breeze, and the ship glided smoothly and without any perceptible motion away over the limpid sea.

When it grew dark, colored lanterns were lighted, and the sailors danced merry dances on the deck. The little mermaid could not help thinking of the first time she rose to the surface of the sea and saw a similar sight of splendor and joy. Light as a swallow in full flight she joined in the dance, and to the sound of cheers and shouting danced as she had never danced before. Her delicate feet seemed to be cut by sharp knives, but the anguish of her heart was so great that she did not feel the pain at all. She knew that this was the last evening she was to see the Prince for whom she had forsaken her people and her home, had given up her beautiful voice, and had daily suffered untold agony, while he remained unaware of it all. This was the last night she would breathe the same air as he, or behold the deep ocean and the star-blue sky. An eternal night without thought or dream awaited her who had no soul, and could not win one. The gaiety and merriment lasted until long past midnight, and the little mermaid laughed and danced with the thought of death in her heart. The Prince kissed his beautiful bride, and she played with his black hair, and arm in arm they went to rest in the splendid tent.

A hushed silence fell upon the ship; only the helmsman stood at the wheel; the little mermaid laid her white arms on the rail and gazed towards the east, waiting to see the red tinge of the dawn—the first rays of the sun, she knew, would kill her. Then she saw her sisters rising out of the sea; they were pale like herself, their long, beautiful hair no longer fluttered in the wind—it had all been cut off.

"We have given it to the witch so that she may bring you help, and save you from dying before dawn. She has given us a knife, look, here it is! Do you see its sharp edge? Before the sun rises you must plunge it into the Prince's heart, and when his warm blood splashes over your feet, they will grow into a fish's tail, and you will become a mermaid again; you will be able to come down to us in the water and live your three hundred years before you turn into dead salt sea-foam. Make haste! Either he or you must die before the sun rises. Our old grandmother has been mourning till her white hair has fallen out as ours fell under the witch's scissors. Kill the Prince and come back! Make haste! Do you see that red streak in the sky? In a few minutes the sun will rise and you must die!" Having said this, they uttered a strange deep sigh and disappeared in the waves.

The little mermaid drew back the purple curtains of the tent, and saw the beautiful bride sleeping with her head on the Prince's breast. She bent down and kissed him on his fair brow, then she looked up at the sky where the first faint flush of dawn became brighter and brighter; she looked at the sharp knife, and again fixed her eyes on the Prince who in his sleep was murmuring the name of his bride. She and she only was in his thoughts. The knife quivered in the mermaid's hand, but then she flung it far out into the waves—they gleamed red where it fell; it seemed as if drops of blood were bubbling up through the water. Once more she looked with dimming eyes upon the Prince; then she threw herself from the ship into the water, and felt her body dissolving into foam.

The sun rose out of the sea. Its rays fell mild and warm upon the death-cold sea-foam, and the little mermaid felt not the hand of

Death. She saw the bright sun, and above her floated hundreds of beautiful ethereal beings, so transparent that through them she could see the white sails of the ship and the rosy clouds of the sky; their voices were music, but so unearthly that no human ear could grasp it, just as no human eye could see their forms. Without wings they floated by their own lightness through the air. The little mermaid saw that she too had a body like theirs, and that it was freeing itself more and more from the foam.

"Towards whom am I floating?" she asked, and her voice sounded like that of the other beings, so ethereal that no earthly music could possibly render it.

"To the daughters of the air," answered the others. "The mermaid has no immortal soul, and can never gain one unless she wins the love of a human being. Her eternal life depends upon a power outside herself. The daughters of the air have no immortal soul either, but they can gain one by their good deeds. We fly to the hot countries where the torrid air of pestilence kills men; we bring cool breezes to them, we spread the fragrance of flowers through the air and send them solace and healing. When we have striven for three hundred years to do all the good we can, we receive an immortal soul and share in the everlasting happiness of mankind. You, poor little mermaid, have striven with your whole heart to do the same. By your sufferings, and by your courage in enduring them, you have raised yourself into the world of the spirits of the air, and now you can gain an immortal soul by good deeds accomplished in the course of three hundred years."

The little mermaid raised her clear translucent arms towards God's sun, and for the first time she felt tears in her eyes.

Noise and bustle had started again on the ship. She saw the Prince and his beautiful wife searching for her; then they gazed with sorrow in their hearts at the bubbling foam, as if they knew that she had thrown herself into the waves. Invisible by now, she kissed the bride on her forehead, smiled at the Prince, and soared with the other children of the air towards the rose-colored cloud floating through space.

"In this way we shall float into the Heavenly Kingdom in three hundred years."

"We may even reach it sooner," whispered one of them. "Invisibly we float into the houses of human beings where there are children, and for every day on which we find a good child who brings joy to his parents, and deserves their love, our time of probation is shortened by God. The child is unaware of it when we float through the room, and if we smile at him in our joy, one year is taken from the three hundred; but if we see a bad and naughty child, then we must weep tears of sorrow over him, and every tear adds one day to our time of probation."

THE SHEPHERDESS AND THE CHIMNEY-SWEEP

HAVE you ever seen one of those really old-fashioned cupboards, black with age, and carved all over with scrolls and foliage? Well, one exactly like that used to stand in a certain sitting-room; it had been inherited from a great-grandmother, and was decorated with roses and tulips from top to bottom. Among the extraordinary-looking flourishes were little stags sticking out their heads with many-pointed antlers; but in the middle of the cupboard there was carved the full-length figure of a man. He was excruciatingly funny to look at, and had the most excruciatingly funny grin—for you couldn't call it a laugh. He had goat's legs, little horns on his forehead, and a long beard. The children always called him "Mr. Field-and-Meadow-Marshal-Major-Company-Sergeant-Billygoat's-Legs," because it was a difficult word to say, and there are not many who are given that title. But fancy anyone having him carved! Anyhow, there he was—always gazing at the table under the mirror, where there stood a lovely china shepherdess. Her shoes were gold, and her frock was charmingly caught up with a red rose, and do you know, she also had a gold hat and a crook. She was ravishing! Close by her stood a little chimney-sweep as black as coal, but also made of china. He was just as neat and clean as anyone else, for you see, he was only a make-believe chimney-sweep; the china-manufacturer might just as well have made a Prince of him, it was all one to him.

There he stood, holding his ladder very daintily, and he had a face as pink and white as a girl's—and that was really a mistake, for he should have had a few black smudges, shouldn't he? He was standing quite close to the shepherdess; they had both been placed where they stood, and having been placed there, they had become engaged. You can see how well they suited each other. They were both young, they were both made of the same kind of china, and were both equally delicate.

Close by stood another figure, three times as big; it was an old Chinaman who could nod his head. He, too, was made of china, and he said that he was the little shepherdess's grandfather—but of course he could not prove it! He insisted that he had authority over her, and that was why he had nodded to Mr. Field-and-Meadow-Marshal-Major-Company-Sergeant-Billygoat's-Legs, when he had asked for permission to marry the little shepherdess.

"That's the kind of husband you ought to have," said the old Chinaman. "I shouldn't be at all surprised if he were made of mahogany. He can make you Mrs. Field-and-Meadow-Marshal-Major-Company-Sergeant-Billygoat's-Legs. He's got that whole cupboard full of silver, let alone what he's put away in secret hiding-places."

"But I don't want to be put into that dark cupboard," said the little shepherdess. "I've heard that he's got eleven china wives in there already."

"Then you can be the twelfth," said the Chinaman. "Tonight, as soon as the old cupboard begins to creak, your wedding shall take place, as sure as I'm a Chinaman!" And with that he nid-nodded and fell asleep.

But the little shepherdess wept and looked at her dearest dear, the china chimney-sweep.

"I'm afraid I shall have to ask you to go out into the wide world with me," she said, "because we cannot stay here."

"I'll do anything you like," said the little chimney-sweep. "Let's start at once; I feel sure I shall be able to support you by my profession."

"I do wish we were safely down from the table," she said. "I

shall never be happy until we are out in the wide world."

Then he cheered her up, and showed her where to put her little feet on the knobs and gilded foliage carved all down the leg of the table; he also used his ladder to help her—and at last there they were, safely on the floor. But when they looked at the old cupboard, there was such a commotion as you never saw! All the carved stags were sticking their heads further out, raising their antlers, and twisting their necks. Mr. Field-and-Meadow-Marshal-Major-Company-Sergeant-Billygoat's-Legs leapt high in the air, and shouted across the room to the old Chinaman, "They're running away! They're running away!"

This scared them a bit, and they jumped quickly into a drawer in the window-seat. It contained three or four incomplete packs of cards, and a little toy theater, fitted up as well as could be. A play was being given, and all the Queens—diamonds and hearts, clubs and spades—sat in the front row, fanning themselves with their tulips, and behind them stood all the Knaves, showing that they had two heads, one at the top and one at the bottom, as playing cards do have. The play was about two people who were not allowed to get married, and it made the shepherdess weep, because it was just like her own story.

"I can't bear it," she said. "I must get out of this drawer." But when they found themselves on the floor again and looked up at the table, the old Chinaman had wakened up and was rocking his whole body backwards and forwards; the lower part of him was one solid piece, you know.

"The old Chinaman is coming!" screamed the little shepherdess, and she was so upset that she fell down on her china knees.

"I've got an idea," said the chimney-sweep. "Let's hide in the big pot-pourri jar in the corner. We can lie there on roses and lavender, and throw salt in his eyes when he comes."

"That isn't enough," she said. "Besides, I know that the old

Chinaman and the pot-pourri jar were engaged once upon a time, and a little tender feeling always remains when you've once been—sort of intimate. No, there is nothing to be done but to go out into the wide world."

"Would you really be brave enough to go out into the wide world with me?" asked the chimney-sweep. "Have you ever thought how large the world is, and that we can never come back here?"

"I have," she said.

The chimney-sweep looked deep into her eyes and said: "My way goes up through the chimney. Would you really be brave enough to crawl with me through the stove and the pipes? After that we shall be inside the chimney, and once there I know exactly what to do. We shall climb so high that they can't get at us, and right at the top there is a hole leading out into the wide world."

So he led her to the door of the stove.

"It looks very black in there," she said, but all the same she followed him through all those pipes where it was as black as night.

"Now we're in the chimney," he said. "And look! look! the loveliest star is shining up there!"

It was a real star in the sky, shining right down to them as if it wished to show them the way. They clambered and they crawled; it was a difficult way to go, and so very very high! But he held her and he helped her, he showed her the best places to put her little china feet, and at last they reached the chimney-top. There they sat down, for they were exhausted, and no wonder!

Above them was the sky all sown with stars, and below them was the city with its many roofs; they gazed far out into the great wide world. The poor shepherdess had never imagined it was like that; she leaned her little head against her beloved chimney-sweep and burst out crying so desperately that the gold peeled off her sash.

"This is too much," she said, "I cannot bear it. The world is too big! I wish I were back on the little table under the mirror. I shall never feel happy until I am there again. I came with you out into the wide world; now don't you think you might take me home again, if you love me the least little bit?"

The chimney-sweep tried to reason with her, talked to her about the old Chinaman, and about Mr. Field-and-Meadow-Marshal-Major-Company-Sergeant-Billygoat's-Legs, but she sobbed so bitterly and kissed her little chimney-sweep so lovingly, that he could not help giving in, though he felt it was a mistake.

So with great difficulty they crawled back down the chimney; they crept through all the pipes—that was not at all nice—and at last they found themselves in the dark stove, where they listened behind the door with all their ears to find out what was going on in the room. Not a soul was stirring; they peeped out—oh, dear! oh, dear! There in the middle of the floor lay the old Chinaman. He had fallen down from the table as he tried to set off after them, and there he lay broken into three pieces; the whole of his back had come off in one, and his head had rolled into a corner. Mr. Field-and-Meadow-Marshal-Major-Company-Sergeant-Billygoat's-Legs was standing where he had always stood, lost in thought.

"It's awful," said the little shepherdess. "Poor old Grandfather has been broken to pieces, and it's all our fault. I shall never get over it." And she wrung her tiny little hands.

"It will be quite easy to have him riveted," said the chimney-sweep. "It will be perfectly easy to have him riveted! Don't get so excited. When his back is glued together, and a strong rivet is put in his neck, he will be as good as ever, and will be able to say all sorts of nasty things to us again."

"Do you really think so?" she said; and then they climbed back on to the table where they used to stand.

"So that's that!" said the chimney-sweep. "We might just as well have spared ourselves all this trouble."

"I do wish, though, that old Grandfather were mended," said the little shepherdess. "Do you think it will be terribly expensive?"

Well, he was mended. The family had his back glued together, he got a strong rivet in his neck, and was as good as new—but nod he could not.

"You *have* grown haughty since you got broken," said Mr. Field-and-Meadow-Marshal-Major-Company-Sergeant-Billygoat's-Legs. "I really don't think it's anything to be so awfully proud of. Am I to have her, or am I not?"

The chimney-sweep and the little shepherdess gave the old Chinaman such a pathetic look; they were so afraid that he might nod—but he could not, and he was not inclined to admit that he had got to wear a rivet in his neck for the rest of his life.

So the china pair remained together. They blessed Grandfather's rivet, and they loved one another, until in the end they fell to pieces.

THE UGLY DUCKLING

IT was so lovely in the country—it was summer! The wheat was yellow, the oats were green, the hay was stacked in the green meadows, and down there the stork went tiptoeing on his red legs, jabbering Egyptian, a language his mother had taught him. Round about the fields and meadows were great forests, and in the midst of those forests lay deep lakes. Yes, it was indeed lovely in the country! Bathed in sunshine there stood an old manor house, surrounded by a deep moat, and from the walls down to the water's edge the bank was covered with great wild rhubarb leaves so high that little children could stand upright under the biggest of them. The place was as much of a wilderness as the densest wood, and there sat a duck on her nest; she was busy hatching her ducklings, but she was almost tired of it, because sitting is such a tedious business, and she had very few callers. The other ducks thought it more fun to swim about in the moat than to come and have a gossip with her under a wild rhubarb leaf.

At last one eggshell after another began to crack open. "Cheep, cheep!" All the yolks had come to life and were sticking out their heads.

"Quack, quack," said the duck, and all her ducklings came scurrying out as fast as they could, looking about under the green leaves, and their mother let them look as much as they liked, because green is good for the eyes.

"How big the world is!" said all the ducklings, for they felt much more comfortable now than when they were lying in the egg.

"Do you imagine this is the whole of the world?" asked their mother. "It goes far beyond the other side of the garden, right into the Rector's field, but I've never been there yet. I hope you're all here," she went on, and hoisted herself up. "No, I haven't got all of you even now; the biggest egg is still there. I wonder how much longer it will take! I'm getting rather bored with the whole thing." And she squatted down again on the nest.

"Well, how are you getting on?" asked an old duck who came to call on her.

"That last egg is taking an awfully long time," said the brooding duck. "It won't break; but let me show you the others, they're the sweetest ducklings I've ever seen. They are all exactly like their father; the scamp—he never comes to see me!"

"Let me look at the egg that won't break," said the old duck. "You may be sure it's a turkey's egg. I was fooled like that once, and the trouble and bother I had with those youngsters, because they were actually afraid of the water! I simply couldn't get them to go in! I quacked at them and I snapped at them, but it was no use. Let me see the egg—of course it's a turkey's egg. Leave it alone, and teach the other children to swim."

"Oh, well, if I've taken so much trouble I may just as well sit a little longer," said the duck.

"Please yourself," said the old duck, and she waddled off.

At last the big egg cracked. "Cheep, cheep!" said the youngster, scrambling out; he was so big and ugly! The duck looked at him: "What a frightfully big duckling that one is," she said. "None of the others looked like that! Could he possibly be a turkey chick? We'll soon find out; he'll have to go into the water, even if I have to kick him in myself!"

The next day the weather was simply glorious; the sun shone on all the wild rhubarb plants. Mother Duck appeared with her family down by the moat. Splash! There she was in the water! "Quack,

quack," she said, and one duckling after another plumped in. The water closed over their heads, but they were up again in a second and floated beautifully. Their legs worked of their own accord; they were all out in the water now, and even the ugly gray creature was swimming along with them.

"That's no turkey!" she said. "Look how nicely he uses his legs, and how straight he holds himself! He's my own flesh and blood, I tell you. He isn't really so bad when you take a good look at him. Quack, quack—come along with me, I'll bring you out into the world and introduce you to the duckyard, but keep close to me or you may get stepped on, and look out for the cat!"

So they made their entrance into the duckyard. What a pandemonium there was! Two families were quarreling over an eel's head; but in the end the cat got it.

"There you are, that's the way of the world!" said Mother Duck, licking her lips, for she did so want the eel's head herself. "Now use your legs," she said. "Move about briskly and curtsey with your necks to the old duck over there; she is the most aristocratic person here, and of Spanish blood, that's why she is so stout; and be sure to observe that red rag round her leg. It's a great distinction, and the highest honor that can be bestowed upon a duck: it means that her owner wishes to keep her, and that she is to be specially noticed by man and beast. Now hurry! Don't turn your toes in; a well-brought-up duckling turns his toes out just as father and mother do—like that. That's right! Now make a deep curtsey with your necks and say, 'Quack, quack!' "

And they did as they were told; but the other ducks all round about looked at them and said out loud, "There now! have we got to have that crowd too? As if there weren't enough of us already; and ugh! what a dreadful-looking creature that duckling is! We won't put up with him." And immediately a duck rushed at him and bit him in the neck.

"Leave him alone," said the mother. "He's not bothering any of you."

"I know," said the duck who had bitten him, "but he's too big and odd. What he wants is a good smacking."

"Those are pretty children you've got, Mother," said the old duck with the rag round her leg. "They are all nice-looking except that one—he didn't turn out so well. I wish he could be made all over again!"

"That can't be done, Your Grace," said Mother Duck. "He's not handsome, but he's as good as gold, and he swims as well as any of the others, I daresay even a little better. I expect his looks will improve, or perhaps in time his size won't be so noticeable. He was in the egg too long, that's why he isn't properly shaped." And she pecked his neck and brushed up the little man. "As it happens he's a drake," she added, "so it doesn't matter quite so much. I think he'll be a strong fellow, and I'm sure he'll make his mark in the world."

"The other ducklings are lovely," said the old duck. "Make yourselves at home, and if you find an eel's head—you may bring it to me."

So at once they felt at home.

But the poor duckling who was the last to be hatched, and who looked so ugly, was bitten and buffeted about and made fun of both by the ducks and the hens. "He's too big!" they all said. And the turkey-cock, who was born with spurs and consequently thought he was an Emperor, blew himself up like a ship in full sail and made for him, gobbling and gabbling till his wattles were quite purple. The poor duckling did not know where to turn; he was so miserable because of his ugliness, and because he was the butt of the whole barnyard.

And so it went on all the first day, and after that matters grew worse and worse. The poor duckling was chased about by everyone;

his own brothers and sisters were downright nasty to him and always said, "I hope the cat gets you, you skinny bag of bones!" And even his mother said, "I wish you were miles away!" And the ducks bit him and the hens pecked him, and the girl who fed them kicked him with her foot.

So, half running and half flying, he got over the fence.

The little birds in the bushes rose up in alarm. "That's because I'm so ugly," thought the duckling, and closed his eyes, but he kept on running, and finally came out into the great marsh where the wild ducks lived. There he lay the whole night long, tired and downhearted.

In the morning the wild ducks flew up and looked at their new companion. "What sort of a fellow are you?" they asked, and the duckling turned in all directions, bowing to everybody as nicely as he could.

"You're appallingly ugly!" said the wild ducks, "but why should we care so long as you don't marry into our family?" Poor thing! as if he had any thought of marrying! All he wanted to do was to lie among the reeds, and to drink a little marsh water.

So he lay there for two whole days, and then came two wild geese, or rather ganders, for they were two young men; they had not been out of the egg very long, and that was why they were so cocky.

"Listen, young fellow," they said. "You're so ugly that we quite like you. Will you join us and be a bird of passage? Close by, in another marsh there are some lovely wild geese, all nice young girls, and they can all say 'Quack.' You're so ugly that you might appeal to them."

Two shots rang out—bang! bang!—both ganders fell dead among the reeds, and the water was reddened with their blood. Bang! bang! was heard again, and whole flocks of wild geese flew up from the reeds, and—bang! bang! bang! again and again. A great shoot was going on. The men were lying under cover all round the marsh, and some of them were even up in the trees whose branches stretched out above the reeds. Blue smoke drifted in among the dark trees and was carried far out over the water. Through the mud came the gun-dogs—splash! splash!—bending down the reeds and rushes on every side. The poor duckling was scared out of his wits, and tried to hide his head under his wing, when suddenly a fierce-looking dog came close to him, with his tongue hanging far out of his mouth, and his wild eyes gleaming horribly. He opened his jaws wide, showed his sharp teeth, and—splash! splash!—off he went without touching the duckling.

"Thank heaven!" he sighed. "I'm so ugly that even the dog won't bother to bite me!"

And so he lay perfectly still, while the shots rattled through the reeds as gun after gun was fired.

It was towards evening when everything quieted down, but the poor duckling dared not stir yet. He waited several hours before he looked about him, and then hurried away from the marsh as fast as he could. He ran over field and meadow, hardly able to fight against the strong wind.

Late that night he reached a wretched little hut, so wretched, in fact, that it did not know which way to fall, and that is why it remained standing upright. The wind whistled so fiercely round the duckling that the poor thing simply had to sit down on his little tail to resist it.

The storm grew worse and worse. Then he noticed that the door had come off one of its hinges and hung so crooked that he could slip into the room through the opening, and that is what he did.

An old woman lived here with her tom-cat and her hen. The cat, whom she called "Sonny," knew how to arch his back and purr; in fact he could even give out sparks, but for that you had to rub his fur the wrong way. The hen had little short legs and was called

"Stumpy." She was an excellent layer and the old woman loved her as her own child.

Next morning they at once noticed the strange duckling; the cat began to purr and the hen to cluck.

"What's the matter?" asked the old woman, looking about her; but her eyes were not very good, and so she mistook the duckling for a fat duck that had lost her way. "What a windfall!" she said. "Now I shall have duck's eggs—if it doesn't happen to be a drake. We must make sure of that." So the duckling was taken on trial for three weeks, but not a single egg came along.

Now the cat was master of the house, and the hen was mistress, and they always said, "We, and the world"; for they imagined themselves to be not only half the world, but by far the better half. The duckling thought that other people might be allowed to have an opinion too, but the hen could not see that at all.

"Can you lay eggs?" she asked.

"No."

"Well, then, you'd better keep your mouth shut!"

And the cat said, "Can you arch your back, purr, and give out sparks?"

"No."

"Well, then, you can't have any opinion worth offering when sensible people are speaking."

The duckling sat in a corner, feeling very gloomy and depressed; then he suddenly thought of the fresh air and the bright sunshine, and such a longing came over him to swim in the water that he could not help telling the hen about it.

"What's the matter with you?" asked the hen. "You haven't got anything to do, that's why you get these silly ideas. Either lay eggs or purr and you'll soon be all right."

"But it's so delightful to swim in the water," said the duckling, "so delightful to get it over your head and dive down to the bottom!"

"Yes, it must be delightful!" said the hen. "You've gone crazy, I think. Ask the cat, the cleverest creature I know, if he likes swimming or diving. I say nothing of myself. Ask our mistress, the old woman, as well; no one in the world is wiser than she. Do you think she would like to swim, or to get the water over her head?"

"You don't understand me," said the duckling.

"Well, if we don't understand you, then who would? You surely don't imagine you're wiser than the cat or the old woman?—not to mention myself, of course. Don't give yourself such airs, child, but be grateful to your Maker for all the kindness you have received. Didn't you get into a warm room, and haven't you fallen in with people who can teach you a thing or two? But you talk such nonsense, it's no fun at all to have you about. Believe me, I wish you well. I tell you unpleasant things, but that's the way to know one's real friends. Come on, hurry up, see that you lay eggs, and do learn how to purr or to give out sparks!"

"I think I had better go out into the wide world," said the duckling.

"Please yourself," said the hen.

So the duckling went away: he swam in the water and dived down into it, but he was still snubbed by every creature because of his ugliness.

Autumn set in. The leaves in the woods turned yellow and brown: the wind caught them and whirled them about; up in the air it looked very cold. The clouds hung low, heavy with hail and snowflakes, and on the fence perched the raven, trembling with the cold and croaking, "Caw! Caw!" The mere thought of it was enough to make anybody shiver. The poor duckling was certainly to be pitied!

One evening, when the sun was setting in all its splendor, a large flock of big handsome birds came out of the bushes. The duckling had never before seen anything quite so beautiful as these birds. They were dazzlingly white, with long supple necks—they were swans! They uttered a most uncanny cry, and spread their splendid great wings to fly away from the cold regions, away to warmer countries, to open lakes. They rose so high, so very high in the air, that a strange feeling came over the ugly little duckling as he watched them. He turned round and round in the water like a wheel, craned his neck to follow their flight, and uttered a cry so loud and strange that it frightened him.

He could not forget those noble birds, those happy birds, and when they were lost to sight he dived down to the bottom of the water; then when he came up again he was quite beside himself.

He did not know what the birds were called, nor where they were flying to, and yet he loved them more than he had ever loved anything. He did not envy them in the least; it would never have occurred to him to want such beauty for himself. He would have been quite content if only the ducks would have put up with him—the poor ugly creature!

And the winter grew so cold, so bitterly cold. The duckling was forced to swim about in the water to keep it from freezing altogether, but every night the opening became smaller and smaller; at last it froze so hard that the ice made cracking noises, and the duckling had to keep on paddling to prevent the opening from closing up. In the end he was exhausted and lay quite still, caught in the ice.

Early next morning a farmer came by, and when he saw him he went on to the ice, broke it with his wooden shoe, and carried him home to his wife. There the duckling revived.

The children wanted to play with him, but he thought they meant to do him harm, so he fluttered, terrified, into the milk-pail, splashing the milk all over the room. The woman screamed and threw up her hands in fright. Then he flew into the butter-tub, and from that into the flour-barrel and out again. What a sight he was! The woman shrieked and struck at him with the tongs. Laughing and shouting, the children fell over each other trying to catch him. Fortunately the door was open, so the duckling dashed out into the bushes and lay there in the newly fallen snow, as if in a daze.

It would be too sad, however, to tell all the trouble and misery he had to suffer during that cruel winter. . . . When the sun began to shine warmly he found himself once more in the marsh among the reeds. The larks were singing—it was spring, beautiful spring!

Then suddenly he spread his wings; the sound of their whirring made him realize how much stronger they had grown, and they

carried him powerfully along. Before he knew it, he found himself in a great garden where the apple trees stood in bloom, and the lilac filled the air with its fragrance, bending down the long green branches over the meandering streams.

It was so lovely here, so full of the freshness of spring. And look! from out of the thicket in front of him came three beautiful white swans. They ruffled their feathers proudly, and floated so lightly on the water. The duckling recognized the glorious creatures, and felt a strange sadness come over him.

"I will fly near those royal birds, and they will peck me to death for daring to bring my ugly self near them. But that doesn't matter in the least! Better to be killed by them than to be bitten by the ducks, pecked by the hens, kicked by the girl in charge of the hen-run, and suffer untold agony in winter."

Then he flew into the water and swam towards the beautiful swans. They saw him and dashed at him with outspread rustling feathers. "Kill me," said the poor creature, and he bowed his head down upon the surface of the stream, expecting death. But what was this he saw mirrored in the clear water? He saw beneath him his own image, but it was no longer the image of an awkward dirty gray bird, ugly and repulsive—he himself was a swan!

It does not matter being born in a duckyard, if only one has lain in a swan's egg.

He felt quite glad to have been through so much trouble and adversity, for now he could fully appreciate not only his own good fortune, but also all the beauty that greeted him. The great swans swam round him and stroked him with their beaks.

Some little children came into the garden to throw bread and corn into the water, and the youngest exclaimed, "There's a new one!" And the other children chimed in, "Yes, there's a new one!" They clapped their hands, danced about, and ran to fetch their father and mother.

Bread and cake were thrown into the water, and everyone said, "The new one is the most beautiful of all! He's so young and handsome!" And the old swans bowed to him.

That made him feel quite embarrassed, and he put his head under his wing, not knowing what it was all about. An overwhelming happiness filled him, and yet he was not at all proud, for a good heart never becomes proud.

He remembered how once he had been despised and persecuted; and now he heard everyone saying that he was the most beautiful of all beautiful birds.

And the lilac bushes dipped their branches into the water before him; and the sun shone warm and mild. He rustled his feathers and held his graceful neck high, and from the depths of his heart he joyfully exclaimed, "I never dreamt that so much happiness was possible when I was the ugly duckling."

THE TINDER-BOX

A SOLDIER came marching down the high-road. Left! Right! Left! Right! He had his knapsack on his back and a sword at his side, for he had been to the wars, and now he was on his way home. As he was marching along, he met an old witch on the high-road. She was the ugliest sight you ever saw—her lower lip hung right down on her chest. Said she, "Good evening, soldier. What a nice sword you've got, and what a big knapsack! You're a proper soldier! Now you shall have as much money as you want."

"That's very kind of you, old witch," said the soldier.

"Do you see that big tree?" said the witch, pointing to the one that stood close to them. "It's quite hollow! Climb up to the top and you'll see a hole; let yourself slide through it and you'll get deep down into the tree. I'll tie a rope round your waist so that I can hoist you up again when you shout for me!"

"What do you want me to do at the bottom of the tree?" asked the soldier.

"Fetch money!" said the witch. "Let me tell you that when you get down to the bottom of the tree, you'll find yourself in a large passage. It's perfectly light because there are hundreds of lamps burning in it. Next you'll see three doors; you can open them all, for the keys are in the locks. If you go into the first room, there in the middle of the floor you'll see a big chest; on top of it sits a dog with a pair of eyes as big as saucers, but never you mind about that! I'll give you my blue checked apron. Spread it out on the floor, then quickly grab the dog, put him on my apron, open the chest, and take as many pennies as you like. They're all copper, but if you'd rather have silver, then you'd better go into the next room. There sits a dog with eyes as big as mill-wheels, but never you mind about that! Put him down on my apron and help yourself to the money. However, if you want gold, you can get that too—and as much as you can carry—when you go into the third room. But I warn you, the dog that sits on the chest there has two eyes, each of them as big as the Round Tower. There's a dog for you, and no mistake! But never you mind about that! Just put him down on my apron, then he won't do you any harm, and you can take as much gold as you like out of the chest."

"That's not a bad idea!" said the soldier. "But what am I to give you in return, old witch? For I suppose you want your share."

"No," said the witch, "I don't want a single penny. I only want you to bring me an old tinder-box which my grandmother forgot the last time she was down there."

"Right you are! Tie the rope round my middle," said the soldier.

"Here it is," said the witch, "and here's my blue checked apron."

So the soldier scrambled up into the tree, let himself drop down through the hole, and there he was, as the witch had said, in the big passage where the hundreds of lamps were burning.

Then he opened the first door. Ugh! there sat the dog with eyes as big as saucers glaring at him.

"You're a handsome fellow!" said the soldier. He set him down on the witch's apron, and took as many coppers as he could carry in his pockets. Then he shut the chest, put the dog back in his place, and went into the second room. Gracious! there sat the dog with eyes as big as mill-wheels!

"You shouldn't glare at me like that!" said the soldier. "You might strain your eyes." Then he set the dog down on the witch's apron, but when he saw the masses of silver coins in the chest, he threw away all the coppers he had and filled both pockets and knapsack with nothing but silver. And now he went into the third room.

Horrors! The dog in there actually had two eyes as big as the Round Tower, and they were turning round in his head like wheels!

"Good evening!" said the soldier, and he saluted, for never in his life had he seen such a dog. But after he had looked at him for a bit he thought to himself, "That will do." Then he lifted him down on the floor and opened the chest. By Jove, what a lot of gold there was! Enough to buy the whole of Copenhagen, as well as all the cake-woman's sugar pigs, all the tin soldiers, whips, and rocking-horses in the world. There was money if ever there was any! So the soldier promptly threw away all the silver coins he had stuffed into his pockets and knapsack, and took gold instead. He filled pockets, knapsack, cap, and boots to the brim so that he could hardly walk. Now he really had got some money! He put the dog back on the chest, slammed the door, and then shouted up through the tree, "Now haul me up, old witch!"

"Have you got the tinder-box?" asked the witch.

"Bother!" said the soldier. "I'd clean forgotten it." And he went straight back to get it. The witch hoisted him up, and there he was once more on the high-road, with his pockets, boots, knapsack and cap all filled with gold.

"What do you want the tinder-box for?" asked the soldier.

"That's none of your business!" said the witch. "You've got your money, now give me the tinder-box!"

"Stuff and nonsense!" said the soldier. "Tell me at once what you want it for, or I'll draw my sword and cut your head off."

"I shan't!" said the witch.

So the soldier cut her head off. There she lay!

But he tied all his money up in her apron, slung the bundle over his shoulder, put the tinder-box in his pocket, and went straight to the town. It was a fine town, and he put up at the very finest inn. He ordered the very finest rooms and the food he liked the best, for he was rich now that he had all that money.

The servant who had to clean his boots could not help thinking that they were rather shabby old things for such a rich man to have, but the soldier hadn't yet bought himself any new ones. Next day, however, he got decent boots and smart clothes. He had now become a fashionable gentleman, and people told him about all the sights of their town, about their King, and what a pretty Princess his daughter was.

"Where is she to be seen?" asked the soldier.

"She's not to be seen at all!" everyone said. "She lives in a big copper castle with lots and lots of walls and towers all round it. Nobody but the King can come and go as he likes because it has been foretold that she'll marry a common soldier, and the King doesn't fancy the idea."

"I should like to see her," thought the soldier, but of course that was absolutely out of the question.

And now he had a jolly good time. He went to the theater, he drove in the Royal Park, and he gave pots of money to the poor. That was a very nice thing to do, for he remembered so well from the old days how awful it was to be without a single penny. Now that he was rich and well-dressed, he suddenly got heaps of friends who all said what a splendid fellow he was, a real gentleman, and that flattered his vanity. But as he was spending a good deal of money every day and never making any, he soon found himself with only twopence left, and had to move from the nice rooms he had occupied and live in a poky little attic right up under the roof. He had to clean his own boots and mend them with a darning needle, and none of his friends came to see him for there were so many stairs to climb.

One evening when it was quite dark and he could not even buy himself a candle, he suddenly remembered there was a piece of one in the tinder-box the witch had sent him down into the tree to get for her. He took out the tinder-box and the candle-end, but the very instant he struck a light and the spark flew from the flint, the door sprang open, and the dog that he had seen down in the tree, with eyes as big as saucers, stood before him and said, "What are your lordship's commands?"

"What's this?" said the soldier. "I call that a jolly fine tinder-box if I can get anything I want so easily. Fetch me some money!" he said to the dog, and pop! he had gone. Pop! he was back again, holding a large bag of pennies in his mouth.

The soldier now realized what a precious tinder-box it was. If he struck once, the dog which sat on the chest with the coppers appeared; if he struck twice, it was the one that had the silver money; and if he struck three times there was the dog with the gold. So the soldier moved back into his nice rooms, put on his smart clothes, and at once all his friends knew him again, and of course were tremendously fond of him.

He suddenly thought to himself, "It seems to me rather queer that one can't get a sight of that Princess! She's supposed to be so very pretty according to what they all say, but what's the use if she's to stay forever inside the big copper castle with all those towers? Can't I manage to see her somehow? Where's that tinder-box of mine?" So he struck a light and pop! there was the dog with eyes as big as saucers.

"I know it's the middle of the night," said the soldier, "but I do so want to see the Princess, if only for a minute."

In a flash the dog was out of the door, and before the soldier had time to think, he was back again with the Princess; she was sitting fast asleep on the dog's back, and she was so lovely that anybody could see she was a real Princess. The soldier could not help it, he simply had to kiss her, for he was a true soldier.

Then the dog ran back with the Princess, but in the morning, when the King and Queen were having breakfast, the Princess said she had had such a strange dream about a dog and a soldier. She had been riding on the dog and the soldier had kissed her.

"That's a pretty tale, I must say!" exclaimed the Queen.

One of the old ladies-in-waiting was ordered to keep watch the following night at the Princess's bedside to see whether it was really a dream, or what else it could be.

The soldier was dying to see the lovely Princess again, so the dog came in the night, picked her up and ran off as fast as he could, but the old lady-in-waiting put on her rubber boots and ran after him just as fast. When she saw them disappear into a large house, she thought, "Now I know where it is," and she drew a large cross on the door with a bit of chalk. Then she went back home to bed, and the dog came back too with the Princess. But when he saw that there was a cross drawn on the door where the soldier lived, he got a bit of chalk as well and drew crosses on all the doors in the whole town, and that was clever of him, for now the lady-in-waiting could not find the right door, when there was a cross on every one of them.

Early in the morning, the King and Queen, the old lady-in-waiting, and all the officers came to see where the Princess had been.

"There it is," said the King, when he saw the first door with a cross on it.

"No, it's there, my dear," said the Queen who saw the next door with a cross on it.

"But here's one, and there's one," they all said; wherever they looked there were crosses on the doors. Then they realized it was no use searching.

The Queen, however, was a very clever woman who could do other things than just drive about in a coach. She took her large gold scissors, cut up a big piece of silk and made a nice little bag of it. She filled it with fine buckwheat flour, tied it on to the Princess's back, and when that was done, she snipped a little hole in the bag so that the buckwheat flour could trickle out wherever the Princess went.

That night the dog came again, took the Princess on his back and ran off with her to the soldier who loved her so very much, and who would have given anything to be a Prince so as to be able to make her his wife.

The dog never noticed how the buckwheat flour was trickling out all the way from the castle as far as the soldier's window up to which he was climbing with the Princess. Next morning it was obvious to the King and Queen where their daughter had been, so the soldier was arrested and clapped into prison. There he sat. Ugh! how dark and dismal it was, and besides they said to him: "Tomorrow you're going to be hanged." It wasn't much of a joke to hear that, and he'd left his tinder-box behind at the inn. Next morning he could see through the iron bars of the little window how people were hurrying out of the town to see him hanged. He heard the drums and saw the soldiers march off. Everybody was running; among the crowd there was a cobbler's apprentice wearing a leather apron and slippers; he was galloping on at such a pace that one of his slippers came off and flew against the wall, where the soldier was peering through the iron bars.

"Hi! my lad! You needn't be in such a hurry," shouted the soldier. "Nothing will happen till I get there, but I wish you would run to my lodging and get me my tinder-box. I'll give you fourpence for your trouble, but you must go like the wind." The cobbler's apprentice was only too anxious to earn the fourpence, so he dashed off to get the tinder-box, gave it to the soldier and—well, just you wait and see.

Outside the town a great gallows had been built: soldiers and hundreds of thousands of people stood round it. The King and Queen sat on a splendid throne just opposite the Judge and the whole Council.

The soldier was already standing on the ladder, but just as they were going to put the noose round his neck, he said that it was customary to grant a criminal one harmless request before he suffered death. He would very much like to smoke a pipe of tobacco—it would be the last pipe he could smoke in this world.

The King had not the heart to refuse him that, so the soldier took his tinder-box and struck a light. One, two, three! Look! There were all the dogs, the one with eyes as big as saucers, the one with eyes like mill-wheels, and the one with eyes as big as the Round Tower.

"Save me and don't let them hang me!" said the soldier. Then the dogs went for the Judge and the whole Council, seized one by the legs, another by the nose, and tossed them so many furlongs up into the air that they fell down and were smashed to pieces.

"Not me, not me!" said the King, but the biggest dog seized both him and the Queen and tossed them up in the air after all the others. Then the soldiers got frightened, and all the people shouted, "Soldier-lad, you shall be our King and marry the beautiful Princess!"

So they put the soldier in the King's coach, and all three dogs danced in front of it and shouted "Hurrah!" The boys whistled between their fingers and the soldiers presented arms. The Princess got out of the copper castle and became Queen, and that suited her down to the ground. The wedding festivities lasted for a week, and all the dogs sat down with the other guests and stared in round-eyed wonder.

THE STORY OF A MOTHER

A MOTHER was sitting watching her little child. She was full of sorrow, full of fear that it would die. The child was deathly pale, its little eyes were closed, it breathed very softly, now and then heavily as if it were sighing, and the mother looked at the darling little soul even more sadly than she did before.

There was a knocking at the door and in came a poor old man; he was wrapped in what seemed to be a great horse-blanket, for that is a very warm thing, and he needed it badly against the winter's cold. Outside everything was covered with ice and snow, and the wind cut one's face like a knife.

As the old man was shivering with cold, and the little child had dropped off to sleep for a moment, the mother put a small mug of beer on the stove and warmed it for him. The old man sat rocking the cradle, while the mother sat down on a chair close beside him, watching her sick child who was breathing so heavily. She lifted its little hand.

"Tell me, you don't think I shall lose him, do you?" she said. "The Lord will not take him away from me, will He?"

And the old man, who was Death himself, nodded in such a strange way that it might just as well have meant yes as no. The mother bowed her head, and tears streamed down her cheeks; her head became heavy, for she had not closed her eyes for three days and nights, and now she slept, but only for a moment; then she wakened with a start, shivering with cold.

"What was that?" she said, looking about everywhere, but the old man had gone, and her child had gone too: Death had taken the child away with him. In the corner the old clock started whirring and whirring, the heavy lead weight ran right down to the floor—plump!—and the clock stopped.

But the poor mother rushed out of the house calling for her child.

Out in the snow sat a woman in long black clothes, and she said, "Death has been in your room, I saw him hurrying away with your little child. He travels faster than the wind, and he never brings back what he has taken away."

"Just tell me which way he went," said the mother. "Tell me which way and I will find him."

"I know the way," said the woman in black, "but before I tell you, you must sing me all the songs you used to sing to your child. I love those songs; I have heard them so often before. I am Night. I saw your tears when you sang them."

"I will sing them all—all," said the mother. "But do not stop me now, I must catch him up, I must find my child!"

But Night sat silent and still, so the mother wrung her hands and sang and wept. Many were the songs she sang, but many more were her tears. At last Night said, "Go into the dark pine wood and turn to the right; that is where I saw Death disappear with your child."

Deep in the woods the roads crossed, and she no longer knew which way to go. There stood a thorn-bush with neither leaf nor flower on it, and no wonder! for it was cold wintry weather and the branches were coated with ice.

"Did you not see Death pass by with my little child?"

"Yes," said the thorn-bush, "but I will not tell you which way he went unless you warm me at your heart. I am freezing to death, and I am turning to ice."

So she pressed the thorn-bush to her breast as tightly as she could to make it really warm, and the thorns pierced deep into her flesh so that her blood came out in great drops, but the thorn-bush grew fresh green leaves and flowers in the cold winter's night—such was

the warmth of a sorrowful mother's heart. The thorn-bush then told her the right road to take.

She came next to a great lake on which were neither ships nor boats. The water was not frozen hard enough to bear her, nor was it open or shallow enough for her to wade through, yet cross it she must to find her child. And so she lay down to drink the lake dry, but that of course was impossible for a human being, though the poor mother thought that perhaps a miracle might happen.

"No, that will never do," said the lake. "You and I ought to come to some agreement. I love to collect pearls, and your eyes are the clearest I have ever seen. If you will cry them out for me, I will carry you over to the great greenhouse where Death lives and looks after the trees and flowers. Each of them is a human life!"

"Oh, what would I not give to reach my child!" said the mother, who was already exhausted with weeping, and she wept more than ever, and her eyes sank down to the bottom of the lake and became two precious pearls. Then the lake lifted her as if she had been in a swing, and in one sweep she was borne to the opposite shore, where there stood a strange house extending for miles and miles. It might have been a mountain with forests and caverns, or a real house made by man, but the poor mother could not see it, for, as you remember, she had cried her eyes out.

"Where shall I find Death, who has taken my little child?" she asked.

"He has not come yet," said the old woman, who was keeper of the graves and custodian of the great greenhouse of Death. "But how have you been able to find your way here, and who has helped you?"

"Our Lord has helped me," she said. "He is merciful, and you will be merciful, too. Where shall I find my child?"

"I do not know him," said the woman, "and as for you, you cannot see. Many flowers and trees have withered this night, and

Death will soon come and transplant them. I suppose you know that every human being has his life-tree or flower according to his nature; they look like other plants, but they have a heart that beats. A child's heart beats too. Be guided by that and you may perhaps recognize your own child's heart-beat. But what will you give me if I tell you what to do next?"

"I have nothing to give," said the grief-stricken mother, "but I will go to the ends of the earth for you!"

"But that is of no use to me," said the woman. "However, you can give me your long black hair. You know yourself that it is beautiful, and I admire it. I will exchange it for my own which is white, and that is better than nothing!"

"Is that all you ask for?" she said. "I will gladly give it to you." And she gave her beautiful black hair in exchange for the old woman's which was white.

Then they went into Death's vast greenhouse, where flowers and trees were growing in weird confusion. There were delicate hyacinths under glass bells, and there were great healthy peonies. Water plants were growing there, a few of them quite fresh, but others sickly-looking, with water-snakes crawling over them, and black crayfish pinching their stems. There were imposing palm trees, oaks and plane trees, parsley and flowering thyme: every tree and every flower had a person's name, for each was a human life, and the name belonged to a person still living in China, Greenland—in fact everywhere in the world. There were big trees crammed into little pots which were almost bursting, and also in several places there were dull little flowers coddled and nursed in rich moss-covered earth. And the grief-stricken mother bent over all the tiniest plants and listened to the human heart beating in each one, and out of millions she at once recognized that of her own child.

"That's it!" she cried, and stretched her hands over a little blue crocus which was drooping feebly to one side.

"Do not touch that flower!" said the old woman, "but stay here, and when Death comes—I am expecting him any moment—stop him from pulling up the plant. Threaten him that you will do the same to the other flowers, and that will frighten him. He is responsible to God for them; not a single one may be uprooted until He gives permission."

Suddenly icy gusts of wind rushed through the place, and the blind mother felt that Death had come.

"How did you find your way here?" he asked. "How could you get here quicker than I?"

"I am a mother," she said.

Death stretched out his long hand towards the little delicate flower, but she held her hands tightly clasped round it, protecting it, though she was terrified lest she should touch the petals. Then Death breathed upon her hands, and she felt his breath colder than the coldest wind, and they fell, quite limp.

"You cannot fight against me," said Death.

"But our Lord can!" she said.

"I only do His will," said Death. "I am His gardener. I take all His flowers and trees and replant them in the great Garden of Paradise, in the Unknown Land, but how they grow there, and what it is like there, I dare not tell you."

"Give me back my child!" said the mother, weeping and imploring. Suddenly she clutched a beautiful flower in each hand, and cried out to Death, "I shall uproot all your flowers, for I am desperate!"

"Do not touch them," said Death. "You say that you are desperate, yet you would cause the same despair to another mother."

"Another mother!" exclaimed the poor woman, immediately dropping the flowers.

"Here, I give you back your eyes," said Death. "I fished them up from the lake—they were shining so brightly. I did not know that they were yours. They are clearer than ever, so take them back and look into the deep well over there. I will tell you the names of the two flowers you were going to uproot, and you will see their whole future, their whole human life, you will see what you were about to disturb and destroy."

And she looked down into the well; it was a joy to see how one of the flowers became a blessing to the world, radiating happiness and goodwill.

Then she saw the life of the other—it was all sorrow and need, horror and misery.

"Both lives are the will of God," said Death.

"Which is the flower destined for misery and which for happiness?" she asked.

"That I refuse to tell you," said Death, "but this much you shall know: one of the flowers was your own child's; it was your child's fate that you saw, your own child's future."

Then the mother shrieked in terror. "Which of them was my child? Tell me! Save my innocent one! Save my child from all that misery! Carry him away rather. Carry him into God's Kingdom! Forget my tears, forget my prayers, forget all that I have said and done!"

"I do not understand you," said Death. "Do you want your child back, or shall I take him with me to that place of which you know nothing?"

Then the mother wrung her hands, fell on her knees and prayed to our Lord: "Don't listen when I pray against Thy will, for Thou knowest best. Don't listen! Don't listen!"

And she bowed her head in submission.

And Death carried her child into the Unknown Land.

THE SHIRT COLLAR

ONCE upon a time there was an elegant gentleman whose whole outfit consisted of a bootjack and a comb, but he also had the most wonderful shirt collar in the world, and it's about this shirt collar that we're to hear a story.

The collar had now arrived at an age when he began to think of getting married, and it so happened that in the wash he found himself next to a garter.

"My word!" exclaimed the collar. "I've never seen anyone so slender, so fine, so soft and so dainty as you. May I ask your name?"

"I won't tell you," said the garter.

"Where do you belong?" asked the collar.

But the garter was overcome with shyness, and found it rather embarrassing to answer such a question.

"I should imagine that you're a belt," said the collar. "I mean a sort of inner belt. I quite realize that you're useful as well as ornamental, my pretty one."

"I forbid you to speak to me," said the garter. "I can't see that I've given you any encouragement."

"The mere fact of being so beautiful is encouragement enough," said the collar.

"Please don't come any nearer," said the garter. "You look so masculine."

"Well, after all, I'm an elegant gentleman," said the collar. "I own a bootjack and a comb." Now that was not true at all, for it was his master who owned them, but he was boasting.

"Keep your distance," said the garter. "I'm not accustomed to such familiarity."

"Prude!" said the collar.

At that very moment he was taken out of the washtub, starched, hung over a chair in the sun, and laid on the ironing board. Then the hot iron appeared on the scene.

"Honored Madam," said the collar, "fascinating little widow, my blood is stirring within me. I shall never be the same again. You're taking the crease out of me! You're burning a hole in me! Oh!—will you be my wife?"

"Rag!" said the iron, and she passed haughtily over the collar, for she fancied she was a steam-engine running on a railway track, pulling carriages behind her.

"Rag!" she said again.

The collar was a bit frayed at the edges, so the cutting-out scissors arrived to snip off the ends.

"Oh!" said the collar, "I can see you're a Première Danseuse. How magnificently you point your toes! I've never seen anything more fascinating. No one in the world can do that like you."

"I know," said the scissors.

"You really ought to be a countess," said the collar. "All I possess is an elegant gentleman, a bootjack, and a comb. Oh, if I only possessed an earldom!"

"As I live and breathe, he is proposing to me!" said the infuriated scissors, and gave him such a snip that he had to be scrapped.

"Now I shall have to propose to the comb," said the collar. "It's very remarkable how you keep all your teeth, my pretty one. Have you never thought of getting married?"

"Of course I have," said the comb. "Didn't you know that I'm engaged to the bootjack?"

"Engaged!" exclaimed the collar.

There was nobody left to propose to, and so he disdainfully turned his back on love-making.

A long time passed, and the collar found himself at the paper-mill in a box where there was a social gathering of rags; the upper ten on one side, and the rag-tag and bob-tail on the other, which is quite as it should be.

Everyone had a great deal to tell, but the collar had the most, for he was a consummate braggart.

"You've no idea how many sweethearts I've had," he said. "They would never give me a moment's peace. After all, I was a stiff and starched gentleman once. I had a bootjack and a comb that I never used. You should have seen me then—you should have seen me when I had a day off! Never shall I forget my first love. She was a belt, so lovely, so soft and charming! She threw herself into a washtub for my sake. There was also a widow; she was red-hot for me, but I gave her the slip and she turned black again. Then there was a Première Danseuse. She gave me the cut which you can still see—a fiery minx, she was! Even my own comb was mad about me, and lost all her teeth from unrequited love. Oh, yes, I've had plenty of experiences like that. But the gart—I mean the belt who threw herself into the washtub, is the one I feel most sorry for. I've a great deal on my conscience, it's about time I was made into white paper."

And that is what actually happened. All the rags were made into white paper, but the collar became that very piece of white paper we see here, the very one on which this story is printed. And that was because he boasted so dreadfully of what he had never been. So let us remember not to behave like that, for who knows? One day we might land in the rag-bag, be made into a piece of white paper, and have our whole life's history, even the most intimate details, printed on the front, and so publish it abroad ourselves—just like the collar.

THE HAPPY FAMILY

YOU know, don't you, that the biggest green leaf in this country is the leaf of the wild rhubarb; if you hold it in front of your little tummy, it's just as good as an apron; and if you put it on top of your head you'll find that in rainy weather it will almost do for an umbrella, for it's so tremendously big. The wild rhubarb plant never grows alone; no, where you see one, you see many; it's a perfect wonder, and all this wonder is food for snails.

The big white snails which in olden days fashionable people used to make into stews to eat, and say, "Umm, how delicious!"—for they really did think that snail-stew tasted delicious—these snails lived on wild rhubarb leaves, and that's why the wild rhubarb had been sown.

Well, there was an old Manor House where snails weren't eaten any more; they had died out, but the wild rhubarb had not. It grew and grew all over the paths and all over the flower-beds; it was impossible to keep it down. The place became a perfect forest of wild rhubarb; here and there stood an apple or plum tree, but except for that nobody would ever have dreamt it was a garden; there was nothing but wild rhubarb plants, and in the midst of them lived the last two old, incredibly old snails.

They themselves did not know how old they were, but they could remember very well that there had once been a great many more of them; that they were the descendants of a family from foreign parts, and that the whole forest had been planted for them and theirs. They had never been out of it, but they knew that there was something else in the world, something that was called the "Manor

House"; up there one was boiled, and then one turned black, and then one was laid upon a silver dish, but what happened after that, nobody knew. However, what it felt like to be boiled and to be laid upon a silver dish, they could not imagine, but it was said to be wonderful and uncommonly stylish. Neither the cockchafer, nor the toad, nor the earthworm, whom they asked, could give them any information, because none of their kind had ever been boiled or laid upon a silver dish.

The old white snails were the most distinguished people in the world—they knew that; the forest was there for their sakes, and the Manor House too, so that they might be boiled and laid upon silver dishes.

They lived a very retired and happy life, and as they had no children, they had adopted a small common snail which they were bringing up as their own; but the little thing would not grow bigger, because he was just a common one. The old people, however, imagined that he was growing; that is to say, Mother—Mother Snail, especially, fancied she could see signs of it. She asked Father, if he could not *see* it, then to *feel* the little shell, and he felt it and admitted that Mother was right.

One day the rain was pouring down in torrents.

"Listen how it drumme-rumme-rums on the rhubarb leaves," said Father Snail.

"My word! Drops are coming through too," said Mother Snail. "They're running right down the stalk! I bet you anything it's going to be sopping wet here. I'm glad we're carrying our good houses on our backs, and that the little one has got one of his own as well. Certainly more has been done for us than for any other creature. It's easy to see that we are the gentlefolk of the world. We were given houses at birth, and the rhubarb forest was planted for our sakes. I should like to know how far it goes, and what lies beyond."

"There is nothing beyond," said Father Snail. "No place can be better than this home of ours; I've got nothing to wish for."

"Oh, I have!" said Mother Snail. "I should like to be taken to the Manor House, and be boiled and laid upon a silver dish—that was done to all our ancestors, and it must be something quite out of the ordinary, believe me."

"The Manor House may have crumbled into ruins," said Father Snail, "or the rhubarb forest may have grown over it so that the people can't get out. Why be in such a hurry? But you always do rush, and the little one is beginning to take after you. See how he's been creeping up that stalk for the last three days! It makes my head ache to look up at him."

"You mustn't scold him," said Mother Snail. "He just crawls at a snail's pace; he'll be a great blessing to us, and we old people have nothing else to live for. But have you ever considered where we shall find a wife for him? Don't you think that deep in the rhubarb forest there may be more of our species?"

"I daresay there may be black ones," said the old man, "black ones with no houses of their own, but that's so vulgar, and besides they do think they're somebody. But let's ask the ants to be our agents, they keep running backwards and forwards as if they really had some business on hand. They may know of a wife for our little snaily."

"I certainly do know the most beautiful bride," said one of the ants, "but I'm afraid it's out of the question, because she's a Queen."

"That doesn't matter," said the old man. "Has she got a house?"

"She's got a castle," replied the ants, "the most wonderful ant-castle with seven hundred corridors."

"Thank you," said Mother Snail. "Our son shall never enter an ant-heap. If that's the best you can do, we'll ask the white gnats to be our agents; they fly far and wide in rain and sunshine; they know the wild rhubarb forest inside out."

"We've got a wife for him," said the gnats. "A hundred man-steps from here there is a little snail, with a house of her own, sitting on a gooseberry bush; she's very lonely and is quite old enough to get married. It's only a hundred man-steps from here."

"Yes, but she must come to him," said the old snails. "He's got a whole forest, and she's only got a bush!"

So little Miss Snail was fetched. It took a week for her to arrive, but that was exactly as it should be, for it proved that she was of the right breed. And then they were married. Six glow-worms provided the illumination as well as they could—apart from this, everything went off very quietly, for the old snails could not stand feasting and dissipation. But a charming speech was made by Mother Snail. Father could not express his feelings. He was too deeply moved.

They gave the young couple the whole wild rhubarb forest as an inheritance, saying, as they had always said, that it was the best place in the world, and that, provided they lived honorably and increased and multiplied, the young people would some day be taken with their children to the Manor House, to be boiled black and laid upon a silver dish.

And when the speech was finished, the old people crept into their houses and never came out again: they had gone to sleep.

The young snail-couple reigned over the forest, and had numerous offspring, but they were never boiled, and never laid upon a silver dish; so they came to the conclusion that the Manor House had crumbled into ruins, and that all the people in the world had died out. As nobody contradicted them of course it was true; and the rain beat on the wild rhubarb leaves to play the drum for them, and the sun shone to color the wild rhubarb forest for them, and they were very happy, the whole family were very, very happy; they really were.

THE LITTLE MATCH-GIRL

IT was so bitterly cold, snow was falling and darkness was gathering, for it was the last evening of the old year—New Year's Eve. In the cold and gloom a poor little girl walked, bareheaded and barefoot, through the streets. She was wearing slippers, it is true, when she left home, but what good were they? They used to be her mother's, so you can imagine how big they were. The little girl lost them as she ran across the street to escape from two carriages that were being driven terribly fast. One slipper could not be found, and a boy ran off with the other, saying that he could use it very nicely as a cradle some day when he had children of his own.

So the little girl walked about the streets on her naked feet, which were red and blue with the cold. In her old apron she carried a whole lot of matches, and she had a packet of them in her hand as well. Nobody had bought any from her, and no one had given her a single penny all day long. She crept along, hungry and shivering, the picture of misery, poor little thing! The snowflakes fell on her long golden hair which curled so prettily about her neck, but she did not think of her appearance now. Lights were shining in every window, and there was a glorious smell of roast goose in the street, for it was New Year's Eve, and she could not think of anything else.

She huddled down in a little heap in a corner formed by two houses, one of which projected further out into the street than the other, but though she tucked her little legs up under her she felt colder and colder. She did not dare to go home, for she had sold no matches nor earned a single penny. Her father would be sure to beat her, and besides it was so cold at home, for they had nothing but

the roof above them and the wind whistled through that, even though the largest cracks were stuffed with straw and rags. Her little hands were almost dead with cold. Oh, how one little match would warm her! If only she dare pull just one from the packet, strike it on the wall and warm her fingers. She pulled one out—scr-r-ratch!—How it spluttered and burnt! It was a warm bright flame like a little candle when she held her hand over it—but what a strange light! It seemed to the little girl as if she were sitting in front of a great iron stove with polished brass knobs and brass ornaments. The fire burnt so beautifully and gave out such a lovely warmth. Oh, how wonderful that was! The child had already stretched out her feet to warm them too, when—out went the flame, the stove vanished, and there she sat with a bit of the burnt match in her hand.

She struck another—it burnt clearly, and where the light fell upon the wall it became transparent like a curtain of gauze. She could see right into the room where a shining white cloth was spread on the table; it was covered with beautiful china, and in the center of it stood the roast goose, stuffed with prunes and apples, steaming deliciously. And what was even more wonderful was that the goose hopped down from the dish, waddled across the floor with carving knife and fork in its back, waddled even straight up to the poor child! Then—out went the match, and nothing could be seen but the thick cold wall.

She struck another, and suddenly she was sitting under the most beautiful Christmas tree; it was much larger and much lovelier than the one she had seen last year through the glass doors of the rich merchant's house. A thousand candles lit up the green branches, and gaily colored pictures, like those in the shop-windows, looked down upon her. The little girl reached forward with both hands—then, out went the match. The many candles on the Christmas tree rose higher and higher through the air, and she saw that they had now turned into bright stars. One of them fell, streaking the sky with light.

"Now someone is dying," said the little girl, for old Granny, the only one who had ever been good to her, but who was now dead, had said: "Whenever a star falls, a soul goes up to God."

She struck another match on the wall; once more there was light, and in the glow stood her old Granny, oh, so bright and shining, and looking so gentle, kind, and loving. "Granny!" cried the little girl. "Oh, take me with you! I know you will disappear when the match is burnt out; you will vanish like the warm stove, the lovely roast goose, and the great glorious Christmas tree!" Then she quickly struck all the rest of the matches in the packet, for she did so want to keep Granny with her. The matches flared up with such a blaze that it was brighter than broad daylight, and her old Granny had never seemed so beautiful nor so stately before. She took the little girl in her arms and flew with her high up, oh, so high, towards glory and joy! Now they knew neither cold nor hunger nor fear, for they were with God.

But in the cold dawn, in the corner formed by the two houses, sat the little girl with rosy cheeks and smiling lips—dead—frozen to death on the last evening of the Old Year. The dawn of the New Year rose on the huddled figure of the little girl, holding the matches, of which a packet had been burnt more than halfway down.

"She was evidently trying to warm herself," people said. But no one knew what beautiful visions she had seen, and in what a blaze of glory she had entered with her dear old Granny into the heavenly joy and gladness of a new year.

THE STEADFAST TIN SOLDIER

ONCE upon a time there were five-and-twenty tin soldiers; they were all brothers, for they were born of the same old tin spoon. They shouldered arms and looked straight in front of them in their fascinating red and blue uniforms. The very first thing they heard in this world, when the lid was taken off their box, was, "Tin soldiers!" A little boy shouted it, and clapped his hands; the soldiers were a present, for it was his birthday, and now he was busy setting them up on the table. Each soldier was the living image of the others, but there was one who was a little bit different. He had only one leg, for he was the last to be cast and the tin had run out. Still, there he stood, just as steadfast on his one leg as the others on their two; and he is the tin soldier we are going to hear about.

On the table where the soldiers had been set up stood a great many other toys, but the thing that caught the eye more than anything else was a wonderful paper castle, with little windows through which you could see straight in to the halls. In front of the castle there were little trees round a tiny looking-glass that was supposed to be a lake. Swans made of wax swam on it, and were mirrored in the glass. This was all very pretty, but the prettiest was a little lady who stood in the open doorway of the castle; she too was cut out of paper, but she had on a skirt of the very finest lawn, and a little narrow blue ribbon over her shoulder like a scarf; in the middle of it was placed a glittering spangle as big as the whole of her tiny face. The little lady held both her arms outstretched—for she was a dancer—and also lifted one of her legs so high that the tin soldier couldn't see it at all, and thought she had only one leg like himself.

"That's the wife for me," he thought, "but she's a very grand lady. She lives in a castle, and I've only got a box, and there are five-and-twenty of us to share it; it's no place for her. All the same I must get to know her." And then he laid himself down full length behind a snuff-box standing on the table. From there he could watch the graceful little lady who kept standing on one leg without losing her balance.

When it was getting late, all the other tin soldiers were put into their box, and the people in the house went to bed. Then the toys began to play, and they played at receiving visitors, at having wars, and giving balls. The tin soldiers rattled in their box, for they wanted to take part in the fun, but they could not get the lid off. The nut-crackers turned somersaults, the slate pencil capered about on the slate; finally there was so much noise that the canary woke up and began to talk—and that in verse, if you please! The only two who did not stir were the tin soldier and the little dancer: she stood firm on the tip of her toe with both arms outstretched; he stood just as steadfast on his one leg, and never took his eyes off her for a moment.

Then the clock struck twelve, and—pop!—up sprang the lid of the snuff-box; but there was no snuff in it, no, there was a little black imp—you see it was a trick-box.

"Tin soldier," said the imp, "kindly keep your eyes to yourself."

But the tin soldier pretended not to hear.

"Just you wait till tomorrow," said the imp.

Well, when tomorrow came and the children got up, the tin soldier was put on the window-sill, and all of a sudden—it was either due to the imp or to the draught—the window flew open, and the soldier fell head first out from the third story. It was a hair-raising fall. He found himself standing on his cap, with his bayonet buried between the paving stones, and his one leg pointing straight up in the air.

The servant and the little boy rushed down immediately to look for him, but though they almost stepped on him, they never saw him. If the soldier had shouted, "Here I am!" they would certainly have found him, but he thought it beneath his dignity to shout when he was in uniform.

Then it began to rain; the drops followed each other faster and faster, until it became a regular downpour. When it was all over, two urchins came along.

"Crikey!" said one of them, "here's a tin soldier! Let's send him sailing!"

So they made a boat out of a newspaper, placed the tin soldier right in the middle of it, and off he sailed, down the gutter; the two boys ran along beside him, clapping their hands. Did you ever see waves like that in the gutter—and did you ever see such a strong current? Now don't forget that it had been raining cats and dogs. The paper boat danced up and down, and sometimes whirled round so rapidly that the tin soldier was shaken from head to foot—but he remained steadfast, never blinked an eyelash, looked straight ahead, and kept on shouldering arms.

Suddenly the boat sailed under a long plank covering the gutter. It was as dark there as if he had been in his box.

"I wonder where I can be going?" he thought. "I bet it's the imp wanting to get even with me! Oh, if only the little lady were here with me in the boat, it could be twice as dark for all I'd care!"

At that very moment there appeared a great water rat who lived under the plank.

"Got your passport?" asked the rat. "Haul it out!"

The tin soldier said nothing, but held his rifle tighter than ever. The boat rushed on and the rat after it, gnashing his teeth horribly, and calling out to sticks and straws, "Stop him! Stop him! He hasn't paid any toll! He hasn't shown his passport!"

But the current became stronger and stronger; the tin soldier could already catch a glimpse of daylight where the plank ended, but he also heard a roaring noise which might very well have frightened the bravest man; for, just imagine! at the end of the plank the water rushed out into a huge canal. The situation was as dangerous for him as shooting a great waterfall would be for us.

By now he had got so near the place that he could not possibly stop. The boat darted out, and the poor tin soldier held himself as stiffly as he could—no one should say of him that he even blinked an eye. The boat whirled round three or four times and filled with water to the very brim; it was bound to sink. The tin soldier was already up to his neck in water. The boat sank deeper and deeper, the paper grew softer and softer. The water now closed over the soldier's head; then he thought of the pretty little dancer whom he would never see again, and in his ears rang the old song:

Here comes a candle to light you to bed,
Here comes a chopper to chop off your head.

Then the paper fell to pieces, and the tin soldier went right through, and was immediately swallowed by a great fish!

Heavens! How appallingly dark it was inside—worse than under the plank! And besides it was terribly cramped, but the tin soldier was as steadfast as ever, and lay there full length with shouldered arms.

The fish bounced about, making the most awful contortions, and finally lay absolutely still. Something like a streak of lightning flashed through it, broad daylight appeared, and a voice was heard exclaiming, "Look who's here!" The fish had been caught, taken to market and sold, and had now landed in a kitchen where the cook cut it open with a knife.

She seized the soldier by his middle and carried him into the sitting-room where everybody wanted to see so remarkable a fellow,

who had traveled about in the inside of a fish. But the tin soldier was not at all proud of it. He was placed on the table, and there—now, isn't that the most extraordinary coincidence?—the tin soldier found himself in the very same room he had been in before! He saw the very same children and the very same toys on the table; the beautiful castle with the pretty little dancer was still there; she was still balancing herself on one leg, and lifting the other high up. She too was steadfast! That moved the tin soldier; he almost wept tin tears—only that isn't done in uniform. He looked at her and she looked at him, but they said nothing.

At that very moment one of the little boys picked up the soldier and threw him into the stove. There was no reason why he should have done that; it was undoubtedly the imp in the snuff-box who was to blame for it.

The tin soldier stood all lit up, and felt a heat that was terrible, but whether it came from the real fire or from love, he did not know. He had lost all his bright colors, but whether that had happened on his voyage, or had been caused by sorrow, nobody could tell. He looked at the little lady, she looked at him, and he felt that he was melting, but still he stood steadfast with shouldered arms. Then suddenly a door opened, the wind caught the dancer, and she flew, like a sylph, into the stove to the tin soldier, blazed up in a flame, and was gone. The tin soldier melted down into a lump, and when next day the servant took out the ashes, she found him in the shape of a little tin heart. But of the dancer nothing remained except the spangle, and that was burnt as black as coal.

THE PRINCESS ON THE PEA

ONCE upon a time there was a Prince; he wanted to get himself a Princess, but she must be a real Princess. So he traveled all over the world to find one, but in every case something was the matter. There were any number of Princesses, but he could never quite make out whether they were real or not—there always seemed to be a catch somewhere. So he came back home and was very unhappy, for he did so want to find a true Princess.

One evening a terrible storm came on; lightning flashed, thunder rolled, and the rain poured down in torrents—it was simply awful! Suddenly there was a knock at the city gate, and the old King went out to answer it.

It was a Princess standing outside, but what a sight the rain and the bad weather had made of her! The water streamed down her hair and down her clothes, it ran in at the toes of her shoes and out at the heels, and yet she said she was a real Princess.

"It won't take us long to find that out," thought the old Queen. However she did not say anything, but went into the bedchamber, took off all the bedclothes, and placed one pea on the bottom boards of the bed. Then she took twenty mattresses and put them on top of the pea, and after that she put twenty feather-beds stuffed with eiderdown on top of the mattresses.

That's where the Princess was to spend the night.

In the morning they asked her how she had slept.

"Oh, dreadfully badly!" said the Princess. "I hardly slept a wink all night. Whatever could have been in the bed? I was lying on something so hard that I'm black and blue all over. It was simply

awful!"

So of course they could see that she was a real Princess, since she had felt the pea right through the twenty mattresses and the twenty feather-beds. No one but a real Princess could have such a tender skin as that.

So the Prince took her for his wife, because now he knew that he had got hold of a real Princess.

And the pea was put on view in the museum, where it is still to be seen—unless somebody has taken it.

Now, wasn't that a real story?

THE RED SHOES

THERE was once a little girl, a dainty and pretty little girl, but because she was very poor she always went barefoot in summer, and in winter wore heavy wooden shoes which made her insteps very red, dreadfully red.

In the heart of the village lived an old shoemaker's widow. She made a little pair of shoes as well as she possibly could, out of strips of old red cloth. They were rather clumsy, but she meant well, as she wanted them to be a present for the little girl. The little girl's name was Karen.

On the very day her mother was buried she was given the red shoes, and wore them for the first time. They were not really suitable for mourning, but as she had no others, she walked in them, barelegged, behind the poor plain straw coffin.

Suddenly a large old carriage drove up with a large old lady in it. She looked at the little girl, and feeling very sorry for her, she said to the parson, "Let me take the little girl and I'll look after her."

Karen thought that it was all because of the red shoes, but the old lady said they were hideous and had them burnt. However she gave her some neat new clothes and had her taught to read and sew. People said she was pretty, but her mirror said, "You are more than pretty, you are lovely."

Now the Queen happened to travel through the country, and she had her little daughter with her—of course she was a Princess. People flocked to the Palace to see them, and Karen was among the crowd. The little Princess stood at the window in a snow-white dress to let herself be admired. She was wearing neither a train nor a golden crown, but she had on a pair of beautiful red morocco shoes. Of course they were far nicer than the ones the shoemaker's widow had made for little Karen. There could be nothing in the world like a pair of red shoes!

When Karen was old enough to be confirmed, she had new clothes and was to have new shoes as well. The fashionable shoemaker in town took the measure of her little feet. He fitted her in his private house, where lovely shoes and shiny leather boots were arranged in great glass cases. The display was very attractive, but it gave no pleasure to the old lady whose eyesight was rather weak. Amongst all the shoes was a pair of red leather ones, exactly like those the Princess had worn. How beautiful they were! In fact the shoemaker said that they had been made for a nobleman's daughter, but they had not fitted very well.

"I suppose they are patent leather, they're so shiny," said the old lady.

"Yes, they *are* shiny," said Karen. The shoes fitted her and they were bought, but the old lady did not know they were red, or she would never have allowed Karen to wear them for her confirmation. However, that's what happened.

Everybody looked at her feet when she walked up the nave towards the chancel. It seemed to her as if those old pictures on the wall tablets, those portraits of clergymen and their wives with ruffs and long black garments, fixed their eyes upon her red shoes. She thought of nothing else when the priest laid his hand upon her head and spoke to her of Holy Baptism, the Covenant with God, and told her that she was now a grown-up Christian.

The organ played a solemn melody, the children sang with their lovely voices, and the old choirmaster sang, but Karen thought of nothing but her red shoes.

By the afternoon the old lady had been told by everybody that Karen had worn red shoes, so she told her that it was very naughty of her, and not at all the proper thing to do, and that hereafter whenever she went to church she must wear black shoes, even if they were old.

The following Sunday there was Holy Communion, and Karen looked at the black shoes and she looked at the red ones—she looked at the red ones again, and finally put them on.

It was beautiful sunny weather; Karen and the old lady followed the dusty path through the cornfield.

At the church door stood an old soldier with a crutch and a funny long beard that was more red than white, in fact it was practically red. He bowed right down to the ground and asked the old lady if he might dust her shoes. Karen also put out her little foot. "My! what beautiful dancing shoes!" said the soldier. "Stick on tightly when you dance!" and he slapped the soles with his hand.

The old lady gave the soldier a penny, and went into the church with Karen.

Everyone stared at Karen's red shoes, and all the portraits stared, and when Karen knelt at the altar and put her lips to the gold chalice, she thought only of the red shoes—it seemed to her as if they were floating before her eyes. She forgot to sing the hymn and she forgot to say the Lord's Prayer.

Then everyone left the church, and the old lady got into her carriage. Karen was about to step in after her when the old soldier said, "Look at the pretty dancing shoes!" Karen could not keep her feet still, she just could not resist dancing a few steps, and when once she had begun, her feet continued to dance—it was as if the shoes had gained control over them. She danced round the corner of the church, she could not help herself; the coachman had to run after her, take hold of her and lift her into the carriage, but her dancing feet kicked the nice old lady violently. Finally they took her shoes off and her legs were still.

At home the shoes were put away in a cupboard, but Karen could not resist looking at them now and then.

Soon after this the old lady lay ill and they said that she could not live. She needed constant attention and careful nursing, and this was naturally Karen's duty. But a big ball was to be given in town and Karen was invited. She looked at the old lady, who in any case could not live, and she looked at the red shoes, for she thought there could be no sin in doing that—she put on the red shoes, thinking there was no sin in doing that either. Then she went away to the ball and started dancing.

When she wanted to turn to the right the shoes danced to the left, when she wanted to dance up to one end of the room the shoes danced down to the other, they danced down the stairs, through the streets and out of the town gate. Dance she did, and dance she must, straight out into the dark forest.

She saw something shining up in the trees, and because of its face she thought it was the moon, but it was the old soldier with the red beard, who nodded to her and said, "Look at the pretty dancing shoes!"

Filled with terror she tried to kick off the red shoes, but they stuck to her feet; she tore off her stockings, but the shoes had grown fast to her feet, and so dance she did, and dance she must, over field and meadow, in rain and sunshine, by day and by night. It was most horrible at night.

She danced through the open gate of the churchyard, but the dead did not dance in there; they had something far more sensible to do. She tried to sit down on a pauper's grave where the bitter tansy grew, but for her there was neither rest nor peace, and as she danced towards the open church door, she saw an angel standing there with long white robes and white wings reaching from his shoulders right to the ground; his face was grave and severe, and in his hand he held a broad and shining sword.

"Dance thou shalt!" he said. "Dance in thy red shoes till thou art pale and cold, till thy body shrivels to a skeleton! Dance from door to door, and wherever proud conceited children live, thou shalt knock at the door till they hear thee and fear thee! Dance, I command thee, dance!"

"Have mercy!" shrieked Karen. But she did not hear what the Angel answered, for the shoes carried her through the gate into the fields, along highway and byway, dancing, ever and ever dancing.

One morning she danced past a door she knew well; within a hymn was being sung; a coffin was carried out covered with flowers. Then she realized that the old lady was dead, and she felt that she herself was forsaken by all and accursed by the Angel of God.

Dance she did, and dance she must, dance through the dark night.

The shoes carried her on over stump and thorn; she was scratched till she bled; she danced across the heath to a lonely little house. She knew that the executioner lived there, and she tapped with her finger on the window-pane and cried, "Come out! Come out! I can't come in, for I'm dancing!"

And the executioner said, "You don't seem to know who I am. I chop off the heads of wicked people, and I can feel my ax beginning to quiver."

"Don't chop off my head," said Karen, "for then I can never repent of my sin, but chop off my feet with the red shoes on!"

Then she confessed her sin, and the executioner chopped off her feet with the red shoes on, and the shoes danced away with the little feet in them over the fields into the depths of the forest.

Then he made her a pair of crutches, and taught her a hymn—the one that penitents always sing. She kissed the hand which had wielded the ax, and went away across the heath.

"I have suffered enough because of the red shoes," she said. "Now I will go to church and show myself to everyone." And she went quickly to the church door, but when she came there the red shoes danced in front of her so that she was frightened and turned back.

The whole week through she was very sad and shed many bitter tears, but when Sunday came she said, "There now, I have suffered and struggled long enough. I think I am just as good as many of the people who sit in church and hold their heads high." She set forth confidently, but no sooner did she reach the churchyard gate than she saw the red shoes dancing in front of her again, and she was terrified. She turned back and repented of her sin with all her heart.

Then she went to the Rectory and begged to be taken into service there; she would be hard-working and do all she could—the wages were not important if only she might have a roof over her head, and be with good people. The Rector's wife felt sorry for her and took her into her service. Karen was serious and industrious. She sat quietly and listened in the evening when the Rector read aloud from the Bible. All the little ones were very fond of her, but when they spoke of frills and finery, and of being as beautiful as a Queen, she would shake her head.

The following Sunday when they went to church, they asked her to go with them, but with tears in her eyes she looked sadly at her crutches. The others went to hear the Word of God. Left alone, she went into her tiny room. It was just big enough for a bed and a chair; she sat down with her hymn-book in her hand, and while she was reading it devoutly, the wind carried the organ notes from the church straight into her room. She raised her face, all wet with tears, and said, "Lord, help me!"

Then the sun shone brightly, and the Angel of God in white robes, the same one whom she had seen that other night at the church door, stood before her. Instead of the sharp sword, he held a beautiful green branch covered with roses. He touched the ceiling with it, raising it high up, and a golden star appeared; then he touched the walls and they opened wide. She saw the organ, she saw the pictures of the Rectors and their wives, she saw the congregation seated in their flower-decorated pews, singing from their hymn-books. For the church itself had come to the poor girl in her narrow little room, or it was she who had been brought to the church. She sat in the pew with the other people from the Rectory, and when they had sung the hymn, they looked up and nodded to her, saying, "It was right of you to come, Karen."

"It was by God's mercy that I came," she said.

The music of the organ pealed forth, and the voices of the children's choir rang out in mellow and lovely tones. The bright rays of the sun streamed warmly through the window to the pew where Karen sat. Her heart was so filled with the sunshine of peace and joy that it broke, and the sunbeams carried her soul to heaven. No one there questioned her about the red shoes.

THE EMPEROR'S NEW CLOTHES

MANY years ago there lived an Emperor who was so exceedingly fond of fine new clothes that he spent all his money on being elaborately dressed. He took no interest in his soldiers, no interest in the theater, nor did he care to drive about in his state coach, unless it were to show off his new clothes. He had different robes for every hour of the day, and just as one says of a King that he is in his Council Chamber, people always said of him, "The Emperor is in his wardrobe!"

The great city in which he lived was full of gaiety. Strangers were always coming and going. One day two swindlers arrived; they made themselves out to be weavers, and said they knew how to weave the most magnificent fabric that one could imagine. Not only were the colors and patterns unusually beautiful, but the clothes that were made of this material had the extraordinary quality of becoming invisible to everyone who was either unfit for his post, or inexcusably stupid.

"What useful clothes to have!" thought the Emperor. "If I had some like that, I might find out which of the people in my Empire are unfit for their posts. I should also be able to distinguish the wise from the fools. Yes, that material must be woven for me immediately!" Then he gave the swindlers large sums of money so that they could start work at once.

Quickly they set up two looms and pretended to weave, but there was not a trace of anything on the frames. They made no bones about demanding the finest silk and the purest gold thread. They stuffed everything into their bags, and continued to work at the empty looms until late into the night.

"I'm rather anxious to know how much of the material is finished," thought the Emperor, but to tell the truth, he felt a bit uneasy, remembering that anyone who was either a fool or unfit for his post would never be able to see it. He rather imagined that he need not have any fear for himself, yet he thought it wise to send someone else first to see how things were going. Everyone in the town knew about the exceptional powers of the material, and all were eager to know how incompetent or how stupid their neighbors might be.

"I will send my honest old Chamberlain to the weavers," thought the Emperor. "He will be able to judge the fabric better than anyone else, for he has brains, and nobody fills his post better than he does."

So the nice old Chamberlain went into the hall where the two swindlers were sitting working at the empty looms.

"Upon my life!" he thought, opening his eyes very wide, "I can't see anything at all!" But he didn't say so.

Both the swindlers begged him to be good enough to come nearer, and asked how he liked the unusual design and the splendid colors. They pointed to the empty looms, and the poor old Chamberlain opened his eyes wider and wider, but he could see nothing, for there was nothing. "Heavens above!" he thought, "could it possibly be that I am stupid? I have never thought that of myself, and not a soul must know it. Could it be that I am not fit for my post? It will never do for me to admit that I can't see the material!"

"Well, you don't say what you think of it," said one of the weavers.

"Oh, it's delightful—most exquisite!" said the old Chamberlain, looking through his spectacles. "What a wonderful design and what beautiful colors! I shall certainly tell the Emperor that I am enchanted with it."

"We're very pleased to hear that," said the two weavers, and they started describing the colors and the curious pattern. The old Chamberlain listened carefully in order to repeat, when he came home to the Emperor, exactly what he had heard, and he did so.

The swindlers now demanded more money, as well as more silk and gold thread, saying that they needed it for weaving. They put everything into their pockets and not a thread appeared upon the looms, but they kept on working at the empty frames as before.

Soon after this, the Emperor sent another nice official to see how the weaving was getting on, and to enquire whether the stuff would soon be ready. Exactly the same thing happened to him as to the Chamberlain. He looked and looked, but as there was nothing to be seen except the empty looms, he could see nothing.

"Isn't it a beautiful piece of material?" said the swindlers, showing and describing the pattern that did not exist at all.

"Stupid I certainly am not," thought the official; "then I must be unfit for my excellent post, I suppose. That seems rather funny—but I'll take great care that nobody gets wind of it." Then he praised the material he could not see, and assured them of his enthusiasm for the gorgeous colors and the beautiful pattern. "It's simply enchanting!" he said to the Emperor.

The whole town was talking about the splendid material.

And now the Emperor was curious to see it for himself while it was still upon the looms.

Accompanied by a great number of selected people, among whom were the two nice old officials who had already been there, the Emperor went forth to visit the two wily swindlers. They were now weaving madly, yet without a single thread upon the looms.

"Isn't it magnificent?" said the two nice officials. "Will Your Imperial Majesty deign to look at this splendid pattern and these glorious colors?" Then they pointed to the empty looms, for each thought that the others could probably see the material.

"What on earth can this mean?" thought the Emperor. "I don't see anything! This is terrible. Am I stupid? Am I unfit to be Emperor? That would be the most disastrous thing that could possibly befall me.—Oh, it's perfectly wonderful!" he said. "It quite meets with my Imperial approval." And he nodded appreciatively and stared at the empty looms—he would not admit that he saw nothing. His whole suite looked and looked, but with as little result as the others; nevertheless, they all said, like the Emperor, "It's perfectly wonderful!" They advised him to have some new clothes made from this splendid stuff and to wear them for the first time in the next great procession.

"Magnificent!" "Excellent!" "Prodigious!" went from mouth to mouth, and everyone was exceedingly pleased. The Emperor gave each of the swindlers a decoration to wear in his button-hole, and the title of "Knight of the Loom."

Before the procession they worked all night, burning more than sixteen candles. People could see how busy they were finishing the Emperor's new clothes. They pretended to take the material from the looms, they slashed the air with great scissors, they sewed with needles without any thread, and finally they said, "The Emperor's clothes are ready!"

Then the Emperor himself arrived with his most distinguished courtiers, and each swindler raised an arm as if he were holding something, and said, "These are Your Imperial Majesty's knee-breeches. This is Your Imperial Majesty's robe. This is Your Imperial Majesty's mantle," and so forth. "It is all as light as a spider's web, one might fancy one had nothing on, but that is just the beauty of it!"

"Yes, indeed," said all the courtiers, but they could see nothing, for there was nothing to be seen.

"If Your Imperial Majesty would graciously consent to take off your clothes," said the swindlers, "we could fit on the new ones in

front of the long glass."

So the Emperor laid aside his clothes, and the swindlers pretended to hand him, piece by piece, the new ones they were supposed to have made, and they fitted him round the waist, and acted as if they were fastening something on—it was the train; and the Emperor turned round and round in front of the long glass.

"How well the new robes suit Your Imperial Majesty! How well they fit!" they all said. "What a splendid design! What gorgeous colors! It's all magnificently regal!"

"The canopy which is to be held over Your Imperial Majesty in the procession is waiting outside," announced the Lord High Chamberlain.

"Well, I suppose I'm ready," said the Emperor. "Don't you think they are a nice fit?" And he looked at himself again in the glass, first on one side and then the other, as if he really were carefully examining his handsome attire.

The courtiers who were to carry the train groped about on the floor with fumbling fingers, and pretended to lift it; they walked on, holding their hands up in the air; nothing would have induced them to admit that they could not see anything.

And so the Emperor set off in the procession under the beautiful canopy, and everybody in the streets and at the windows said, "Oh! how superb the Emperor's new clothes are! What a gorgeous train! What a perfect fit!" No one would acknowledge that he didn't see anything, so proving that he was not fit for his post, or that he was very stupid.

None of the Emperor's clothes had ever met with such a success.

"But he hasn't got any clothes on!" gasped out a little child.

"Good heavens! Hark at the little innocent!" said the father, and people whispered to one another what the child had said. "But he hasn't got any clothes on! There's a little child saying he hasn't got any clothes on!"

"But he hasn't got any clothes on!" shouted the whole town at last. The Emperor had a creepy feeling down his spine, because it began to dawn upon him that the people were right. "All the same," he thought to himself, "I've got to go through with it as long as the procession lasts."

So he drew himself up and held his head higher than before, and the courtiers held on to the train that wasn't there at all.

THE DARNING NEEDLE

ONCE upon a time there was a darning needle who was so grand that she imagined she was a sewing needle.

"Be very careful of what you're handling," said the darning needle to the fingers that picked her up. "Don't let me fall! If you drop me on the floor I may never be found again, I'm so fine, you know!"

"Not so fine as all that!" said the fingers, and they squeezed her tightly round her middle.

"Look! Here I come with my suite!" said the darning needle, trailing a long thread after her, but there was no knot at the end of the thread.

The fingers guided the needle towards the cook's slipper. The leather was torn and needed mending.

"I call this rough work," said the darning needle. "I shall never get through. I'm going to break! I'm going to break!" And she really did break. "You see," she said, "I am too delicate."

"She's no good now," said the fingers, but they still had to hold on to her. The cook dropped some sealing-wax on the darning needle and stuck her in the front of her dress.

"Ha! ha! Now I'm a brooch," said the darning needle. "I always knew that I should get on in the world. When one has the makings of something, one always becomes something!"

She laughed inwardly—for you can never see outwardly when a darning needle laughs. There she sat, looking right and left, as proudly as if she were riding in a state coach.

"May I presume to ask if you are made of gold?" she enquired of the pin, her neighbor. "You are quite good-looking and you have a head of your own, but it's rather small. You must do something about developing it; you see, we can't all have our extremities adorned with sealing-wax."

And the darning needle drew herself up so proudly that she fell off the dress and down into the sink at the very moment that the cook was busy rinsing it.

"Now we're off on a journey!" said the darning needle. "I hope to goodness I'm not going to get lost." But lost she was.

"I'm too fine for this world," she exclaimed as she sat in the gutter. "Still I know what I'm worth, and there is always a certain satisfaction in that." The darning needle sat bolt upright and never lost her good spirits.

All kinds of things floated over her, sticks, straws, and bits of old newspapers.

"Look at them drifting along!" said the darning needle. "They all seem to be missing the point. I am the point! Here I sit. See, there goes a stick! He hasn't an idea in his head but 'Stick' and that's just what he is. There goes a straw, look how he turns and twists about! Don't think so much of yourself—you might bump into the curb. There goes a newspaper floating by! Everything that was printed on his pages has long been forgotten, but he is still puffed up with it. I sit quietly and patiently here; I know what I am, and I shall remain what I am."

One day something was glittering for all it was worth close by; the darning needle fancied it must be a diamond; it turned out to be a bit of a broken bottle, but since it glittered, the darning needle spoke to it and introduced herself as a brooch.

"I suppose you are a diamond!"

"Well, yes, something of the sort!"

Each one now believed the other to be a thing of almost priceless value, and so they talked together of the world and its conceit.

"I used to live in a box belonging to a young lady—and that young lady was a cook," said the darning needle. "She had five fingers on each hand, and I never saw anything like the conceit of those five fingers. All they had to do was to hold me, take me out of the box, and put me back in the box."

"Were they at all brilliant?" asked the bit of glass.

"Brilliant?" said the darning needle. "Indeed not! They were stuck-up! They were five brothers, belonging to the 'Finger' family. They stood proudly beside one another, and were all of different heights. The first of the five, 'Tom Thumb,' was short and plump; he stood outside the ranks and had only one joint in his back; he could only make one bow, but he said that if he were cut off a man's hand, that whole man would be no good as a soldier. 'Lick-pot,' the second, stuck himself into sweet and sour, and pointed at the sun and moon. He was the one who guided the pen when they wrote. 'Middleman,' the third, looked over the heads of the others. 'Goldband' wore a gold belt round his middle; and little 'Twiddle-de-dee,' the fifth, did nothing at all and was proud of it. There was bragging and nothing but bragging, and that's why I went down the sink."

"And now we sit here, glittering away," said the bit of glass.

At that very moment it was carried off by a torrent of water which poured into the gutter and made it overflow.

"There now, he's been moved on," said the darning needle. "I remain here; I'm too refined to move, but I pride myself on it, and that's respectable enough!" And she sat there proudly, lost in thought.

"I'm so very fine that I could almost believe myself to have been born of a sunbeam—besides the sun always seems to seek me out in the water. Yes, I'm so fine that my mother cannot catch me. If I had my old eye which broke off, I think I should cry—but no, I won't—it isn't done."

One day some ragamuffins were messing about in the gutter finding old nails, coins, and things of that sort. Such filth! but that was their idea of a good time.

"Ow!" shouted one of them; he had pricked himself on the darning needle. "What a nasty brute!"

"I'm not a brute, I'm a young lady," said the darning needle, but nobody heard her. The sealing-wax had come off and she had turned black, but black makes one look slimmer, so she imagined herself finer than ever.

"Here comes an eggshell sailing along," said the boys, and they stuck the darning needle into the shell.

"A white frame for my black beauty!" said the darning needle. "That's most becoming! I shall be noticed now. I only hope I shan't be sea-sick. That would break me, I'm sure!" But she was not sea-sick, and she did not break.

"A good way of avoiding sea-sickness is to have a steel stomach, and always to bear in mind that you are something more than a mere mortal. Now I'm all right. The finer you are, the more you can stand."

"Crack!" went the eggshell as a heavily loaded cart went over it.

"Good heavens, what a squeeze!" said the darning needle. "I'm getting sea-sick all the same. I'm breaking! I'm breaking!"

But she did not break, though the cart had passed over her; she was lying there lengthwise in the gutter—so let's leave her there.

THE NIGHTINGALE

IN China, as of course you know, the Emperor is a Chinese, and all the people round him are Chinese too.

It is a great many years since all this happened, but that's just why the story is worth hearing before it is forgotten.

The Emperor's Palace was the most marvelous one in the world, made wholly and entirely of fine porcelain, so costly, but so fragile and delicate that you had to take mighty good care whenever you touched it. In the garden the strangest flowers were to be seen, and the most glorious of them all were hung with little silver bells, which tinkled so that nobody should pass by without noticing them. Yes, everything in the Emperor's garden was most ingeniously thought out. And it was so big that even the gardener did not know how far it extended. If you kept on walking, you came at last to the most wonderful forest with lofty trees and deep lakes. The forest went down to the edge of the fathomless blue sea; large ships could sail close in under the branches of the trees, among which there lived a nightingale. Her song was so entrancing that even the poor fisherman, who had many other things to attend to, would stop and listen to the nightingale as he was drawing in his nets at night.

"Now isn't that lovely!" he said, but he had to attend to his work, and he forgot the bird. However, the following night, when the nightingale sang again, and the fisherman came back to the same place, he repeated, "Now, isn't that lovely!"

Travelers from all over the world came to the Emperor's city. They admired the city as well as the Palace and the garden, but when they heard the nightingale everyone said the same: "That's the most fascinating of all."

When they returned home, the travelers talked about their visit; and the learned men wrote many books about the city, the Palace, and the garden, but the nightingale was by no means forgotten—on the contrary, they praised her above everything else, and those who could write in verse wrote the most beautiful poems about the nightingale in the forest by the deep sea.

These books went all over the world, and some of them finally reached the Emperor. Sitting in his golden chair he read and read. Every now and then he nodded his head contentedly, for he was delighted with the masterly descriptions of the city, the Palace, and the garden; "But the nightingale is really the most fascinating of all," they said.

"What!" said the Emperor. "The nightingale? It's funny I should never have heard of her. Is it possible that there is such a bird in my Empire, and in my very own garden? No one has ever told me so. Fancy having to find that out from books!"

Then he called his gentleman-in-waiting, who was so haughty that if a person of inferior rank had the audacity to address him, or to ask him questions, he answered nothing but "Peh!" and that means nothing at all.

"I understand that we have a most remarkable bird here called a nightingale," said the Emperor. "They say she is the most fascinating thing in my great Empire. Why have I never been told of this bird?"

"I have never heard of her before," said the gentleman-in-waiting. "She has never been presented at Court."

"I command her to come and sing for me tonight," said the Emperor. "Just imagine! The whole world knows that I possess this marvel, and I myself know nothing about it!"

"I have never heard of her before," repeated the gentleman-in-waiting, "but I am going to look for her, and I shall find her, too."

But where was the nightingale to be found? The gentleman-in-waiting kept running up and down all the stairs in the Palace, through the halls and the corridors, but none of the people he met had ever heard of the nightingale. So he ran back to the Emperor, and told him that undoubtedly it was just something that had been made up by the people who write books. "Your Imperial Majesty must not believe all that is written. It's pure invention, and what they call the black art."

"But the book in which I have read this," said the Emperor, "was sent to me by the high and mighty Emperor of Japan, and therefore cannot be all lies. I insist upon hearing the nightingale; she must be here tonight. I have bestowed my most gracious favor upon her—but if she does not appear, the entire Court will be punched in the stomach after supper."

"Tsing-pe!" said the gentleman-in-waiting, and he started again on his chase upstairs and downstairs, through halls and corridors; half the Court went with him, for none of them were particularly keen on being punched in the stomach after supper.

People were asking right and left about this remarkable nightingale which was known the whole world over, except to the members of the Court.

At last they found a poor little girl in the kitchen. She said, "Oh, the nightingale! I know all about her. My, how she sings! Every evening I am allowed to take scraps from the table to my poor sick mother who lives down by the shore. On my way home, when I stop to rest in the forest, I hear the nightingale sing. Tears come into my eyes, and I feel as if my mother were kissing me."

"Little kitchen-maid," said the gentleman-in-waiting, "I will get you a permanent place in the Palace kitchen, and obtain permission for you to see the Emperor dine, if you will only lead us to the nightingale, for she has been commanded to appear at Court this evening."

So they all went into the forest where the nightingale usually sang; half the Court went as well.

As they walked along a cow began to moo.

"Oh!" exclaimed the courtiers. "That's her! What extraordinary power for such a small creature! I'm sure I've heard her before."

"No, it's a cow mooing," said the little kitchen-maid. "We are still a long way from the place."

Then they heard frogs croaking in the pond.

"Beautiful!" sighed the Chinese Court-chaplain. "Now I can hear the nightingale; it sounds like little church bells."

"No, it's the frogs," said the little kitchen-maid, "but I think we shall soon hear her."

Then the nightingale began to sing.

"That's the nightingale," said the little girl. "Listen, listen! There she sits," she added, pointing to a little gray bird up in the branches.

"Is it possible?" exclaimed the gentleman-in-waiting. "I should never have thought she was like that. How common she looks! But she has probably lost her color seeing herself surrounded by so many distinguished personages!"

"Little nightingale!" called out the kitchen-maid. "Our gracious Emperor would so much like to hear you sing."

"With the greatest of pleasure," she replied, and sang so that it was a pure delight to hear her.

"It sounds like glass bells," remarked the gentleman-in-waiting, "and look how her little throat throbs! It's strange that we've never heard her before. That bird will be a great success at Court."

"Shall I sing once more before the Emperor?" asked the nightingale, who thought that His Imperial Majesty was present.

"Most excellent little nightingale," said the gentleman-in-waiting, "I have great pleasure in commanding you to appear at a Court function this evening, where you will delight His Imperial Majesty with your enchanting song."

"My song sounds better in the open," answered the nightingale, but she went with them willingly when she heard it was the Emperor's wish.

At the Palace everything had been beautifully polished; the walls and floors, which were all made of porcelain, sparkled in the light of thousands of golden lamps; most magnificent flowers with little jingling bells were placed in the corridors; there was such a coming and going, such a draught that all the little bells were set jingling and jangling. It was impossible to hear one's own voice.

In the center of the great reception hall, near the Emperor's throne, a golden perch had been placed for the nightingale. The entire Court was present, and the little kitchen-maid was allowed to stand behind the door, as she had now been appointed Imperial Court Cook.

They were all dressed in their best clothes, and they stared at the little gray bird to whom the Emperor was nodding graciously.

And the nightingale sang so beautifully that tears came into the Emperor's eyes and rolled down his cheeks. And then the nightingale sang still more beautifully and melted his very heart, and the Emperor was so pleased that he wanted the little bird to wear his golden slipper round her neck, but the nightingale declined the honor with thanks: her reward had already been ample.

"I have seen tears in the Emperor's eyes; nothing could be more precious to me! An Emperor's tears possess a mysterious power. Heaven knows I have been sufficiently rewarded." And she sang again with that sweet entrancing voice of hers.

"It has the most delightful touch of coquettishness we've ever heard," said the ladies present, and they filled their mouths with water to produce a jug-jugging sound whenever anyone spoke to them. It made them fancy they were nightingales themselves; even the footmen and the chambermaids let it be known that they also were quite pleased, which means a great deal, for these people are the most difficult to satisfy. There was no doubt about it, the nightingale was a huge success.

From that time she was to remain at Court, and have her own cage, with permission to go out for a walk twice a day and once at night. Twelve servants were to accompany her, each one holding tightly on to a silken ribbon fastened to the bird's leg. There was no fun at all in that kind of outing.

The whole town was talking about the wonderful bird, and when two people met, one of them could hardly say "Night . . ." before the other said "Gale!"—and then they sighed, and understood one another.

It even went so far that eleven pork-butchers' children were named after the nightingale, but not a single one of them had a note of music in him.

One day a large parcel arrived for the Emperor, on which was written "Nightingale."

"That's a new book about our famous bird, I'm sure," said the Emperor; but it wasn't a book, it was a small *objet d'art* lying in a box—an artificial nightingale, copied from the living bird, but covered all over with diamonds, rubies, and sapphires. When it was wound up, it could sing one of the airs sung by the real nightingale, while its tail flicked up and down, glittering with silver and gold. Round its neck was a ribbon with the inscription: "*The nightingale of the Emperor of Japan is poor compared with that of the Emperor of China.*"

"It's wonderful!" they all said; and the one who had brought the artificial bird was immediately given the title of "Chief-Imperial-Nightingale-Bringer."

"Now let's hear them together," said someone. "What a duet that will be!"

So they had to sing together, but it did not turn out very well, because the real nightingale sang in her own way, while the other bird's song was purely mechanical. "We can't lay the blame on the artificial bird," said the music-master. "It keeps perfect time, and sings exactly according to my method."

Then the artificial bird had to sing by itself. It was just as great a success as the real bird, and besides it was much prettier to look at, because it sparkled like so many bracelets and brooches.

Three-and-thirty times it sang its one and only tune, and still it was not the least bit tired. The courtiers would willingly have heard it all over again, only the Emperor thought that now the real nightingale should sing a little—but where was she? No one had noticed that she had flown out of the open window, away to her own green forests.

"What on earth is the meaning of this?" asked the Emperor, and all the courtiers were furious, and declared that the nightingale was a most ungrateful creature. "Fortunately we still have the best bird," they said; so the artificial one had to repeat for the thirty-fourth time its single tune, but they had not yet managed to learn it perfectly, because it was very difficult. The music-master praised the artificial bird to the skies; he assured them that it was better than the real nightingale, not only because of its diamond-studded exterior, but also because of its mechanical interior.

"For you see, ladies and gentlemen, and Your Imperial Majesty above all, with the real nightingale one can never be sure what is coming, but with the artificial bird everything has been set once and for all, and will remain set once and for all. The mechanism can be explained; one can take it to pieces and demonstrate what human skill can do, how the cylinders are disposed, how they go round, and how one thing is the result of another."

"Then it is exactly as I imagined it!" exclaimed everyone, and the music-master was authorized to show the bird to the people on the following Sunday.

"They ought to hear it too," said the Emperor.

They did hear it, and were as merry as if they had had a drop too much tea, for that is the Chinese all over. "Oh!" was heard on all sides, and everyone held up the finger we call "Lick-pot," and nodded his head.

But the poor fisherman who had heard the real nightingale said, "Well, it sounds quite nice, it's almost like the real bird, but there's something lacking, I don't know what."

However, the real nightingale was banished from the Empire.

The artificial bird had its place on a silken cushion near the Emperor's bed, and all the presents of gold and precious stones which the bird had received were lying round it. It had now been given the title of "High Imperial Bedside-table Singer, Class No. 1 on the left." The Emperor considered that side the most distinguished because of the heart, for even an Emperor's heart is on the left. And the music-master wrote twenty-five volumes about the artificial bird; they were all very long-winded and learned, full of the most difficult Chinese words—and yet everybody said they had read and understood them, otherwise they would of course have been stupid, and would have been punched in their stomachs.

In this way a whole year passed. The Emperor, the Court, and all the other Chinese knew by heart every tremolo and every trill of the artificial bird's song, and that was why they preferred it. They were able to join in the singing, and they did so.

The street urchins sang "Zee, zee, zee, gloo, gloo, gloo!" and the Emperor sang it too. They thought it was perfectly fascinating.

One evening, when the artificial bird was in the midst of its song, and the Emperor was listening to it from his bed, something suddenly clicked inside the bird, something snapped—"R-R-R-R—" The wheels whirled round and round, and the music stopped. The Emperor jumped quickly out of bed and summoned his physician, but what use was he? Then the watchmaker was brought, and after a great deal of discussion and examination, he repaired the bird as well as he could; but he said it must not be wound up too often, for the cogs were almost worn out and it was impossible to put in new ones to make the music go as smoothly as before.

It was a sad state of affairs! Once a year only was the artificial bird allowed to sing, and even that was almost too much of a strain, but on these occasions the music-master made a little speech, elaborated with all the most difficult words, declaring that the song was just as good as ever, and then of course it was just as good as ever.

Five years had gone by, when the whole country was suddenly stricken with a great sorrow—for at the bottom of their hearts the people were very fond of their Emperor; now he was ill, it was said, and could not possibly live. A new Emperor had already been chosen, and people stood in the street and asked the gentleman-in-waiting how it fared with the Emperor.

"Peh!" he said, and shook his head.

Cold and pale lay the Emperor in his great magnificent bed; the whole Court believed him dead, and everyone hastened to greet the new Emperor. The valets ran out to gossip, and the chambermaids gave a big tea-party. Thick carpets had been laid down in all the halls and corridors to muffle the sound of footsteps: a profound silence had fallen upon the Palace.

But the Emperor was not dead yet. Stiff and pale he lay in his magnificent bed with the long velvet curtains and heavy gold tassels. High up a window stood open, and the moon shone down on him and on the artificial bird.

The poor Emperor could hardly breathe; it seemed to him that something was sitting on his chest. He opened his eyes and saw that it was Death. He had put on the golden crown; in one hand he held the Emperor's golden sword, and in the other his gorgeous banner.

From between the folds of the big velvet curtains strange-looking faces peered out, some quite horrifying, others gentle and mild. These were all the bad and good deeds of the Emperor watching him now that Death was sitting on his heart.

"Do you remember this? Do you remember that?" they whispered one after the other. And they told him so many things that a cold sweat broke out on his brow.

"No, no, I never knew about any of those things," said the Emperor. "Music! music! Let the great Chinese drum be sounded to drown all these voices!"

But they continued to whisper, and Death nodded in the Chinese fashion to every word that was said.

"Music, more music!" cried the Emperor. "Dearest little golden bird, sing, I beg you, sing! I have given you gold and precious stones, I hung my golden slipper round your neck myself; sing, I beg you, sing!"

But the bird remained silent—there was no one to wind it up, and so it could not sing; but Death kept on staring at the Emperor from his great hollow eye-sockets. The silence became deeper and more terrifying.

Suddenly through the window was heard the sweetest of songs. It was the little living nightingale that was sitting on a branch outside. She had heard of her Emperor's distress, and had come to bring him hope and comfort with her song. As she sang, the phantoms became paler and paler, the blood flowed quicker and quicker through the Emperor's frail body, and Death himself listened and said, "Sing on, little nightingale, sing on!"

"Yes, if you will give me the magnificent golden sword, if you will give me the gorgeous banner, if you will give me the Emperor's crown."

Then Death handed over each of these treasures for a song, and the nightingale continued her singing. She sang about the quiet churchyard where the white roses bloom, where the elder-tree fills the air with its fragrance, and where the fresh green grass is bedewed with the tears of sorrowing mourners. Death was seized with a longing for his quiet garden, and vanished like a cold white mist out of the window.

"Thank you! thank you!" said the Emperor. "You heavenly little bird, I know full well who you are. It was you I banished from my Empire, and yet your song has chased the evil visions from my bed, and driven Death from my heart. How can I reward you?"

"You have rewarded me; tears came to your eyes when I sang to you the first time; I shall never forget what that meant to me. Those are the jewels that warm a singer's heart. But go to sleep now, and wake up well and strong again. I will sing to you." And she went on singing. At last the Emperor fell into a sweet slumber, a sweet soothing slumber.

The sun was shining through the window on him when he awoke, strong and well. Not one of his servants had yet come to his room, for they all believed him to be dead; but the nightingale was still singing.

"You must stay with me always," said the Emperor. "You shall only sing when you feel like it, and I will break the artificial bird into a thousand pieces."

"Don't do that," said the nightingale. "It did all that it was capable of doing. Keep it as you did before. I cannot settle down and live in the Palace, but do let me come whenever I like. In the evening I will sit on that branch just outside your window and sing so that you may be glad and also thoughtful. I will sing about happy people and about those who suffer, I will sing about the good and the evil around you which are kept hidden from you. The little song-bird flies far and wide, to the fisherman's hut or the farmer's house, to all who are a long way from you and your Court. I love your heart better than your crown, and yet the crown has an odor of sanctity about it. I will come and I will sing to you, but you must promise me one thing."

"Whatever you ask," said the Emperor. And there he stood in his Imperial robes which he had put on himself, holding the sword heavy with gold up to his heart.

"One thing only I beg of you—let no one know that you have a little bird who tells you everything, then all will go even better."

And the nightingale flew away.

The servants came in to attend to their dead Emperor—yes, there they stood—and the Emperor said, "Good morning!"

THE SNOW QUEEN

A TALE IN SEVEN STORIES

First Story

Which Concerns the Mirror and Its Fragments

LISTEN! Now we are going to begin. When the story is ended we shall know a lot more than we do now.

It was all the work of a wicked troll, one of the wickedest of them, in fact "Old Nick" himself. One day he was in high good humor, for he had made a mirror which had the peculiarity of reducing the reflection of everything good and beautiful to almost nothing, while everything worthless and ugly became even more worthless and ugly than before. The most beautiful landscapes when seen in the mirror looked like boiled spinach, and the best of men became hideous, or stood on their heads and had no stomachs. Their faces were so distorted that it was impossible to recognize them, and if you had a single freckle you might be sure that it would look as if it had spread all over your nose and mouth. "That's great fun!" said Old Nick. If a good pious thought passed through anyone's mind, the mirror reflected it as a leering grin, and the devil was convulsed with laughter at his most original invention. All those who went to the troll-school—he had a troll-school, you know—rushed about telling everybody that a miracle had happened. For the first time, they declared, you could see what the world and its people really looked like. They ran everywhere with the mirror, and at last there was not a single country nor a single person that had not been distorted. They even attempted to fly up into heaven to make fun of the angels and the Lord God. The higher they flew with the mirror the worse it leered; they could hardly hold it. They flew higher and higher, nearer and nearer to God and the angels. The grinning mirror shook so terribly that it slipped out of their hands and crashed down to earth, where it was shattered into hundreds of millions and billions and—many many more pieces, and now it did much greater damage than before. Some of the splinters were scarcely as big as grains of sand, and they went whirling about all over the wide world. When they flew into people's eyes they stuck there, causing them to see everything crooked, or to notice only the ugly side of things, for every single little speck of glass retained the power of the whole mirror.

A few people even got a splinter of it into their hearts, and that was terrible indeed, for then their hearts became exactly like a lump of ice. Some of the pieces were so large that they could be used as window-panes, but it was better not to look at one's friends through that kind of window. Other fragments were made into spectacles, and when people put them on so as to see clearly and be fair in their judgment, the trouble began. The Evil One was so tickled with it all that he split his sides with laughter; but tiny specks of glass were still whirling about in the air.

And now we shall hear what happened.

Second Story
A Little Boy and a Little Girl

In the big city, so overcrowded with houses and people that there is not space enough for everybody to have even a tiny garden, and most people must content themselves with flowers in pots and boxes, there were two poor children who had a garden a little bigger than a flower-pot. They were not brother and sister, but they loved each other just as much as if they were. Their parents lived next door to one another, up in two attics. These attics had dormer windows facing each other across the gutter which separated the roof of one house from that of its neighbor. You had only to stride over the gutter to get from one window to the other. The parents had a big window-box outside each window, in which grew such vegetables as they needed, and a little rose-tree as well. Each box had one tree, and it throve splendidly.

One day it occurred to the parents to place the boxes right across the gutter in such a way that they almost reached from one window to the other, and looked for all the world like two hedges of flowers. The pea-plants hung down over the boxes, and the rose-trees, throwing out long shoots, draped themselves round the windows like garlands, reaching out towards one another; it looked almost like a triumphal arch of green leaves and flowers. As the boxes were very high, the children knew that they were not to clamber up on to them, but they were often allowed to step out of their own windows and sit together on their little stools under the roses. In that little paradise of theirs they had a glorious time playing.

Of course there was no amusement of that sort during the winter. The windows were often completely frozen over, but then the children warmed pennies on the stove, held the heated coin against the frozen pane, and lo! there appeared a most perfect peephole, as round as round could be. From behind each peephole gazed out the loveliest child's eye you ever saw. It was the little boy and the little girl behind the window. His name was Kay, and her name was Gerda.

In summer-time one jump was enough to bring them together, but in winter they had to run all the way downstairs and all the way up again before they could meet.

Outside the snow was whirling.

"Look at the white bees swarming," said the old grandmother.

"Have they got a Queen-bee too?" asked the little boy, for he knew that there was one among the real bees.

"Yes, they have," said Grandmother. "She's always to be found where the swarm is thickest. She's the biggest of them all, and never remains still on the earth, but always returns to the black cloud. Many a winter's night she flies down through the streets of the town and looks through the windows; then they freeze over in the most peculiar way, as if they were decorated with flowers."

"Oh, yes, we've seen that," said the children, and so they knew it was true.

"Can the Snow Queen come in here?" asked the little girl.

"Just let her try!" exclaimed the boy. "I'll put her on the hot stove and melt her." But the grandmother stroked his hair and told some other stories.

That evening, when Kay was at home and half undressed, he clambered up on to the chair by the window and peeped through the little hole. A few snowflakes were falling, and one of them, the very biggest, remained on the edge of one of the flower-boxes. The snowflake grew larger and larger: at last it took the shape of a woman clothed in the finest white gauze, which looked as if it had been made of millions of star-like flakes. She was beautiful and delicate, but she was all ice—glimmering, glittering ice. Nevertheless she was alive: her eyes flashed like two clear stars, but there was neither peace nor rest in them.

She nodded towards the window and beckoned with her hand. The little boy got frightened and jumped down from the chair. At that very moment it seemed as if a great bird flew past the window.

Next day the weather turned clear and frosty—then a thaw set in—and spring appeared. The sun shone and over the whole countryside came a quiver of green, the swallows built their nests, the windows were flung wide open, and the children sat once more in their little garden in the gutter, high up above all the other floors.

That summer the roses bloomed as they had never bloomed before. The little girl had learnt a hymn with a parable about the Christ Child and the roses; they reminded her of her own. She sang to the little boy, and then they both sang:

"*As the roses bloom in the valley, sweet,*
So the Christ Child there ye shall truly meet."

And the little ones held each other by the hand, kissed the roses, and looked up at God's bright sunshine and spoke to it, as if the Christ Child were there. What beautiful summer days those were! How lovely it was among the fresh rose-trees which never seemed to stop blooming!

Kay and Gerda were looking at the picture-book of birds and beasts, when suddenly—at the very moment that the big church clock struck five—Kay cried out, "Ow! Something has pricked my heart, and now I've got something in my eye!"

The little girl put her arms round his neck. He blinked his eyes; no, there was nothing there.

"I think it's gone," he said, but it had not gone. It was just one of those specks of glass which had flown from the mirror—the troll-mirror you remember, that horrid mirror which made everything great and good that was reflected in it seem small and ugly, but made everything wicked and bad seem magnified, and every flaw more noticeable. Poor Kay! a splinter had also found its way into his heart; it would soon turn into a lump of ice. He suffered no pain now, but the splinter was still there.

"What are you crying for?" he asked. "It makes you look so ugly. There's nothing the matter with me."

"How horrid!" he suddenly shouted. "That rose is all worm-eaten, and look, that one is quite crooked. Come to think of it, those roses are just as nasty as they can be—they're as bad as the boxes they're growing in." And then he kicked the boxes and tore off the two roses.

"What are you doing, Kay?" cried the little girl, and when he noticed how frightened she was, he snatched off another rose and ran inside through his own window, away from dear little Gerda.

Later on, when she came with the picture-book, he said it was only fit for a baby in arms. When Grandmother was telling stories, he always interrupted with a "but," and, if he could manage it, he would walk behind her, put on a pair of spectacles, and mimic her. It was a wonderful imitation, and people thought it great fun. Very soon he could copy the speech and the walk of everybody who lived in the street.

Kay could imitate to perfection whatever was peculiar or ugly about them, and people said, "He's got a good head on him, that lad!" But it was the bit of glass that had flown into his eye, and the splinter that had lodged in his heart, which made him tease even little Gerda who loved him with all her heart and soul.

The games he played now were very different from what they used to be; they were quite intellectual. One winter's day, when the snowflakes were whirling, he went outside with a great magnifying-glass, and opened out his blue coat-tails to the falling flakes. "Now look through the glass, Gerda," he said. Every snowflake had become much larger and looked like a beautiful flower or a ten-pointed star; it was wonderful!

"Isn't that curious?" said Kay. "These are much more interesting to look at than the real flowers, and there's not a single flaw in them—they're quite perfect until they begin to melt."

A few minutes afterwards Kay appeared with thick gloves on, and carrying his sledge on his back. He shouted right into Gerda's ear, "They've said I can go sledging in the big square where all the other boys are playing"—and off he went.

In the square the boldest boys often tied their sledges to the farmers' carts, and so had a good ride. It was great fun. While they were happily at play, a big sleigh appeared. It was all painted white, and in it someone was sitting wrapped up in a rough white fur coat, and wearing a rough white fur cap. The sleigh drove twice round the square; quickly Kay looped the rope of his little sledge on to it and was pulled along. They drove on faster and faster, straight into the next street. The driver turned round and nodded kindly to Kay as if they were old friends. Each time he wanted to unfasten his little sledge the driver nodded again, and he remained where he was, and so they drove right out of the town gate. Then the snow began to fall so heavily that the boy could not see his hand before his face as they sped on. Suddenly he dropped the rope in order to get away from the big sleigh, but it was no use—his little sledge could not be freed, and on they went like the wind. He started shouting, but nobody heard him, and the snow whirled and the sleigh flew. Every now and then it gave a jump; they seemed to be flying over hedges and ditches. The boy was terrified, he tried to say his prayers, but could remember nothing but the multiplication table. The snowflakes became larger and larger, until they looked like great white hens. All of a sudden they flew to one side, the big sleigh stopped, and the person who was driving it stood up. The fur coat and cap were made entirely of snow. It was a woman, tall and slender, and glittering white. It was the Snow Queen.

"We haven't done badly at all," she said. "But don't tell me you are cold. Creep into my bearskin." And she placed him beside her in the sleigh, and wrapped the fur round him. He felt as if he were sinking into a deep snowdrift.

"Are you still cold?" she asked, and kissed him on the forehead. Ugh! Her kiss was colder than ice. It penetrated right into his heart which was already half turned into ice. He thought he was going to die—but only for a moment, then a sense of relief came, and he did not notice the cold any more.

"My sledge! don't forget my sledge!" was his first thought. So it was fastened to one of the white hens, and the bird flew behind them with the sledge on its back. The Snow Queen kissed Kay once more, and immediately he forgot little Gerda, and the grandmother, and everyone at home.

"I'm not going to kiss you any more," she said. "If I did, I should kiss you to death." Kay looked at her. She was so beautiful. He could not imagine a brighter or more lovely face. She did not seem to be all ice now as she did when she sat outside the window and beckoned to him. In his eyes she was perfect. He was not at all frightened; he told her that he could do mental arithmetic even with fractions; that he knew the areas of all the countries, and the answer to "What is their population?" And she went on smiling. Then he began to suspect that he did not know so very much after all. Bewildered, he gazed into space. She flew away with him, flew high up on to the black cloud, while the storm howled and roared —it sounded very much like old folk-tunes. They flew over woods and lakes, over sea and land; below them the icy wind went whistling, wolves howled, black screaming crows flew low over the glistening snow, but over it all shone the moon, large and clear, and on that Kay gazed during the long, long winter's night. By day he slept at the feet of the Snow Queen.

Third Story
The Flower Garden of the Woman Who Could Work Magic

How was little Gerda getting on without Kay? Where was he? Nobody knew, nobody could give any information. The boys could only say that they had seen him fasten his little sledge to a beautiful big sleigh which had driven through the street and disappeared out of the town gate. Nobody knew where he was; many tears were shed, and little Gerda cried her heart out. It was rumored that he was dead, that he had been swallowed up by the river near the town. How long and dreary were those winter days!

Spring came with warmer sunshine.

"Kay is dead and gone," said little Gerda.

"I don't believe it," said the sunshine.

"He's dead and gone," she said to the swallows.

"We don't believe it," they answered, and finally little Gerda did not believe it herself.

"I'm going to put on my red shoes," she said one morning, "the ones Kay has never seen, and then I'll go down to the river and ask about him."

It was early in the morning; she kissed her grandmother who was still asleep, put on the red shoes, and stole away all alone out of the town gate down to the river.

"Is it true that you've taken my little playmate? I'll give you my red shoes if you'll give him back to me."

And it seemed to her that the waves were nodding in such a strange way. Then she took off her red shoes—her dearest treasure—and threw them into the river, but they remained near the bank and were brought back to her by the wash of the little waves. It seemed as if the river refused to take her dearest treasure, because it had not got her little Kay. However, she thought that she might not have thrown them far enough, so she climbed into a boat that lay among the reeds, went to the further end and threw her shoes overboard; but the boat was not tied and her movements made it slip away from the land. She noticed this and hurried to get out, but before she could reach the other end of the boat it was already some distance from the bank, and was drifting faster and faster downstream.

She got frightened and started crying, but no one heard her except the sparrows, and they could not carry her ashore, but they flew along the river's edge, chirping as if to comfort her, "Here we are! Here we are!"

The boat floated along with the stream, and little Gerda sat quite still in her stocking feet; her little red shoes floated along behind her, but could not catch up with the boat as it sped away. Both sides of the river were beautiful with old trees and lovely flowers, and slopes dotted with grazing sheep and cows; but not a single soul was to be seen.

"Perhaps the river will carry me to little Kay," thought Gerda, and she became more cheerful. She stood up and for a long time looked at the beautiful green banks. Then she came to a great cherry orchard in which there was a little house with strange blue and red windows. It had a thatched roof, and outside were two wooden soldiers who presented arms to everyone who sailed past.

Gerda called out to them; she thought they were alive, but of course they did not answer. She got quite close to them because the river was carrying the boat straight towards the bank.

Gerda called louder. An old, old woman then came out of the house, leaning on a crooked stick, and wearing a large sun-hat painted with the most beautiful flowers.

"You poor little child!" said the old woman. "However did you manage to get out on to the great strong current and let yourself be carried away into the wide world?" And the old woman waded right out in to the water, hooked the boat with her stick, drew it towards the bank, and lifted little Gerda out.

She was glad to be on dry land again, though she was a little afraid of the strange old woman.

"Now come and tell me who you are, and how you came here," she said.

So Gerda told her everything. The old woman shook her head and said, "Hm, hm!" And when Gerda had finished her story, and asked her if she had not seen little Kay, the old woman said no, he hadn't come her way, but he was sure to come. She told her not to be downhearted, but to taste her cherries and see her flowers, which were more interesting than any picture-book, for each of them could tell a story. Then she took Gerda by the hand and they went into the little house, and the old woman locked the door.

The red, blue, and yellow windows sat high up under the roof. The daylight coming through was such a strange mixture of all kinds of colors; but on the table was a bowl with the most wonderful cherries, and Gerda, who was not afraid any more, ate as many as she liked. While she was eating, the old woman combed her hair with a golden comb, her pretty hair hanging in sunny curls about her little round friendly face that had the bloom of a rosebud.

"I've been longing for a sweet little girl like you," said the old woman. "We shall get along ever so well together." And while she was combing her hair, Gerda forgot her foster-brother Kay more and more, for, you know, the old woman was well versed in witchcraft, though she was not really a bad witch! She only "hocus-pocused" a bit for her own pleasure, and just now she wanted very much to keep little Gerda with her, so she went out into the garden, stretched her crooked stick towards all the rose-trees, and even the most beautiful ones disappeared into the black earth, leaving never a trace to show where they had been. The woman was afraid that they would remind Gerda of her roses at home, and of Kay, and make her run away.

Then she led her out into the flower garden. Never had Gerda known such fragrance and such beauty! Every conceivable flower of every season was there in full bloom. No picture-book could have been gayer or prettier. Gerda jumped for joy, and played about till the sun set behind the tall cherry trees. Then she was put into a lovely bed with red silken eiderdowns stuffed with blue violets, and she slept there dreaming as gloriously as any Queen on her wedding morning.

The next day she played again with the flowers in the warm sunshine—and so she did for many a day. Gerda knew every flower, but, however many there were, it always seemed to her that one was missing, though she did not know which one it was. One day she sat looking at the old woman's sun-hat with the painted flowers, the prettiest of which was a rose. The old woman had forgotten to take this one off her hat when she conjured the others down into the earth. But that's what happens when you don't keep your wits about you!

"What! aren't there any roses here?" said Gerda, and she ran in among the flower-beds, searching and searching, but there was not a single rose to be found. Then she sat down and wept; her hot tears fell just on the spot where a rose-tree had disappeared, and when those warm tears had moistened the earth, the tree sprang up again, blossoming as beautifully as before. Gerda put her arms round it, kissed the roses, and thought of the beautiful ones at home, and of course of little Kay.

"Oh, how I have been delayed!" said the little girl. "I started out to find Kay—don't you know where he is?" she asked the roses. "Do you think he's dead and gone?"

"He's not dead," said the roses. "We've been down in the earth where all the dead people are, but Kay was not there."

"Thank you," said little Gerda, and she went to the other flowers, looked into their hearts and asked, "Don't you know where little Kay is?"

But every flower stood in the sun, dreaming its own fairy tale or its story. Gerda listened to many, many of them, but none of the flowers knew anything about Kay.

What did the tiger-lily say?

"Do you hear the drum? Boom, boom! There are only two notes, always boom, boom! Listen to the women's dirge! Listen to the cry of the priests! The Hindu woman stands in her long red robe on the pyre, the flames rise up round her and her dead husband, but she is thinking of the living man down there in the crowd, of him whose eyes are burning hotter than the flames, whose fiery glances have penetrated her heart deeper than the flames which will soon burn her body to ashes. Can the flame of the heart perish in the flame of the funeral pyre?"

"I don't understand that at all," said little Gerda.

"That's my story," said the tiger-lily.

What does the convolvulus say?

"High above the narrow mountain path looms an ancient castle. The thick ivy climbs up the old red walls reaching to the balcony where stands a fair maiden. She leans over the balustrade and gazes far down the road. No rose bends more gracefully on its stem than she; no apple blossom, wafted by the wind, is lighter than she. How her costly gown rustles! 'Will he never come?' "

"Is it Kay you mean?" asked little Gerda.

"I'm only telling you my own story, my own dream," answered the convolvulus.

What does the little snowdrop say?

"Between the trees hangs a board held up by two long ropes; it is a swing. Two pretty little girls in dresses white as snow, and with long green silken ribbons fluttering from their hats, are swinging away merrily. Their brother, who is taller than they, is standing on the swing with his arms round the ropes to steady himself. In one hand he holds a little saucer, in the other a clay pipe; he is blowing bubbles. High and low, high and low flies the swing, and the bubbles float about in ever-changing colors. One of the bubbles still clings to the bowl of the pipe, swaying in the breeze. High and low, high and low flies the swing. A little black dog, light as the bubbles, stands on his hind legs, begging to be taken on to the swing. Backwards and forwards it flies—the dog rolls over, barks and gets angry; the children tease him, the bubbles burst; a swinging board, a dancing foam-picture is my song."

"The story you tell me may be very pretty, but you tell it so sadly, and you never mention Kay."

What do the hyacinths say?

"There were three fair sisters, transparent and delicate: the first had on a red dress, the second a blue one, and the third was all in white. Hand in hand they danced by the calm lake in the bright moonlight. They were not elves, but human beings. The air was heavy with the scent of flowers, and the maidens disappeared into the forest. The scent became stronger—three coffins, with three beautiful maidens in them, glided from the depths of the forest across the lake. Fire-flies flew about gleaming like little flickering lights. Are the dancing maidens asleep or are they dead? The scent of the flowers tells of their death; the evening bell tolls for the dead."

"You make me feel very sad," said little Gerda. "Your scent is so strong I can't help thinking of those dead maidens. Oh, dear! Is little Kay really dead? The roses have actually been down in the ground, and they say no!"

"Ding, dong," tolled the hyacinth bells. "We're not ringing for little Kay; we don't know him. We're merely singing our song, the only song we know."

Gerda went up to the buttercup shining in the midst of the glistening green leaves. "You're such a bright little sun," she said. "Tell me, do you know where I can find my playmate?" And the buttercup shone so brightly, and it looked at Gerda. What song would the buttercup sing? That song was not to be about Kay either.

"On the first day of spring, God's sun shed its warmth upon a little courtyard; its rays spread over the wall of the neighboring house. Close by grew the first yellow flowers, shining like gold in the warm sun. Old Grandmother sat out of doors in her chair; her pretty granddaughter, a poor servant-girl, was returning home from a short visit; she kissed her grandmother, and there was gold, a heart's gold, in that blessed kiss. Gold on her lips, gold of the flower, gold above in that morning hour! That's my little story," said the buttercup.

"Poor old Granny!" sighed Gerda. "I'm sure she is longing for me, and grieving for me as she grieved for little Kay. But I'm soon going home again, and then I shall take Kay with me. It's no use asking the flowers. They only know their own songs, they've got no news to tell me."

Then she tucked up her little frock so that she could run faster, but the white narcissus brushed against her leg as she jumped over it. That stopped her; she looked at the tall flower, bent down over it, and asked, "Do you happen to know anything?"

And what did the narcissus say?

"I can see myself! I can see myself!" said the narcissus. "Oh, how strong my fragrance is! Up in the garret stands a little dancer, half dressed. She stands first on one leg, then on both, and flicks her toe at the whole world. She is a mere vision. She pours water from a teapot on to a bit of stuff she is holding. It is her bodice—cleanliness is a good thing, you know! On a hook hangs her white frock which has also been washed in the water from the teapot, and dried on the roof. She puts it on and ties her saffron-yellow kerchief round her neck, and the dress seems all the whiter. Look at her balancing herself on one leg! Look how erect she stands on a single stem! I can see myself! I can see myself!"

"I don't care about that," said Gerda. "What a thing to tell me!" and then she ran to the end of the garden.

The gate was locked, but she wiggled the rusty latch till it got loose, and the gate sprang open; then little Gerda ran barefoot out into the wide world. Three times she looked back, but no one pursued her. At last she could run no more, so she sat down on a big stone, and when she looked about her, lo! summer was over; it was late autumn. You would never have suspected it in the beautiful garden where there was sunshine all the time, and where the flowers of all the seasons were in bloom.

"Good heavens! How I have dawdled!" said little Gerda. "Autumn has come already, I daren't rest any longer." And she got up to walk on.

Oh, how sore and tired were her poor little feet! And all around it looked so cold and bleak. The long willow leaves were quite yellow, and the mist dripped from them like drops of water; one leaf after another fell; only the blackthorn still bore its fruit, a fruit that puckered up your mouth.

Oh, how gray and gloomy it looked, out in the wide world!

Fourth Story
The Prince and Princess

Gerda had to rest again. Right in front of her a big crow started hopping about on the snow; he had been sitting watching her for a long time, turning and bending his head; and then he said, "Caw! caw! Caw'd day! Caw'd day!"

He could say it no better, but he meant to be kind to the little girl, and asked where she was going, all alone like that in the wide world. "Alone!" That was a word she understood only too well, and she felt how much it expressed. Then she told the crow the whole story of her life, and asked if he had not seen Kay. The crow nodded his head thoughtfully and said, "Maybe I have, maybe I have!"

"What! do you really think you have?" cried the little girl, almost smothering him with kisses.

"Gently, gently!" said the crow. "It might have been little Kay, but if so, I'm afraid he has forgotten you for the Princess."

"Does he live with a Princess?" asked Gerda.

"Yes. Listen!" said the crow. "But it's so difficult for me to speak your language. If only you understood 'Crowish,' it would be easier for me to tell you all about it."

"I'm sorry I've never learnt it," said Gerda, "but Granny knows it, and she knows 'Gibberish' too. I wish I'd learnt it!"

"Never mind," said the crow. "I'll tell you as well as I can, but I'm afraid it's going to be pretty bad all the same." Then the crow told her all he knew.

"In the Kingdom where we are now, there's a Princess who is most terribly clever, and no wonder, for she has read all the newspapers in the world and then forgotten them again, which shows you how clever she is! The other day she was sitting on her throne—and that's no great fun either, they say. Well, then almost unconsciously she began to hum a tune, and that just happened to be:

'Why shouldn't I marry me, why? ah, why?'

" 'Now that's an idea!' she said; so she made up her mind to get married, but she wanted a husband who knew how to answer when he was spoken to, someone who did not only stand there looking superior, for that's so boring! So she had the gong sounded to collect all her ladies-in-waiting, and when they heard what she wanted, they were delighted. 'Oh, we *are* pleased,' they said. 'We were thinking exactly the same thing the other day!' I assure you that every word I'm telling you is true," said the crow. "I've got a tame sweetheart who goes about the Palace, and she's told me everything." Of course his sweetheart was a crow, for birds of a feather flock together.

"All the newspapers were at once published with a border of hearts and the initials of the Princess, and it was announced in them that any handsome young man might come to the Palace and talk to the Princess, and the one who talked as if he were quite at home there, and was the best talker, the Princess would choose for her husband. Yes, yes," said the crow, "you must believe me, for it's as true as I sit here! Suitors began to arrive in great numbers—there was a hustle and a bustle everywhere, but nothing happened on the first or second day. They were all talkative enough when they were in the streets, but once inside the Palace gates, where they saw the guards in silver-braided uniforms, and the lackeys in gold-braided liveries lining the stairs, and the reception halls all lit up, they were dumbfounded. When they stood in front of the throne where the Princess was sitting, they could think of nothing to say but the last word she had said herself, and she did not care to hear it repeated.

It was just as if all the people in the room had been given snuff-plasters on their stomachs which had paralyzed their faculties, but as soon as they were out in the streets again, nothing could stop their chatter. There was quite a long line of them from the town gate as far as the Palace. I saw it myself!" said the crow. "They got hungry and thirsty, but not even a glass of lukewarm water was sent out to them from the Palace. It's true that a few of the most sensible had brought sandwiches with them, but they did not share them with their rivals. They thought to themselves, 'Just let him look hungry, and the Princess will have none of him!' "

"But Kay, little Kay," asked Gerda, "when did he come? Was he among all those people?"

"Give me time! give me time! We are soon coming to him. It was on the third day that a little fellow came swaggering along up to the Palace without either horse or carriage. His eyes sparkled like yours and he had beautiful long hair, but his clothes were a bit shabby."

"That was Kay!" Gerda burst out joyfully, clapping her hands. "I've found him at last!"

"He carried a little knapsack on his back," said the crow.

"No, it must have been his sledge," said Gerda. "He had it with him when he went away."

"It might have been," said the crow. "I didn't take much notice of it, but I know from my tame sweetheart that when he passed through the Palace gate and saw the bodyguards in silver, and the lackeys on the stairs in gold, he wasn't the least bit embarrassed. He only nodded to them and said, 'It must be very boring just to stand on the stairs; I'd rather go inside!' The halls were ablaze with lights; Privy Councilors, Knights of the Elephant, and Ambassadors were walking barefoot, carrying gold salvers. It was enough to overawe anyone. His boots squeaked most dreadfully, but still he wasn't a bit frightened."

"I'm sure that was Kay," said Gerda. "I know he had new boots on, I've heard them squeak in Granny's room."

"Yes, I should think they did squeak," said the crow, "and quite unabashed, he walked straight up to the Princess, who was sitting on a pearl as big as a spinning-wheel. All the ladies-in-waiting with their maids and their maids' maids, and all the gentlemen-in-waiting with their footmen and their footmen's footmen who kept pages, were standing round, and the nearer they stood to the door, the haughtier they looked. The footmen's footman's boy, who always wore slippers, was almost more than one could bear to look at, so proudly did he stand in the doorway."

"It must have been awful," said little Gerda. "And yet Kay has won the Princess!"

"If I had not been a crow, I should have married her myself, even though I am engaged. They say he spoke as well as I do when I speak 'Crowish'—I have that from my tame sweetheart. He was unabashed and looked so handsome; he had not come with the idea of wooing the Princess, but simply to hear her wisdom. That appealed to him and he appealed to her."

"It must have been Kay," said Gerda. "He was so clever that he could do mental arithmetic with fractions. Oh! won't you take me to the Palace?"

"It's easy enough to talk," said the crow, "but how are we to manage it? I'll speak to my tame sweetheart about it, she might be able to advise us—but I may as well tell you that a little girl like you will never be admitted."

"Oh, yes, I shall," said Gerda. "When Kay hears that I've arrived, he'll come out at once and fetch me."

"Wait for me at that stile," said the crow, and he waggled his head and flew off.

It was completely dark before he returned. "Caw, caw," he said. "She sends her kind regards and a little loaf of bread for you. She took it from the kitchen; there's plenty there and you must be hungry! It's impossible for you to get into the Palace with those bare feet; the guards in silver and the lackeys in gold would never allow it. But don't cry, we'll manage to get you in somehow. My sweetheart knows a little back staircase which leads up to the Princess's bedchamber, and she also knows where she can find the key."

Then they went into the garden, and from there into the great avenue where the leaves were falling one by one, and when the lights in the Palace were put out one by one, the crow led little Gerda to a back door which stood ajar.

Oh, how her heart was beating with fear and longing! It was just as if she were going to do something wrong, and yet she only wanted to know if it really was little Kay. No, there could be no doubt; she fancied she could actually see his bright eyes and his long hair. She had such a vivid recollection of his charming smile—the smile he used to have when they sat at home together under the rose-tree. Surely he would be glad to see her, and to hear what a long way she had come for his sake, and how sad they had all been at home when he did not return. She was trembling with fear and joy.

There they were on the stairs. A little lamp was burning on a cupboard. In the middle of the landing stood the tame crow, twisting and turning her head to look at Gerda who curtseyed as Granny had taught her.

"My fiancé has spoken so charmingly of you, little lady," said the tame crow. "Your *Vita,* as people call it, makes a most touching story, I must say! If you will take the lamp, I will precede you. We will go straight ahead to avoid meeting anyone."

"It seems to me there is someone close behind us," said Gerda, and something swished by; it looked like shadows on the wall, shadows of horses with flying manes and skinny legs, of huntsmen, and ladies and gentlemen on horseback.

"Those," said the lady crow, "are only the dreams which come to take the thoughts of the Prince and Princess a-hunting. That is a good thing, for it will give you a better chance to look at them while they are asleep. But if you should ever rise to a state of honor and dignity, promise me that you will show a grateful heart."

"That was quite uncalled for," said the wild crow.

Then they came into the first hall; it was hung with rose-tinted satin, embroidered with flowers. Even here the dreams were flying past with such speed that Gerda could not distinguish the lords and ladies. Each hall was more beautiful than the last; it was enough to bewilder anyone.

Now they were in the bedchamber. The ceiling looked like the crown of a great palm-tree with leaves of crystal, costly crystal, and down towards the center of the floor hung a thick golden stem from which two lily-shaped beds unfolded. One was white, and in that lay the Princess; the other was red, and that was the one in which Gerda had to look for little Kay. She bent aside one of the red leaves, and saw a little brown neck—surely it was Kay! She called out his name very loudly—held the lamp close to him; the dreams rushed back into the room on horseback; he awoke, turned his head, and—it was not little Kay! It was only about the neck that the Prince looked like Kay, though he was young and handsome. The Princess peeped out from her white lily bed and asked whatever was happening. Then little Gerda cried and told her the whole story, and all that the crows had done for her.

"You poor little thing!" said the Prince and Princess, and they praised the crows, and said they were not at all angry with them, but hoped they would not do it again. However, they should be rewarded this time.

"Would you like to fly about as freely as you please?" asked the Princess, "or would you prefer a permanent position as 'Court Crows,' with the rights to the kitchen scraps?"

Both crows curtseyed and asked for permanent positions, for they thought of their future, and said it would be useful to have something put by for a "showery rainy day," as they called it.

The Prince got out of his bed and let Gerda sleep in it, and he could not have done more. She folded her little hands and thought, "How kind men and birds are!" Then she shut her eyes and slept peacefully. All the dreams came rushing back again, looking like angels drawing a little sledge on which Kay sat, nodding gaily. This was only a dream, and of course it vanished as soon as she woke up.

The next day she was dressed in silk and velvet from top to toe. She was invited to stay at the Palace and enjoy herself, but she begged only for a little horse and carriage, and a pair of little boots. She wanted to drive out into the wide world and look for Kay.

They gave her a pair of boots and a muff, and dressed her up most charmingly, and when she was ready to leave, there was a new coach of pure gold at the door, on which the coat-of-arms of the Prince and Princess shone like a star. Coachman, lackeys, and outriders—yes, there were outriders too—all wore golden crowns. The Prince and Princess themselves helped her into the coach, and wished her all the luck in the world. The wild crow, who was now married, accompanied her the first twelve miles, and sat beside Gerda, as it did not agree with him to ride backwards. The other crow stood in the gateway flapping her wings. She did not go with them as she was suffering from a headache, as she had been eating too much ever since she obtained the permanent position at Court. The coach was lined with sugared pastry twists, and the box-seats were filled with fruits and ginger nuts.

"Good-by! Good-by!" cried the Prince and Princess. Little Gerda wept and the crow wept too while they were driving the first few miles. Then he said good-by, and that was the hardest parting of all. He flew up into a tree and flapped his great black wings as long as he could see the coach, glittering like the bright sunshine.

Fifth Story
The Little Robber Girl

They drove on through the dark forest, but the coach gleamed like a torch, dazzling the robbers. It was more than they could bear. "It's gold! It's gold!" they shouted, and they rushed forward and seized the horses, killed the little postillions, the coachman, and the footmen, and dragged Gerda out of the coach.

"What a plump dainty morsel! She must have been fattened on nuts," said the old robber-hag, who had a long beard and eyebrows that hung down over her eyes. "She's like a little fatted lamb. What a titbit she will be!" she said, drawing her shining glittering knife, and scaring little Gerda almost out of her wits.

"Ow!" yelled the old hag at that very moment. Her little daughter, who was riding pick-a-back, had bitten her ear—the child was as wild and naughty as they make them. "You loathsome brat!" screamed the mother. However, she was prevented from knifing Gerda.

"She shall play with me," said the little robber-girl. "She shall give me her muff and her pretty dress, and sleep with me in my bed." And the brat bit her mother again so hard that she jumped and spun round with pain. All the robbers roared with laughter and said, "Look at her dancing with her whelp!"

"I want to get into the coach," said the little robber-girl. She insisted on having her own way, for she was terribly spoilt and terribly pig-headed. So she and Gerda got in, and the coach drove off at full speed, over scrub and thorn, deeper into the forest. The little robber-girl was only as big as Gerda, but she was much stronger, had broader shoulders and a darker skin, and her eyes were coal black—they had almost a sad look. She put her arms round

Gerda's waist and said, "They shan't knife you as long as I don't get angry with you. Surely you must be a Princess."

"No," said little Gerda, "I'm not." And she told her all that had happened to her, and how fond she was of little Kay. The robber-girl gazed at her earnestly, gave a little approving nod and said, "They shan't knife you even if I do get angry with you, because then I shall do it myself." So she dried Gerda's eyes, and stuck both her own hands into her soft warm muff.

At last the carriage stopped; they had arrived in the courtyard of an old robber castle. The walls were cracked from top to bottom, ravens and crows flew out of the empty casements; immense bull-dogs, that looked as if they would be able to devour a man in one gulp, jumped about, but they did not bark, for that was forbidden. A big fire was burning on the stone floor of the smoky old hall; the smoke drifted along the ceiling, trying to find a way out. A huge caldron of soup was boiling, and hares and rabbits were turning on the spit.

"Tonight you shall sleep with me and all my little pets," said the robber-girl. Then they had something to eat and drink, and went over to a corner where straw and mats were spread out. On the beams and rafters above were perched nearly a hundred pigeons that seemed to be asleep, but they stirred just a bit when the two little girls came in. "These are all mine," said the robber-girl, seizing the one nearest to her. She held it by its legs and shook it until it flapped its wings. "Kiss it!" she cried, thrusting it in Gerda's face. "Up there, behind bars, sit the bad boys from the woods," she went on, pointing to a hole high up in the wall. "Bad boys they are, those two, and they'd fly away at once if they weren't locked up properly. And here is my old sweetheart, Moo," she said, dragging out by the horns a reindeer, wearing a polished copper ring round its neck, by which it was tied up. "We must keep a tight hold on him, or he'd run away from us. Every single evening I tickle his neck with my sharp knife—that makes him quiver all over with fright!" The little girl drew a long knife from a crack in the wall, and lightly caressed the reindeer's neck with it. The poor animal kicked out, but the robber-girl only laughed, and pulled Gerda down into the bed with her.

"Do you keep the knife beside you while you're asleep?" asked Gerda, rather terrified.

"I always sleep with a knife," said the little robber-girl. "You never know what may happen. But now tell me again what you told me before, about little Kay, and why you went out into the wide world." And Gerda told her story all over again, and the wood-pigeons cooed in their cage, while the other pigeons slept. The little robber-girl put her arm round Gerda's neck, holding her knife in the other hand; soon she was fast asleep, that was plain enough from the sound. But Gerda could not close her eyes, for she did not know whether she was going to live or die. The robbers sat round the fire, drinking and singing, and the old robber-hag was turning somersaults. It was dreadful for the little girl to have to see such goings-on.

Then the wood-pigeons said, "Coo, coo—we've seen little Kay. A white hen was carrying his sledge, while he himself was sitting in the Snow Queen's sleigh, skimming over the tree-tops as we sat in our nests. She breathed upon us young ones, and every single one died except us two, coo, coo."

"What are you saying, you up there?" asked Gerda. "Where was the Snow Queen going? What do you know about it?"

"She was most likely heading for Lapland, as they always have snow and ice there. Just ask the reindeer that is tied up with a rope."

"There is ice and snow in that country; it's a glorious place to live in," said the reindeer. "You can prance about wherever you like on those vast glittering lowlands. There the Snow Queen has her summer tent, but her permanent Palace is up near the North Pole on the island called Spitzbergen."

"Oh, Kay, little Kay!" sighed Gerda.

"Lie still, do you hear, or you'll get my knife into you," said the robber-girl.

In the morning Gerda told her all that the wood-pigeons had said, and the little robber-girl looked quite serious, nodded her head and answered, "That's good! That's good! Do you know where Lapland is?" she asked the reindeer.

"Who should know if I don't?" said the reindeer, with sparkling eyes. "That's where I was born and bred. I have pranced about in the snow-fields up there."

"Listen!" said the robber-girl to Gerda. "You see that all our men-folk are out, but the old hag is still here, and here she'll stay. Later on in the morning she'll take a swig out of the big bottle, and then have a little snooze; as soon as that happens, I'll do something for you."

So she jumped out of bed, threw her arms round her mother's neck, pulled her mustache and said, "Good morning, my dear old Nanny-goat, good morning!" and her mother tweaked her nose until it became red and blue—but it was all done for love.

As soon as her mother had drunk out of the big bottle and had dozed off, the robber-girl went up to the reindeer and said, "A funny feeling is coming over me that I should like to tickle you several times more with my sharp knife, you're so amusing when I do; but never mind. I'll untie you and lead you out, so that you can run to Lapland; but you must put your best foot foremost and carry this little girl to the Snow Queen's Palace, where her playmate is. You heard what she told me, of course, for she spoke loud enough, and I know you were eavesdropping."

The reindeer pranced for joy. The robber-girl lifted little Gerda up on its back, and was thoughtful enough to tie her on firmly; she even gave her a little cushion to sit on. "That's right," she said.

"Here are your fur boots, put them on, for it will be very cold, but I'm going to keep your muff, it's such a lovely one. All the same, I don't want you to be cold, so here are Mother's big mittens, they'll reach right up to your elbows. Put them on—now your hands look exactly like my dirty old mother's!"

And Gerda wept for joy.

"I don't like to hear you sniveling," said the little robber-girl. "You ought to be looking quite happy now. Here, take these two loaves of bread and this ham, so that you won't starve." They were then tied on to the reindeer's back as well; the little robber-girl opened the door, called in all the big dogs, cut the rope with her knife, and said to the reindeer, "Now, run! but take good care of the little girl."

Gerda stretched out her bemittened hands towards the little robber-girl and said good-by. Then the reindeer darted off at lightning speed over bush and scrub, right through the great forest, and over swamps and wastes. The wolves howled and the ravens croaked. "Ssh-sw-ssh!" came repeatedly from the sky; it seemed as if it were sneezing streaks of blood-red light.

"Those are my dear old Northern Lights," said the reindeer. "Look how they glow!" And then it ran faster than ever, day and night. The loaves were eaten, and the whole ham—and then they found themselves in Lapland.

Sixth Story

The Lapp Woman and the Finn Woman

They stopped at a little hovel, and what a wretched hovel it was! The roof sloped down to the ground, and the door was so low that the family had to crawl on their stomachs to get in and out. No one was at home but an old Lapp woman, who was frying

fish over a whale-oil lamp. The reindeer told her Gerda's story, but began with its own, because it seemed so much more important. Gerda was so numb with cold that she could not utter a word.

"You poor creatures!" said the Lapp woman. "You've got a long way to go yet. You'll have to travel hundreds of miles right into the wastes of the Finmark, because that's where the Snow Queen has gone on her holiday, and she burns blue flares every single night. I'll scribble a line on a dried cod, for I have no paper. I want you to take it to the Finn woman up in those regions, for she will be able to direct you better than I can."

When Gerda had been warmed and refreshed with food and drink, the Lapp woman wrote a few words on the dried cod, told Gerda to take great care of it, and tied her on to the reindeer again, and off they went.

All night long the air was full of spitterings and sputterings—the most beautiful blue Northern Lights were burning.

At last Gerda and the reindeer arrived in the Finmark, and knocked on the Finn woman's chimney, for she had not even a door. The hovel was so hot and stuffy that the Finn woman went about almost naked. She was short and very grubby. At once she loosened little Gerda's dress and took off her mittens and boots, otherwise she would have been far too hot. Then she put a piece of ice on the reindeer's head, and read what was written on the codfish. She read it three times, and when she knew it by heart, she popped the fish into the soup caldron, for there was no reason why it should not be eaten—she did not believe in waste.

The reindeer told its own story first, and then little Gerda's. The Finn woman blinked her intelligent eyes, but said nothing. "You're so clever," said the reindeer. "I know that you can tie all the winds of the world together with a bit of thread. If the skipper unties one knot, he gets a good wind; if he unties the second, it blows hard; and if he unties the third and fourth knots, such a gale breaks loose that forests are destroyed. Won't you give this little girl a drink so that she may have the strength of twelve men, and overpower the Snow Queen?"

"The strength of twelve men!" said the Finn woman. "Humph! A lot of good that would be!" Then she went to a shelf, took down a large rolled-up skin and unrolled it. Curious characters were written upon it, and the Finn woman read till beads of perspiration trickled down her forehead.

But the reindeer again implored her to do something for little Gerda, and Gerda looked at the Finn woman with such beseeching eyes, full of tears, that she began blinking again, and drew the reindeer into the corner, where she whispered to it while she put another piece of ice on its head.

"It's true that little Kay is with the Snow Queen, and finds everything to his taste and liking. He thinks it is the best place in the world—but that's because he's got a splinter of glass in his heart, and a little chip of it in his eye. They will have to come out, or else he will never be human again, and the Snow Queen will keep him in her power."

"But can't you give little Gerda something to take which will give her power over everything?"

"I can't give her greater power than she already has! Don't you see how great that is? Don't you see how men and beasts are bound to serve her? Don't you see how well she has been able to get on in the wide world in her bare feet? We mustn't tell her of this power—it lies in her heart. It lies in the fact that she is a sweet innocent child. If she herself can't reach the Snow Queen and get the glass out of Kay's heart and eye, we can't help her! The Snow Queen's garden begins about ten miles away. Carry the little girl as far as that. Put her down by the big bush covered with red berries that stands in the snow, and don't waste time gossiping, but hurry back to me." Then the Finn woman lifted little Gerda up on to the reindeer, which ran off at full speed.

"Oh, I've left my boots and mittens behind!" Gerda cried when she got out into the biting cold, but the reindeer did not dare to stop. It ran on till it came to the bush with the red berries; there it put Gerda down and kissed her on the mouth, while great bright tears trickled down the animal's face. Then it ran back as fast as it could.

There stood poor Gerda without shoes, without mittens, far out in the icy-cold wastes of the Finmark. She ran as fast as her legs would carry her. A whole regiment of snowflakes came towards her. They did not fall from the sky, for it was quite clear and a-shimmer with bright Northern Lights. The snowflakes danced along the ground, and the nearer they came the bigger they grew. Gerda remembered very well how big and strange they had appeared when she looked at them through the magnifying glass. But here they were much bigger and more terrifying, they were alive, they were the vanguards of the Snow Queen, and had the most extraordinary shapes. Some of them looked like horrible huge hedgehogs, others looked like bundles of knotted snakes sticking out their heads on all sides, others looked like little fat bears with their hair standing on end; all were shining white, all were live snowflakes.

Then little Gerda said the Lord's Prayer, but the cold was so great that she could see her own breath; it looked like a cloud of smoke coming out of her mouth; her breath became more and more dense, shaping itself into little white angels that grew bigger and bigger as soon as they touched the ground. All wore helmets and carried shields and spears in their hands. More and more of them appeared, and when Gerda had finished her prayer she was surrounded by a whole legion. They struck at those ugly snowflakes with their spears, smashing them into a thousand pieces, and after that little Gerda walked fearlessly and cheerfully on. The angels stroked her hands and feet which made her feel the cold less, and then she walked briskly towards the Snow Queen's Palace.

But now let us see how Kay is getting on. Gerda was the last person he was thinking of, and least of all did he suspect that she was standing just outside the Palace.

Seventh Story

What Happened in the Queen's Palace, and Later

The walls of the Palace were made of drifting snow, and the windows and doors of biting winds. There were more than a hundred halls, shaped by the drifting of the snow. The largest of them stretched out for many miles, and all were lit up by the bright Northern Lights. These halls were tremendous—so empty, so icy-cold, so dazzling. There was never any gaiety here, not even the smallest dance for the bears, at which the storm winds could make the music, and the polar bears walk on their hind legs and show off their good manners. There was never a party where they played at muzzle-slapping and paw-clapping, and never did the white fox-girls forgather to enjoy a bit of gossip over their coffee. Empty, vast, and icy-cold were the Snow Queen's halls. The Northern Lights glowed at such regular intervals that one could reckon exactly when they would be at their highest and lowest. In the midst of the immense empty snow hall was a frozen lake, cracked into a thousand pieces, and each piece so resembled all the others that it looked like a real work of art. When at home the Snow Queen sat in the very center, and then she said she was sitting on the "Mirror of Reason," which according to her was the only one that counted in this world.

Little Kay was quite blue with the cold, indeed almost black, and his heart was practically a lump of ice. But he was not aware of it, because the Snow Queen had kissed away the icy chill.

He was busy fitting together a few flat sharp-edged pieces of ice, and trying to shape them into some kind of pattern, for he wanted to make something out of them, just as we do when we make Chinese puzzles with little squares of wood. Kay was arranging patterns, and most intricate ones, in that game known as the "Puzzle of Ice-cold Reason." To him these figures appeared very remarkable and of the greatest importance because of the chip of glass in his eye. He put together patterns to form a written word, but he could never manage to spell out the one word he had in his mind—the word "Eternity"; for the Snow Queen had said, "If you can find out how to make that figure, you shall be your own master, and I will give you the whole world, and a new pair of skates." But he could not.

"Now I'm going to fly away to the warm countries," said the Snow Queen. "I want to have a look into the black caldrons"—she meant the volcanoes, Etna and Vesuvius, as we call them. "I must touch them up with white a bit; it's so refreshing after all those lemons and grapes." And away she flew.

Kay sat all alone in the empty ice-hall that stretched out for miles and miles. He looked at the pieces of ice, and thought and thought for all he was worth. He sat so stiff and still that he seemed to be frozen to death.

Just then little Gerda came into the Palace through the great gates which were the cutting winds, but she said her evening prayers and the winds calmed down as if lulled to sleep. She walked into the big empty hall, caught sight of Kay, knew him at once, flew towards him and flung her arms round his neck, held him fast and shouted, "Kay! darling little Kay! At last I've found you!"

But there he sat, quite still, stiff and cold. Then Gerda shed hot tears which fell upon his breast and penetrated right into his heart. They thawed the lump of ice, and dissolved the splinter of glass that was lodged in it. He looked at her and she sang:

"As the roses bloom in the valley, sweet,
So the Christ Child there ye shall truly meet."

Kay burst into tears. He cried and cried so hard that his tears washed the tiny chip of glass out of his eye. Now he recognized her and exclaimed with joy, "Gerda! darling little Gerda! Where have you been so long? And where have I been?" He looked all round and said, "How cold it is here! How vast and empty!" He clung to Gerda who laughed and cried for joy. Their happiness was so heavenly that even the pieces of ice danced merrily, and when they grew tired, they lay down and formed the exact word that the Snow Queen had told Kay to find—so now he would become his own master, and she would give him the whole world and a new pair of skates.

Gerda kissed his cheeks and the color came back into them, she kissed his eyes and they shone like hers. She kissed his hands and feet and he became well and strong again. The Snow Queen might come home now—there stood his order of release, written in glittering ice.

They took one another by the hand and walked out of the great Palace. They talked of Grandmother, and of the roses on the roof. Wherever they went the winds dropped and the sun burst forth. When they reached the bush with the red berries, the reindeer was waiting for them. It had brought a younger one whose udders were full of warm milk for the children, and it kissed them on the mouth. Then they carried Kay and Gerda first to the Finn woman's hovel, where they warmed themselves in her hot room and received instructions for their homeward journey, then on to the Lapp woman who had made them new clothes, and had put her own sleigh in order for them.

Both the reindeer ran beside them and came with them as far as the frontier of the country, where the first green buds were peeping forth. There they took leave of the reindeer and the Lapp woman: "Good-by!" said everybody. And now the first little birds began to twitter, the forest had green buds, and out from it a young girl came riding towards them on a beautiful horse which Gerda recognized—it had been harnessed to the golden coach. The young girl wore a bright red cap, and carried pistols in her belt. It was the little robber-girl, who had grown tired of staying at home. She was riding northwards first, to see if she liked it there, and if not, she could always go somewhere else. She recognized Gerda at once, and Gerda recognized her. It was a merry meeting.

"You're a nice one for gadding about," she said to little Kay. "I'm just wondering if you deserve to have someone running to the ends of the earth for your sake." But Gerda patted her cheek, and asked about the Prince and Princess.

"They've gone away to foreign lands," said the robber-girl.

"But the crow?" asked Gerda.

"Oh, the crow is dead," she answered. "His tame sweetheart is now a widow, and wears a bit of black wool tied round her leg. She feels terribly sorry for herself, but that's all nonsense. Now do tell me all that has happened to you, and how you managed to get hold of Kay."

And Gerda and Kay both told their story.

"Well, that's that," said the robber-girl, and she shook hands with them and promised that if she ever passed through their town, she would come up and call on them. Then she rode away into the wide world. Kay and Gerda walked on, hand in hand, and all the way, as they were going, spring appeared with flowers and bursting buds. Church bells were ringing; they recognized the high towers, and the big city—the very city they used to live in. They walked into it, straight to Grandmother's door, up the stairs and into the room, where everything was exactly as they had left it. The old clock was ticking—tick, tock—the hands were marking the time; but just as they passed through the door, they realized that they had become grown-up people. The roses from the boxes in the gutter under the roof peeped in at the open windows, where Kay and Gerda once more found their own two little stools. They sat down on them and held each other by the hand. The memory of the cold empty splendor of the Snow Queen's Palace had vanished like a bad dream. Grandmother was sitting there in God's blessed sunshine, reading aloud from the Bible, "Except ye become as little children, ye shall not enter into the Kingdom of Heaven."

Kay and Gerda looked into each other's eyes, and all at once they understood the meaning of the old hymn:

"Ah! search for the places lowly and meek,
With tears, in the dust, for the Saviour seek;
Then the Christ Child there ye shall truly meet,
For the roses bloom in the valley, sweet."

And there they both sat, grown up, and yet children—children at heart—and it was summer, warm heavenly summer.

THE JUMPERS

THE flea, the grasshopper, and the jumping goose * once wanted to see which of them could jump the highest, so they invited the whole world, and anybody else who wished to come to the treat. When they were all together in the room, one could see that they were three fine specimens of jumpers.

"Well, I'm giving my daughter to the one who jumps the highest," said the King, "for it seems so stingy to let these gentlemen jump for nothing."

The flea was the first to come forward; he had such nice manners, and bowed right and left, for he had blue blood in his veins; he only moved in human society, and that means a lot.

Next came the grasshopper. He was certainly considerably heavier than the flea, but still he carried himself rather well, and wore green, the very uniform he was born with. Moreover this gentleman said that he was descended from an old, old family in the land of Egypt, and that here in this country he was very highly esteemed; he had been brought straight from the fields and put into a card-house three stories high, made of nothing but Kings and Knaves turned face inwards; as for the doors and windows, they were cut out of the middles of the Queens of Hearts.

"I can sing so well," he said, "that sixteen native crickets, who

* "Jumping goose"—in Danish "Springgaas." This was an old-fashioned Danish plaything, made from the breast-bone of a goose. A piece of string was tied round the projecting ends of the bone at the back, and a peg was twisted tightly in the string to form a spring. A lump of cobbler's wax was fixed to the under side of the bone and the end of the peg stuck into it, but the tension of the string soon released the peg, and the "goose" jumped.

have chirped and chirped ever since they were born, and yet have never been given a card-house, are so consumed with envy and vexation since hearing me, that they have grown even thinner than they were before."

So now both of them, the flea and the grasshopper, had explained to everybody's satisfaction who they were, and why they thought they were quite good enough to marry a Princess.

The jumping goose said nothing, but people remarked that he was thinking all the more, and the Court dog had only to take one sniff at him to guarantee that the jumping goose was a pedigree bird.

The old Alderman, who had received three decorations for holding his tongue, declared he knew definitely that this goose was endowed with magic powers, for you could tell from his back whether the winter would be mild or severe, and you can't tell that even from the back of the man who writes the Almanac.

"Well, I shan't say anything," said the old King. "I just potter about thinking my own thoughts."

And now the jumpers took the field.

The flea jumped so high that nobody could see how high it was, and so they decided that he hadn't jumped at all, and that was the bad part of it.

The grasshopper jumped only half as high as the flea, but he sprang straight into the King's face, and the King said it was disgusting.

The jumping goose hesitated for a long time; at last people began to think that he couldn't jump at all.

"I hope he hasn't fainted," said the Court dog, and gave him another sniff, when—plomp!—the goose gave a little crooked jump right into the lap of the Princess who was sitting on a low golden footstool.

Then the King said, "The highest jump is the jump up to my daughter, so that settles it! But it took brains to find it out, and the

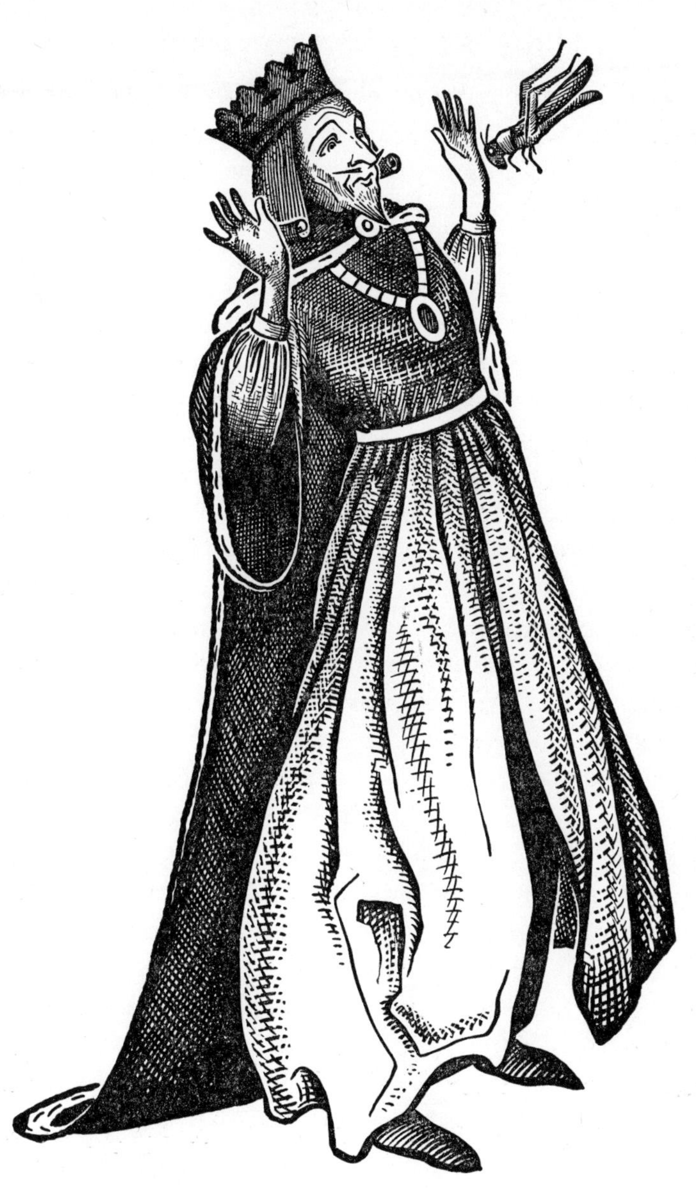

jumping goose has proved that he has brains. He knows what he is about!"

And so he won the Princess.

"I made the highest jump, all the same," said the flea. "But what do I care? Let her have that miserable goose-carcase with his peg and his wax! I made the highest jump, all the same, but you get no attention in this world unless you have a good physique."

And then the flea went away to fight in foreign parts, where it is said that he was killed.

The grasshopper went out into a ditch and meditated on the way of the world; and he too said, "A good physique, that's the thing! A good physique, that's the thing!" Then he sang his own sad little ditty, from which we have taken this story; and it needn't be the gospel truth, even if it is in print.

THE SHADOW

YOU have no idea how the sun can burn in hot countries. There, people turn mahogany brown, and in the very hottest countries they get baked into Negroes. However, it was only to one of the moderately hot countries in the South that a learned man had come from one of the cold ones. He fancied that he would be able to get about there as he did at home, but he soon realized his mistake. He and all sensible people were obliged to stay inside. The shutters and doors remained closed all day long; it looked as if the whole house were asleep or abandoned. True, the narrow street with the tall houses where he lived was built in such a way that it was exposed to the sun from morning till night; it was simply unbearable! The learned man from the cold countries, who was young and clever, felt as if he were sitting in a white-hot oven. This exhausted him and he became quite thin; even his shadow shrank and became much smaller than it was at home. Not until evening when the sun had set did these two begin to recover.

It was a real pleasure to see. As soon as the candle was brought into the room, the shadow stretched itself up the wall, and even along the ceiling, getting taller and taller until it regained its strength.

The learned man went out on to the balcony to stretch himself, and as the stars gradually appeared in the beautiful clear sky, he felt that he was coming to life again. In southern countries every window has a balcony, and on all of them people began to come out, because one does need a breath of fresh air even if one is accustomed to being mahogany-colored! Things grew very lively up above and down below. Shoemakers, tailors and all the rest of them moved on to the pavement, out came tables and chairs, candles were lit—there must have been more than a thousand of them. One talked and another sang; they strolled up and down; carriages drove past; donkeys trotted along with their tinkling bells—ting-a-ling-ling. There were funeral processions and hymn-singing. Street urchins sent off squibs, and church bells rang. A street full of fascinating life!

Only in that one house, opposite the one in which the learned stranger lived, there was no sign of life, yet somebody did live in it, for flowers were standing on the balcony. Despite the hot sun, they were in full bloom and that would never have been possible unless they were watered, so somebody must be watering them, therefore there must be people in the house. In fact towards evening the door was opened, but it was dark over there—at any rate in the front room. From the inner rooms came the sound of music. The learned stranger thought this music very wonderful; but it was quite possible that his imagination alone made him think so, for to him everything in the South seemed wonderful, if only there had been no sun.

The stranger's landlord said he did not know who had taken the house opposite, because nobody was ever seen over there. And so far as the music was concerned, he found it very tiresome. "It's exactly as if someone were practicing a piece he couldn't quite manage—always the same piece over and over again! 'I shall get it right in time,' he seems to say, but he doesn't, however long he practices."

One night the stranger woke up. He was sleeping with the French windows open, the wind played with the curtain, and he fancied that a strange radiance came from the balcony opposite. All the flowers were as brilliant as gorgeous-colored flames, and in the midst of the flowers stood a beautiful slender maiden. It seemed as if a radiance came from her also. It positively hurt his eyes, because he opened them too wide when he awoke from his sleep.

With one leap he was out of bed, tiptoeing behind the curtain—but the maiden had gone; the brilliance had gone; the flowers no longer glimmered, but stood there just as usual. The door was ajar, and from the inner room the music sounded so soft and so lovely that it made one feel quite romantic. It all seemed like magic—but who lived there? Where was the private entrance? The entire ground floor was given up to shops, and people had really no business to use them just as passages.

One evening, later on, the stranger was sitting on his balcony, and behind him in the room the candle was burning. This naturally moved his shadow over to the wall of the house opposite. Of course, there it sat among the flowers on the balcony; and when the stranger moved the shadow also moved, as a shadow does.

"I believe my shadow is the only living thing over there," said the learned man. "Look how nicely it sits among the flowers! The door is ajar; I wish the shadow would have sense enough to step inside and look round, and come back and tell me what it saw! Yes, you ought to make yourself useful," he said jokingly. "Be good enough to walk in! Well, are you going to?" And he nodded to the shadow, and the shadow nodded back at him. "Now go, but don't get lost!" And the stranger stood up, and the shadow on the balcony opposite stood up too, and the stranger turned—and the shadow did likewise. If anyone had looked closely enough, he would have noticed that the shadow passed through the half-open French window opposite, at the very moment that the stranger went into his room and dropped the long curtain behind him.

Next morning, the learned man went out to drink his morning coffee and to read the papers.

"What's this?" he said, coming out into the sunshine. "I've got no shadow! Then it really did go last night and never came back. What a nuisance!"

It annoyed him, not only because the shadow had gone, but also because he knew that there was a story about a man without a shadow, a story that was known to everybody in the cold countries, and if the learned man returned home and told his own story, they would say he was just repeating the old one; and after all, he was a man with original ideas! He decided, then and there, not to say a word about it, which was certainly very sensible of him.

That evening he again went out on his balcony. Quite rightly he had put the candle behind him because he knew that a shadow always uses its master for a screen, but he could not coax it out. He made himself short, he made himself long, yet there was no shadow, and no sign of a shadow appeared. He said, "Ahem! ahem!" but that was no help. It was most irritating; however in southern countries everything grows very quickly, and after a week he noticed with great pleasure that when he walked in the sun a new shadow was growing out from his feet; the root had evidently remained. After three weeks he had quite a decent shadow, and when he started on his way home to the northern countries, it grew more and more on the journey, and was finally so long and so large that half of it would have been plenty!

The learned man got home at last, and wrote books about what is true in the world, what is good, and what is beautiful. Days went by, years went by, in fact many, many years went by.

One evening, while he was sitting in his room, there came a gentle tapping at the door. "Come in," he called out, but nobody came; he opened the door, and in front of him stood a person so extraordinarily thin that it made him feel quite uneasy. However, this person was very well dressed and undoubtedly somebody important.

"Whom have I the honor of addressing?" asked the learned man.

"I thought you wouldn't know me," answered the distinguished stranger. "I've grown such a substantial body that I'm now made of real flesh and wear clothes. You never expected to see me in such a state of prosperity, did you? Don't you recognize your old shadow?

You probably thought I should never come back. I've been getting on very nicely since last I was with you; I've become very rich in every way. If I wanted to buy my freedom I could easily do so." And he rattled a bunch of valuable seals dangling from his watch, and slipped his hand through the thick gold chain he wore round his neck. My! how the diamond rings glittered on his fingers! and mark you, they were all real, too.

"Well, really, I can't get over it," said the learned man. "What in the world does all this mean?"

"Nothing commonplace, I can assure you," said the Shadow, "but you are not a commonplace person, and I have, as you very well know, blindly followed in your steps from childhood. As soon as you thought I was experienced enough to make my way alone in the world, I went away, and have been successful beyond all expectation. But a kind of longing came over me to see you once more before you die—you know you will have to die some day! I also wanted to see this country once more, because, after all, one always has a soft spot for one's native land. I know you have got another shadow now. Do I owe either of you anything? Be kind enough to let me know."

"Is it really you?" asked the learned man. "Why, how extraordinary! I should never have thought that one's old shadow could come back in the form of a human being."

"Tell me what I owe," said the Shadow again, "for I hate to be under any kind of obligation."

"How can you talk like that?" said the learned man. "What obligation could there possibly be? You are as free as anyone else. I'm delighted to hear about your success! Sit down, my friend, and give me some idea how all this happened, and what you saw in the house on the other side of the street in that warm country."

"Yes, I'll tell you all about it," said the Shadow, and he sat down. "But only on condition that if you happen to meet me anywhere in this town, you won't tell anybody that I used to be your shadow. I mean to get married, as I have more than enough to support a family."

"Don't worry," said the learned man, "I shan't tell anybody who you really are. Here's my hand on it. I promise. A man is as good as his word."

"A word is as good as his—shadow," continued the Shadow, who had no other way of putting it.

It was really quite striking how human it appeared to be, all dressed in black, and in the very finest broadcloth at that, patent-leather boots, and a hat that could be pressed together till it was nothing but a crown and a brim, besides the things that we already know about—the seals, gold chain, and diamond rings. It was a real pleasure to see how extremely well dressed the Shadow was, and because of this it appeared completely human.

"Now listen to me," said the Shadow, pressing his patent-leather boots for all he was worth down on the sleeve of the learned man's new shadow that lay like a faithful poodle at his feet. The Shadow did this either out of arrogance, or perhaps because he wanted to make the new shadow stick to his own feet. The shadow that was lying there kept perfectly still, listening to every word, for it was anxious to know how one could become free, and work up to being one's own master.

"Do you know who lived in that house opposite?" asked the Shadow. "Ah, me! It was the loveliest creature in the world—it was the Muse of Poetry! I spent three weeks in the house, and it had just the same effect on me as if I had lived there for three thousand years, and had read all that had ever been written in poetry or prose; you can take my word for it. I have seen everything and I know everything!"

"The Muse of Poetry!" exclaimed the learned man. "Yes, yes, she often lives like a hermit in great cities. The Muse of Poetry! Yes, I saw her myself for one single brief moment, but then sleep lay heavy on my eyes. She stood on the balcony, as bright as the brightest Northern Lights. Tell me, tell me! You were on the balcony, you went through the door, and then—?"

"Then I was in the ante-room," said the Shadow. "You were always looking across at that ante-room. There was no light there, but only a kind of dusk. Through an open door you had a view of other doors opening on to a whole vista of great rooms and halls. They were lit up so brilliantly that I should have been annihilated by that flood of light had I penetrated into the room where the maiden lived, but I was cautious, I took my time—that's what one should do."

"And tell me, old chap, what did you see there?" asked the learned man.

"I saw everything, and I am going to tell you about it—but—I want you to understand that it is not because I am stuck-up, but—as a free man, and with my knowledge of things, besides my established position and my flourishing circumstances, I do wish you would address me with less familiarity."

"I'm so sorry," said the learned man. "It's an old habit that is difficult to break. You're perfectly right and I will remember to treat you with respect. But now—sir—tell me everything you saw."

"Everything!" said the Shadow. "For I saw everything and I know everything."

"What did it look like in that inner room?" asked the learned man. "Was it like the green forest? Was it like some holy church? Were the rooms like the starry sky when one stands on the mountain-tops?"

"Everything was there," said the Shadow. "I didn't actually go the whole way in, I remained in that front room, in the dusk, but I had an excellent view from there. I saw everything and I know everything! I was at the Court of The Muse of Poetry—in the ante-

room!"

"But what did you see there? Did all the ancient Gods march through the halls? Did the old heroes fight there? Did lovely children play there and tell about their dreams?"

"I repeat that I was there, and you may be very sure that I saw everything that was to be seen. If you had come over, you would not have changed into a human being as I did. And, moreover, I learnt to understand my innermost nature, my ego, my relationship with the Muse of Poetry. Yes, when I was with you I did not think of these things, but you remember how strangely I used to grow at every sunrise and sunset? In the moonlight I seemed almost more distinct than you did yourself. I did not then understand my own nature, but in the ante-room it became clear to me. I was human. I emerged fully developed, but you were no longer in the warm country. As a man I was ashamed to appear as I did; I needed boots, clothes, and all that human veneer which distinguishes a human being. I took refuge—I can confide in you, you will not put it in any book—I took refuge under the skirt of the cake-woman at the corner of the street, and hid myself there. She did not realize whom she was hiding. It was evening before I ventured out, but then I ran about the streets in the moonlight, and stretched myself along the wall—that does tickle my back so delightfully! I ran up and I ran down; I looked through the highest windows and into reception rooms and attics. I peeped where nobody else could peep, and I saw what nobody else saw, and what nobody else was supposed to see. On the whole it is a wicked world. I would not choose to be a man if it were not considered worth while to be one. I saw the most incredible things being done by wives, husbands, parents, and amongst those little darlings of model children. I saw," said the Shadow, "what no one was supposed to know, but what they would all like to know, namely all the goings-on next door. If I had published a newspaper it would have been widely read, I can tell you! But instead I wrote straight to the people concerned, and it created a terrible upheaval in all the towns through which I passed. They were afraid of me, and at the same time they were remarkably fond of me. The Professors made me Professor; the tailors rigged me out in new clothes—so now I am well supplied; the Master of the Mint struck coins for me, and the women thought me handsome. So I became the man I am. And now I must say good-by. Here is my card. I live on the sunny side of the street, and am always at home on rainy days." And the Shadow went away.

"What a strange story!" said the learned man.

Days and years passed by, and the Shadow returned again.

"How are you getting on?" he asked.

"Alas!" said the learned man. "I am writing about the True, the Good, and the Beautiful, but nobody cares to hear about such things. I feel quite desperate, for I take it very much to heart."

"I don't," said the Shadow. "I'm getting fat, and that's what one should try to be. You don't understand the world, and that makes you ill. You'll have to travel. I'm going for a journey this summer; will you come with me? I should like to have a traveling companion. Will you come with me as my shadow? I shall be very happy to take you, and I'll pay all the expenses."

"That's going a bit too far," said the learned man.

"Well, I don't know about that," said the Shadow. "It would do you a lot of good to travel. If you'll be my shadow, the trip won't cost you anything."

"That's too much!" said the learned man.

"Well, it's the way of the world," said the Shadow, "and you won't be able to change it either." And away he went.

The learned man was not feeling at all well. Sorrow and care followed him, and whatever he said about the True, the Good, and the Beautiful mattered just about as much to most people as roses do to a cow. Finally he was really ill.

"You're getting to look like a shadow," people said to him, and the learned man shivered, for he thought there might be some truth in it.

"You must go to some watering-place," said the Shadow who had come to visit him. "There's nothing else to be done. I'll take you with me for old time's sake. I'll pay all the expenses of the trip, and you shall write about it and do your best to be a bit entertaining on the journey. I must go to a watering-place because my beard isn't growing as it should—that's also a kind of disease. A beard is so essential! Now do be reasonable and accept my offer. Remember! we're traveling as friends."

So they set out on their journey. The Shadow was master now, and the master became the shadow. They drove together, they rode together, and they walked side by side, in front of one another, or behind one another, according to the position of the sun. The Shadow always managed to take the place of the master, and the learned man was not very particular about it, for he was good-natured as well as extremely kind and easy-going. One day he said to the Shadow, "As we have now become traveling companions, and even grew up together, don't you think we should call each other by our Christian names? It sounds more intimate, doesn't it?"

"That's a capital idea!" said the Shadow who was really the master. "What you say is very frank and well-meant, and I in return am going to be just as well-meaning and frank. Being a learned man, you know very well how strange life is. Certain people cannot bear to touch brown paper, it makes them sick. Others almost have a fit when a nail is scratched on a window-pane. I, for my part, have a similar feeling when I hear you call me by my Christian name; I feel myself dragged down to the position I held when I was first with you. You see, it's a question of feeling, not of pride. I cannot permit you to use my Christian name, but I will gladly call you by yours—and so we meet half-way."

And from that moment the Shadow addressed his former master by his Christian name.

"It's really too much that I should have to say 'Sir' to him while he calls me by my Christian name," thought the learned man, but he had to put up with it.

Eventually they arrived at a watering-place, where they met many strangers, and among them a lovely Princess who suffered from being able to see too clearly, which is so alarming.

She at once noticed that the newcomer was a very different person from all the rest. "They say he is here to make his beard grow, but I see the real reason—he cannot cast a shadow!"

Her curiosity was aroused, so she started a conversation with the stranger on the promenade. Being a Princess, she had no need to stand on ceremony, but said outright to him, "I know what is the matter with you. You cannot cast a shadow."

"Your Royal Highness must be in considerably better health," replied the Shadow. "I know what your complaint was—it was that your eyesight was too keen; but that is no longer the case, for the fact is that I have a most unusual shadow. Can't you see the person who always follows me about? Other people have an ordinary shadow, but I do not care for what is ordinary. People often provide their servants with liveries of better material than they wear themselves, and that is why I thought of dressing up my shadow as a human being. You see, I have even given him a shadow of his own. It is very expensive, but I like to have something unique."

"Is it possible?" thought the Princess. "Can I really have been cured? This is the best watering-place in the whole world. Water has nowadays quite miraculous healing powers. But I am not going away now that things are beginning to get amusing. This stranger pleases me very much. I hope his beard won't grow, because if it does, he will leave at once."

That evening the Princess and the Shadow danced together in the great ballroom. She was light, but he was still lighter; never had she met with such a partner. She mentioned the country from which she came, and he knew all about it, for he had been there once while she was away. He had looked through every window from basement to attic. He had seen this and that, and could therefore answer the Princess, and could hint at things at which she marveled. Beyond doubt, he was the wisest man in the whole world. His knowledge fascinated her to such a degree that when they danced together again, she fell in love with him. The Shadow was only too well aware of this, for her gaze almost pierced right through him.

They danced once more, and she was on the point of telling him of her love, but she did not want to be too hasty; she was thinking of her country and her Kingdom, and of the many people over whom she had to rule. "He must be a clever man," she said to herself, "and that is a good thing. He dances to perfection—that is also a good thing—but I am wondering if his knowledge goes deep enough, for it is just as important. He must be examined."

And little by little she began to put the most difficult questions to him, questions she could not have answered herself, and the Shadow made a wry face.

"You cannot answer that question?" asked the Princess.

"I learnt it in my kindergarten days," said the Shadow. "I believe that even my shadow, standing near the door over there, could answer it."

"Your shadow!" said the Princess. "That would be very strange!"

"I am not certain that he can," said the Shadow, "but I am inclined to believe it. He has followed me and listened to me for so many years that surely he must be able to. But Your Royal Highness will permit me to remind you that he is very proud of passing for a man, so if you want him to give a good answer, he must be in a good temper, in fact he must be treated just as a human being."

"I like that," said the Princess.

So now she approached the learned man at the door, and talked to him about the sun and moon, about people—what they look like, and what they really are—and he answered her most wisely and well.

"What an extraordinary man that must be to have such a learned shadow," she thought. "It would be a real blessing for my country and people if I chose him for my consort. I will!"

And they soon came to an agreement—the Princess and the Shadow, but no one was to know anything about it until she returned to her Kingdom.

"No one, not even my shadow," said the Shadow, and he had his own special reason for this.

At last they were in the country over which the Princess ruled when she was at home.

"Listen, my friend," said the Shadow to the learned man, "now that I am as happy and powerful as anyone can be, I'll do something very special for you. I want you to stay with me in my Palace, to drive with me in the royal carriage, and have a hundred thousand golden guineas a year; but in return for that you must allow yourself to be called a shadow by everyone. You must not say you were ever a man, and once a year, when I sit on my balcony in the sunshine to let people gaze at me, you must lie at my feet as becomes a shadow. I may as well tell you that I'm going to marry the Princess. The wedding will take place this evening."

"I can't stand any more," exclaimed the learned man. "I won't do it! I won't have it! That would be deceiving the entire country and the Princess too. I'm going to tell the whole story—that I am the man, and that you are the shadow, and that you are just masquerading."

"No one will believe you," said the Shadow. "Be reasonable, or I shall call the guard."

"I'll go straight to the Princess," said the learned man.

"But remember, I shall go first," said the Shadow, "and you'll go to prison."

That is exactly what happened, for the guards obeyed the one they knew was to marry the Princess.

"Why, you are trembling!" said the Princess when the Shadow came into her room. "Has anything happened? You must not be taken ill tonight, just when we are going to be married."

"I have been through the most terrible experience that can happen to anyone," said the Shadow. "Just fancy! You know a miserable shadow-brain can't stand very much—fancy! my shadow has gone mad; he believes that he is the man, and that I—just imagine!—that *I* am his shadow!"

"How dreadful!" said the Princess. "I hope he has been locked up."

"Indeed he has. I am afraid he will never recover."

"Poor Shadow!" said the Princess. "He is very unhappy. It would be a real act of charity to relieve him of the little bit of life he still has. In fact, after thinking it over carefully, I do believe it will be necessary to put him quietly out of the way."

"That seems rather hard," said the Shadow, almost with a sigh, "for he was a faithful servant."

"You have a very noble character," said the Princess.

In the evening the whole town was brilliantly illuminated, and cannon were fired, boom! boom! and the soldiers presented arms. What a wedding that was! The Princess and the Shadow stepped out on to the balcony to show themselves to the people, and to hear the last roar of cheers.

The learned man heard nothing of all this, for he had already been put out of the way.

THE SWINEHERD

ONCE upon a time there was a poor Prince who owned a Kingdom: it was quite a tiny one, but still large enough to enable him to marry—and marry he would. We must admit that it was rather daring of him to say to the Emperor's daughter, "Will you have me?" But that's just how daring he was, for his name was famous throughout the world. Hundreds of Princesses would gladly have said, "Yes, and thank you for asking me!" But did she?

Well, we shall see.

By the grave of the Prince's father there grew a rose-tree. Oh, such a lovely rose-tree! It blossomed only once every five years, and then it had only one single flower, but that was a rose whose fragrance was so wonderful that it made you forget all your cares and troubles.

The Prince also had a nightingale which could sing as though all the world's beautiful melodies were hidden in its little throat. This rosc and this nightingale were to be his gifts to the Princess, and so they were put in two large silver caskets and sent to her. The Emperor had them carried before him as he went into the great hall, where the Princess and her ladies-in-waiting were playing at receiving visitors—they never did anything else—and when she saw the large caskets with the gifts, she clapped her hands in sheer delight. "Oh, if it were only a tiny little kitten!" she said—but out came the beautiful rose.

"Fancy! how prettily it is made!" said all the ladies-in-waiting.

"It's more than pretty," said the Emperor, "it's lovely!" But the

Princess felt it, and almost burst into tears.

"Fie, Papa!" she said. "It's not artificial—it's *real!*"

"Fie!" repeated all the ladies, "it's real!"

"Well," said the Emperor, "let's see what the other casket contains before we lose our tempers."

Then the nightingale appeared. It sang so beautifully that they could find nothing to say against it at first.

"Superbe!" "Charmant!" exclaimed the ladies, for they all spoke French, each one worse than the other.

"How that bird reminds me of our late Empress's musical-box!" said an old courtier. "Yes, yes, it's exactly the same tone, the same interpretation."

"Exactly!" said the Emperor, and he wept like a little child.

"You don't mean to say that it's a real bird?" said the Princess.

"Indeed it *is* a real bird," said the messengers who had brought it.

"Then let it go," said the Princess, and on no account would she allow the Prince to come into her presence.

But he was not to be put off so easily. He smeared his face with brown and black, pulled his cap down over his eyes, and knocked at the door.

"Hullo! How do you do, Emperor?" he said. "Could you give me a job here at the Palace?"

"Well—we get so many people applying for work," said the Emperor. "But let me see—I do want someone to look after the pigs, because we've got such a lot of them."

And so the Prince was made "Swineherd by appointment to His Majesty."

He was given a wretched little room near the pigsties, and there he had to live. He worked hard all day long, and by evening he had made a pretty little pot edged with tinkling bells, and as soon as the pot boiled the bells tinkled beautifully, and played the old tune:

"Ach, du lieber Augustin,
Alles ist weg, weg, weg!"

But the most ingenious part of it all was that when you put your finger into the steam from the pot, you could smell at once what food was being prepared in every kitchen in the town. What was a mere rose compared with that!

Now the Princess came walking by with all her ladies-in-waiting, and when she heard the tune she stood still and looked very pleased, because she too could play "Ach, du lieber Augustin." It was the only tune she knew, and she played it with one finger.

"Oh! that's the tune I know," she said. "Why, he must be an educated swineherd! Listen! Go and ask him the price of that instrument."

One of the ladies was obliged to run into the piggery, but she was careful to put on a pair of pattens first.

"How much do you want for that pot?" asked the lady.

"I want ten kisses from the Princess," answered the swineherd.

"Well, I never!" exclaimed the lady.

"And I won't take less," said the swineherd.

"Well, what does he say?" asked the Princess.

"I really can't repeat it," said the lady. "It's too shocking!"

"Then you can whisper it to me!" And the lady whispered.

"Oh, isn't he naughty!" said the Princess, and she walked away at once, but after having gone a few steps, she heard the bells ring out again so prettily:

"Ach, du lieber Augustin,
Alles ist weg, weg, weg!"

"Listen, ask him if he will take ten kisses from my ladies, instead," said the Princess.

"No, thank you!" said the swineherd. "Ten kisses from the

Princess, or I keep my pot!"

"Now, isn't that annoying!" said the Princess. "Well, then—you'll have to stand in front of me so that we shan't be seen."

The ladies placed themselves in front of her, spread out their big hoop skirts, and the swineherd got ten kisses, and she got the pot.

And then the fun began!

The whole evening and all day long the pot was kept boiling. There was no dinner cooked in the entire town which they didn't know about—from the Lord Chamberlain's down to the cobbler's. The ladies danced about and clapped their hands.

"We know who's going to have soup and pancakes, we know who's going to have boiled rice and hash! Isn't it thrilling?"

"Most thrilling!" said the Mistress of the Robes.

"Yes, but don't breathe a word about it," said the Princess, "because I am the Emperor's daughter."

"Heaven forbid!" they all said.

But the swineherd, that is to say the Prince—of course they didn't know he wasn't a real swineherd—hadn't let the day go by without making something. This time he had made a rattle. When he twirled it you could hear all the waltzes, jigs and polkas that had been known since the creation of the world.

"But it's superb!" said the Princess as she passed by. "Never have I heard anything more lovely! Listen! Go and ask him the price of that instrument—but mind, I'm not going to do any more kissing!"

"He demands one hundred kisses from the Princess," said the lady who had been in to ask.

"Well, he must be mad!" said the Princess, and she walked on. But when she had gone a few steps, she stopped. "After all, one must patronize the arts," she said. "I am the Emperor's daughter. Tell him he can have ten kisses as yesterday. The rest he may take from my ladies-in-waiting."

"Oh! but we should hate that!" said the ladies.

"Nonsense!" answered the Princess. "If I can kiss him, I'm sure you can. Remember I give you board and wages." And the lady had to return to the piggery.

"One hundred kisses from the Princess," said the swineherd, "or the bargain is off."

"Hide me!" said the Princess—and the ladies-in-waiting placed themselves in front of her, and he began taking his kisses.

"What on earth is going on down at the piggery?" asked the Emperor, who had come out on to his balcony. He rubbed his eyes and put on his spectacles.

"Bless me, if it isn't the ladies-in-waiting up to their tricks again! I'd better go and see."

Then he pulled up his slippers which he had trodden down at the heels. My stars, how he hurried!

As soon as he came down into the yard he walked very softly. The ladies were busy counting the kisses to see fair play, so that there should be neither too many nor too few; they hadn't the faintest suspicion of the Emperor's presence.

He raised himself on tip-toe.

"Well, I declare!" he said, when he saw them kissing, and he smacked them on the head with his slipper, just as the swineherd got kiss number eighty-six.

"Out you go!" said the Emperor, for he was very angry. And both Princess and swineherd were put outside his Empire.

There she stood crying, while the swineherd fumed, and the rain poured down.

"Poor miserable me!" said the Princess. "If only I had accepted the handsome Prince! I am very, very unhappy!"

Then the swineherd stepped behind a tree, wiped the brown and black from his face, threw away his shabby clothes, and appeared in his princely splendor, so magnificent that the Princess, in spite of herself, curtseyed very low.

"I have come to despise you, my beauty," he said. "You refused an honorable Prince, you did not appreciate the rose or the nightingale, but you kissed a swineherd for the sake of a miserable tinkling toy. You have got just what you deserve!"

Then the Prince went into his Kingdom, shut the door and bolted it, and for all he cared, she might stay outside and sing:

"Ach, du lieber Augustin,
Alles ist weg, weg, weg!"

LITTLE CLAUS AND BIG CLAUS

THERE were two men in one village, both of whom had the very same name. They were both called Claus, but one of them owned four horses, and the other only one, so to tell them apart, people called the man who had four horses Big Claus, and the man who had only one horse Little Claus. Now we are going to hear what happened to these two, for this is a true story.

The whole week through, Little Claus had to plow for Big Claus, and lend him his one horse; in return, Big Claus lent him all his four horses, but only once a week, and that was on Sundays. Hooray! How Little Claus did crack his whip over all the five horses, for they were as good as his own on that one day. The sun was shining so beautifully, and all the bells were ringing for church; the people were dressed in their Sunday best and, with their hymn-books under their arms, were going to hear the parson preach, and they looked at Little Claus plowing away with all the five horses. He was so happy that he cracked his whip again and shouted, "Gee up, all my good horses!"

"I don't want you to shout that," said Big Claus. "Only one of the horses is yours, remember!"

But when some more people passed by on their way to church, Little Claus forgot he wasn't to say it, so he shouted again, "Gee up, all my good horses!"

"Look here, kindly stop that," said Big Claus; "for if you say it again I'll knock your horse on the head, and kill him on the spot, and that will be the end of him."

"All right, I won't say it again," said Little Claus, but when another lot of people went by and nodded "Good morning," it pleased him so much, and he thought it looked so very grand to be plowing with five horses, that he cracked his whip once more and shouted, "Gee up, all my good horses!"

"I'll gee up your horses for you!" said Big Claus, and he took the tether-peg mallet and gave Little Claus's only horse such a knock on the head that it fell down, stone dead.

"What a shame! Now I haven't got any horse at all!" said Little Claus, and he began to cry. By and by he flayed the horse, took the hide and let it dry thoroughly in the wind. Then he stuffed it into a bag which he slung over his shoulder, and went off to the town to sell it.

He had a very long way to go, and had to pass through a huge dark forest. Presently a terrible storm came up. He lost his way, and before he could find it again evening had come, and it was too far for him to get either to the town or back home again before night fell.

Close to the road there was a large farmhouse; the shutters had already been put up over the windows, but still a ray of light escaped at the top. "I suppose they won't mind letting me spend the night here," thought Little Claus, and he knocked at the door.

The farmer's wife opened it, but when she heard what he wanted, she told him to clear out. Her husband was away, and she wasn't having any strangers on the place.

"Very well, then I shall have to sleep out of doors," said Little Claus, and the farmer's wife slammed the door in his face.

Close by stood a big haystack, and between this and the house was a little shed with a flat thatched roof.

"I can sleep up there," said Little Claus when he saw the roof. "It will make a fine bed. I hope the stork won't fly down and bite my legs!" A real live stork, you know, was standing on the roof where it had its nest.

So Little Claus climbed up on to the shed, where he tossed and turned about until he found a comfortable position. The wooden shutters didn't quite fit the windows at the top, and so he was able to look straight into the room.

There was a large table laid with wine and a joint, and such a delicious-looking fish. The farmer's wife and the parish clerk were sitting at table all alone; she kept helping him to wine, and he kept helping himself to the fish—for it was one of his pet dishes.

"If only I could get a bite of that!" said Little Claus, and he poked his head quite close to the window. Heavens, what a glorious cake he could see now! That was a feast and no mistake!

Suddenly he heard someone riding along the road towards the house. It was the woman's husband coming home.

He was an excellent man, but he had one strange affliction—he couldn't for the life of him bear the sight of a parish clerk; if he ever set eyes on one he got mad with rage. Now that's why the parish clerk had come to pass the time of day with the farmer's wife, knowing that her husband would be away; and the good woman had put before him all the best food she had in the house. All of a sudden they heard the husband coming, and they were so frightened that the woman begged the clerk to creep into a great empty chest which stood in one of the corners. He did as he was told, for he knew very well that the poor afflicted husband couldn't bear the sight of a parish clerk. The woman quickly hid the delicious food and wine away in her oven, for if her husband had seen it he would certainly have asked what it all meant.

"Oh, dear," sighed Little Claus up on the shed, when he saw all the food disappear.

"Is that anybody up there?" asked the farmer, looking up at Little Claus. "What are you lying there for? You'd better come inside with me."

Little Claus then told him how he had lost his way, and asked if he might stay the night.

"Why, certainly!" said the farmer; "but first let's have a bite to eat."

The farmer's wife welcomed them in a most friendly way, laid the long table, and gave them a large bowl of porridge. The farmer was hungry and set to with right good will, but Little Claus couldn't help thinking about the delicious joint, the fish, and the cake which he knew were in the oven.

He had put the bag with the horse-hide under his feet—for you remember he had left home to sell the horse-hide in the town. He had no appetite at all for porridge, so he trod on the bag and the dry hide gave quite a loud squeak.

"Ssh!" said Little Claus to his bag, but at the same time he trod on it again, and it squeaked much louder than before.

"Why, what on earth have you got in your bag?" asked the farmer.

"Oh, it's a wizard," said Little Claus. "He tells me that we shouldn't be eating porridge, when he's conjured the whole oven full of meat, fish, and cake."

"You don't say so!" said the farmer, and in less than no time he had opened the oven and seen all the delicious food his wife had hidden—but he thought it was the wizard in the bag who had conjured it there. The wife didn't dare say a word, but at once put the food on the table, and then they had their fill of the meat, the fish, and the cake.

Little Claus again trod on his bag and made the hide squeak.

"What does he say now?" asked the farmer.

"He says," answered Little Claus, "that he's also conjured us three bottles of wine, and that they are in the oven too." Then the wife had to bring out the wine she had hidden, and the farmer drank and got quite merry. He thought what fun it would be to have a wizard like the one Little Claus had in his bag.

"Can he conjure the devil up too?" asked the farmer. "I should like to see him, for now I'm just in the mood for it."

"Certainly," said Little Claus. "My wizard can do anything I ask him to. Can't you?" he said, and he trod on the bag so that it squeaked again. "Did you hear? He said 'Yes!' But the devil is so terrifying to look at that I should advise you not to try."

"Oh, I'm not a bit afraid. I wonder what he looks like."

"Well, he's going to appear in the shape of a parish clerk."

"Ugh!" said the farmer. "How horrible! You know I can't bear the sight of parish clerks. But never mind—so long as I know it's the devil, I can stand it better. I've plucked up my courage now, but don't let him come too near."

"Just let me ask my wizard," said Little Claus, treading on the bag and putting his ear up against it.

"What does he say?"

"He says you must open the chest over there in the corner, and you'll see the devil all right crouching inside, but mind you hold on to the lid, otherwise he'll slip out."

"Will you help me to hold it?" asked the farmer, going to the chest in which his wife had hidden the real clerk, who was trembling with fear.

The farmer lifted the lid ever so little and peeped under it. "Ugh!" he gasped out, jumping backwards. "I did see him, he looked exactly like our own clerk. It was too awful!"

So they had to have another go at the wine, and then another one after that, and there they sat drinking till late into the night.

"You must sell me that wizard," said the farmer. "Ask as much as you like for him. I'll give you a whole bushel of money right away."

"No, I couldn't do that," said Little Claus. "Just think how useful this wizard can be to me."

"Oh, but I must have him," said the farmer, and he went on

insisting.

"Well," said Little Claus, giving in at last, "as you've been kind enough to give me a night's lodging, all right. You shall have the wizard for a bushel of money, but you must give me full measure."

"Don't worry about that," said the farmer, "but you'll have to take the chest away with you. I won't keep it in the house another hour. He might still be in it."

So Little Claus gave the farmer the bag with the dried hide in it, and got a whole bushel of money—and full measure too—in exchange for it. The farmer also gave him a big wheelbarrow to take away the money and the chest.

"Good-by," said Little Claus, and off he went with his money, and the chest with the clerk still in it.

On the other side of the wood ran a deep river; the current was so strong that it was hardly possible to swim against it. A fine new bridge had been built over it. Little Claus stopped halfway across, and said loud enough for the clerk to hear him: "What good is that stupid chest to me? It's heavy enough to be full of stones. I shall be tired out if I wheel it any longer; I'll just throw it into the river; if it sails home to me, well and good; but if it doesn't, no matter!"

Then he took hold of it with one hand and lifted it up a little as if he meant to throw it into the water.

"Stop! stop!" shouted the clerk inside. "Let me out first!"

"Oh!" exclaimed Little Claus, pretending to be frightened. "He's still there! I'd better be quick and push the chest into the river, and let him drown."

"Oh, no, no!" screamed the clerk. "I'll give you a whole bushel of money if you don't."

"Well, that's another story," said Little Claus, opening the chest. The clerk crept out at once, pushed the empty chest into the water and went off home, where Little Claus got his bushel of money.

He'd already got one from the farmer, so now he had his whole wheelbarrow quite full of money.

"Anyway, I call that a good price for my horse," he said to himself when he got home to his room and emptied all the money in a great heap on the floor.

"Big Claus will be as cross as two sticks when he hears what a lot I've made out of my one and only horse, but I'm not going to tell him the whole truth about it."

Then he sent a boy over to Big Claus to borrow a bushel measure.

"What can he want with that?" thought Big Claus, and he smeared tar underneath it, so that a little of whatever was being measured might stick to it. And that's exactly what happened, for when the measure was returned to him there were three new silver coins sticking to the bottom.

"What's this?" said Big Claus, and came rushing over to Little Claus. "How did you get all that money?"

"Oh, I got it for my horse-hide which I sold last night."

"My word, that's a thundering good price, I must say!" exclaimed Big Claus; then he ran home, took an ax and knocked all his four horses on the head, ripped off their hides and drove off to the town with them.

"Hides! hides! Who'll buy hides?" he shouted through the streets.

The shoemakers and tanners came running up and asked him how much he wanted for them.

"A bushel of money apiece!" said Big Claus.

"Are you mad?" they all said. "Do you think we've got money by the bushel?"

"Hides! hides! Who'll buy hides?" he shouted again, and to everyone who asked him the price, he answered, "A bushel of money."

"He's trying to make fools of us," they all said, and the shoemakers took their straps, and the tanners their leather aprons, and began to belabor Big Claus.

"Hides; hides!" they mocked at him. "Yes, we'll give your hide a good tanning! Out of the town with him!" they shouted, and Big Claus ran away as fast as he could, for he'd never had such a beating in his life before.

"Well," he said when he got home, "Little Claus shall pay for this. I'll slay him for it."

Now at Little Claus's home the old grandmother had died; true enough, she had been very bad-tempered and nasty to him, but all the same he was very sorry, so he took the dead woman and put her into his own warm bed, to see if she might not possibly come to life again. She was to lie there all night, while he himself meant to sit in the corner and sleep in a chair, as he had often done before.

As he sat there in the night, the door opened and Big Claus came in with an ax. He knew well enough where to find Little Claus's bed, so he went straight up to it and knocked the dead grandmother on the head, thinking she was Little Claus.

"There now," he said, "you won't fool me any more." And he went home again.

"What a wicked man he is, wanting to kill me," said Little Claus. "It's lucky for the old dame that she was dead already, otherwise he would have finished her off."

Then he dressed his old grandmother up in her Sunday best, and having borrowed a horse from his neighbor, harnessed it to his cart, and planted her bolt upright on the back seat in such a way that she couldn't possibly fall out when the horse began to trot—and off they bowled through the woods. When the sun rose, they were outside a big inn. Little Claus pulled up and went in to get something to eat.

The innkeeper had heaps and heaps of money, and was quite a good sort, but he was very hot-tempered, almost as if he were filled with pepper and snuff.

"Good morning," he said to Little Claus. "You've got into your

Sunday best early today."

"Yes," said Little Claus. "I'm going to town with my old grandmother. She's out there in the cart; I can't get her to come in. Would you mind taking her a glass of mead? But you'll have to speak pretty loud, for she's hard of hearing."

"Right you are!" said the innkeeper, and he filled a large glass full of mead and took it out to the dead grandmother, who had been propped up in the cart.

"The young man has sent you a glass of mead," said the innkeeper, but the dead woman never uttered a word; she just sat stock still.

"Can't you hear?" shouted the innkeeper as loud as he could. "The young man has sent you a glass of mead!"

Once more he shouted the same thing, and then again for the fourth time, but as she never even stirred, he lost his temper and flung the glass right into her face, so that the mead ran down her nose, and she tumbled over backwards into the cart, for she was only propped up, and not tied at all.

"Hi! What are you doing there?" shouted Little Claus, rushing out and grabbing the innkeeper by the throat. "You've killed my grandmother. Just look, there's a great hole in her forehead."

"Oh, what a tragedy!" cried the innkeeper, clasping his hands in despair. "It's all because of my hot temper. Dear Little Claus, I'll give you a whole bushel of money, and have your grandmother buried as if she was my own; but mum's the word, or they'll cut my head off, and that's very unpleasant, you know."

So Little Claus got another bushel of money, and the innkeeper buried the old grandmother as if she'd been his own.

When Little Claus came back home with all the money, he immediately sent his boy over to Big Claus to borrow a bushel measure.

"What the devil does this mean?" exclaimed Big Claus. "Didn't I kill him after all? I'd better go and find out for myself." And he went over to Little Claus with the measure.

"Where in the world did you get all that money from?" he asked, opening his eyes wider and wider when he saw the money that had been added to the heap.

"It was my grandmother you killed, not me," said Little Claus, "so I have just sold her for a bushel of money!"

"My word, that's a thundering good price!" said Big Claus, so he hurried home, took an ax, and quickly killed his own old grandmother. Then he put her in his cart, drove to the surgery in town, and asked the doctor if he wanted to buy a dead body.

"Who is it? and where did you get it from?" asked the doctor.

"It's my grandmother," said Big Claus. "I've killed her to get a bushel of money."

"Good Lord!" said the doctor. "You must be raving, man! You'd better not say that, or they'll have your head off." And then he told him point-blank what a terribly wicked thing he had done, and what a scoundrel he was, and that he ought to go to prison. At this Big Claus got so frightened that he dashed straight from the surgery into his cart, whipped up the horses and galloped off home. But the doctor and everyone else thought he must be mad, so they let him drive wherever he liked.

"You shall pay for this," said Big Claus, once he had reached the high-road. "Yes, indeed, you shall pay for this, Little Claus." So as soon as he got home he took the biggest sack he could find, went over to Little Claus and said, "You've fooled me again. First I killed my horses, and now I've killed my old grandmother. It's all your fault, but you shan't make a fool of me any more." Then he grabbed Little Claus by the middle, thrust him into the sack, threw him over his shoulder and shouted, "Now I'm going to take you out and drown you!"

The river was a long way off, and Little Claus wasn't at all light to carry. The road went past the church, where the organ was playing, and the people were singing very beautifully. Big Claus put down the sack with Little Claus inside it, close to the church door, and thought it might be quite a good thing to go in and hear a hymn before he went any further. There was no chance for Little Claus to get out of the sack, and everybody else was in church, so in he went.

"Oh, dear, oh, dear!" sighed Little Claus in the sack. He twisted and turned about, but he couldn't manage to loosen the cord. At that very moment an old cattle drover with chalk-white hair passed by, leaning on a big stick. He was driving a whole herd of cows and bullocks in front of him, and they bumped into the sack in which Little Claus was sitting, and pushed it over.

"Oh, dear!" sighed Little Claus. "I'm so young to go to heaven already."

"And poor me," said the drover, "I'm so old and yet I can't get there!"

"Open the sack!" shouted Little Claus. "Crawl in and take my place, and you'll be in heaven before you know it."

"That's just what I want!" said the cattle-drover, and he untied the sack for Little Claus, who jumped out at once.

"You'll take care of the cattle for me, won't you?" said the old man, and he crawled into the sack. Little Claus tied it up again and went off with all the cows and bullocks.

Soon after this, Big Claus came out of church and threw the sack over his shoulder again. He couldn't help noticing that it had got very light, for the old drover was not more than half the weight of Little Claus.

"How light he is to carry now! I'm sure it must be because I've been listening to a hymn." Then he went to the broad deep river, threw the sack with the old drover in it into the water, and shouted after him, thinking of course that it was Little Claus, "There now! You shan't fool me any more."

So he started off for home, but when he came to the cross-roads he met Little Claus coming along with all his cattle.

"I'll be blowed!" said Big Claus. "Didn't I drown you?"

"To be sure you did!" said Little Claus. "You threw me into the river less than half an hour ago."

"But where on earth did you get all these fine cattle from?" asked Big Claus.

"They're sea cattle," said Little Claus. "I'm going to tell you the whole story, and I'm going to thank you for drowning me. I'm at the top of the tree now. I'm really rich, I tell you. I was scared to death in the sack when the wind whistled about my ears as you threw me down from the bridge into the cold water. I sank straight to the bottom, but I didn't hurt myself, for the finest soft grass grows down there. I fell on that, and the sack was opened at once. The loveliest maiden in snow-white garments, and with a green wreath on her wet hair, took my hand and said, 'Is that you, Little Claus? Here are some cattle for you to begin with. Four miles farther up the road there's another drove of them which I will also give you for a present.' Then I discovered that the river was a great high-road for the sea-people. Down there at the bottom they walked and drove straight in from the sea, and far up into the land, where the river is lost to sight. It was lovely down there with flowers and the freshest of grass. Fishes darted past my ears as birds do in the air up here. I can't tell you how nice-looking the people were, and what a lot of cattle there were grazing along the ditches and fences!"

"But why have you come back to us so soon?" asked Big Claus. "I shouldn't have done that if it was so beautiful down there."

"Why," said Little Claus, "that's where I've been very clever! Don't you remember what I told you? The sea-maiden said that four miles farther up the road—and by the road she meant the river, for she can't get anywhere else—there was another drove of cattle waiting for me. But I know how the river meanders in and out; it would be a terribly roundabout way. No, the shortest way, if you can manage it, is to come up on land and go straight across to the river again. It saves about two miles, and so I get quicker to my sea-cattle."

"Oh, you are a lucky fellow," said Big Claus. "Do you think I shall get some sea-cattle too, if I go down to the bottom of the river?"

"I'm sure of it," said Little Claus, "but I can't carry you in the sack to the river, you're too heavy. If you'll go there yourself and crawl into the sack, I'll throw you in with the greatest of pleasure."

"Thanks very much," said Big Claus, "but if I don't find any sea-cattle when I get down there, I'll give you such a walloping as you'll never forget."

"Now don't be a bad boy!" So they went down to the river.

When the thirsty cattle saw the water, they ran as fast as they could to reach it and drink.

"Look what a hurry they're in," said Little Claus. "They're longing to go down to the bottom again."

"Yes, but help me first," said Big Claus, "or you'll get a good beating." And then he crawled into the big sack which had been lying across the back of one of the bullocks. "Put a stone in it, or I'm afraid I shan't sink," said Big Claus.

"You'll sink fast enough," said Little Claus, but still he put a good big stone in the sack, tied the rope tight, and gave it a good push—plump! There was Big Claus out in the river, and he sank straight to the bottom.

"I'm afraid he won't find his cattle," said Little Claus, and he drove home the ones he had.

THE FIR TREE

DEEP in the forest there stood such a pretty little fir tree. It grew in a nice spot; the sun could reach it, there was fresh air in abundance, and all around it were many taller comrades, firs as well as pines. But the little fir tree was in a great hurry to grow up. It paid no attention to the warm sunshine or the fresh air, and it took no notice of the farmers' children who went about chattering, and picking strawberries or raspberries. Often they would sit down by the little tree, with whole jugfuls of raspberries, or holding strawberries threaded on long straws, and exclaim, "Isn't that baby tree the sweetest thing you ever saw!" But the fir tree did not like to hear that at all.

The next year it had added a long section to its growth, and the following year one still longer. You can always tell a fir tree's age by the number of new sections it has.

"Oh, I wish I were as tall as the others!" sighed the little tree. "Then I could spread my branches far and wide, and from my top see what the world looks like. The birds would build their nests in my branches, and when the wind was blowing, I should be able to nod with as much dignity as the others."

It found no pleasure in the sunshine, nor in the birds, nor in the rosy clouds that went sailing over it morning and evening.

In winter, when the ground was covered with glistening white snow, a hare would often come hopping along, and jump right over it. How annoying that was! But two winters passed by, and in the third it was so tall that the hare was obliged to run round it.

"Oh, if I could but grow and grow, become tall and old! That's

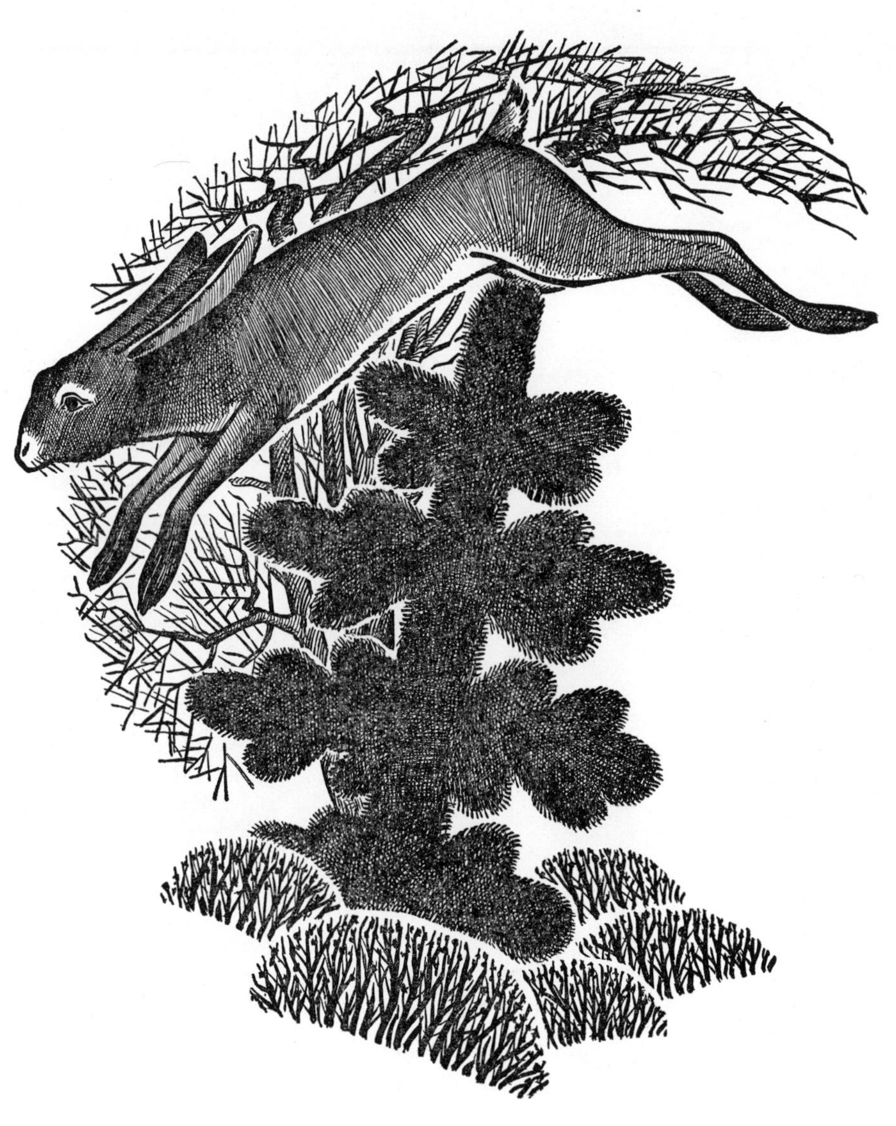

the only thing worth living for," thought the tree.

In the autumn the woodcutters would come and fell a few of the tallest trees; this happened every year, and the young fir, which was now quite grown up, trembled with fear when it saw the splendid big trees fall to the ground with a crash. Their branches were lopped off so that they looked all naked and thin; one could hardly recognize them. They were loaded on to timber-wagons, and horses dragged them away out of the forest.

Where were they going? What would happen to them?

In the spring, when the swallows and the stork arrived, the tree asked them, "Do you know where the other trees were taken? Did you meet them?"

The swallows knew nothing about it, but the stork looked thoughtful, nodded his head, and said, "Yes, I think I did meet them. Coming away from Egypt, I saw many new ships with splendid new masts. I daresay those were the trees you mean; they had a smell of fir about them. They wanted to be remembered to you; they looked grand, very grand."

"If only I too were big enough to fly over the sea! Tell me, what is this sea really, and what does it look like?"

"That would take too long to explain," said the stork, and he walked away.

"Enjoy your youth! Rejoice in your healthy growth, and in the young life that is within you!" said the sunbeams.

And the wind kissed the tree, and the dew wept tears over it, but the fir tree did not understand.

With the coming of Christmas, quite a number of very young firs were chopped down, some of them neither so tall nor so old as our tree, which was still restless and impatient to get away. These young firs, just the most beautiful ones, were not stripped of their branches—they were loaded on to timber-wagons and horses dragged them away out of the forest.

"Where are they going?" asked the fir tree. "They are no taller than I am, in fact one of them was much smaller—why were they allowed to keep all their branches? Where are they going?"

"We know! We know!" chirped the sparrows. "We've peeped in at the windows down in the town. We know where they're going to. The greatest pomp and splendor imaginable awaits them there! We've peeped in at the windows, and we've seen them planted in the middle of a nice warm room, and decorated with the most beautiful things—gilded apples, gingerbread, toys, and many hundreds of bright candles!"

"And then?" asked the fir tree, quivering through all its branches. "And then? What happens then?"

"We haven't seen anything more than that, but it was too wonderful for words!"

"Was I born for such a glorious destiny, I wonder?" exclaimed the tree, trembling with delight. "That is even better than crossing the sea. I'm sick with longing. If it were only Christmas now! I'm as tall and well-grown as those trees which were taken away last year. Oh, if I were only loaded on to the wagon! Oh, that I were in that warm room in the midst of so much pomp and splendor! And then—? Then something still better, still more beautiful will happen, or why should they take such trouble to decorate me? Something still greater, still more splendid is bound to happen—but what? Oh, how I ache, how I yearn! I don't know myself what is wrong with me."

"Rejoice in me," said both the air and the sunshine. "Rejoice in your fresh youth out here in the open!"

But it did not rejoice at all. It grew and grew; winter and summer it stood there, ever green, dark green. The people who looked at it said, "What a beautiful tree!" And the following Christmas it was the first to be felled. The ax struck deep into its marrow, and with a profound sigh the tree fell to the ground. It suffered pain, it felt faint, and could not think of any happiness, for it was sad at parting from its home, from the place where it had grown up; it knew that it would never again see its dear old friends, the little bushes and flowers round about—perhaps not even the birds. It was anything but pleasant to say good-by.

The tree did not recover until it found itself unloaded in a yard with other firs and heard a man say, "This one's a beauty. This is the one we want."

Then two servants in smart livery arrived, and carried the fir tree into a beautiful great reception room. All round the walls hung portraits, and beside the tiled stove stood big Chinese jars with lions on their covers. There were rocking chairs, silk-covered sofas, large tables littered with picture books, and toys worth loads and loads of money—at least so the children said.

And the fir tree was planted in a big tub filled with sand; but no one could see it was a tub, for it was covered with green cloth, and stood on a great many-colored carpet. How the tree trembled! What was going to happen? Men servants and young ladies began to decorate it. On the branches they hung little nets cut out of colored paper, every net filled with sweets; gilded apples and walnuts hung down as if they grew there, and more than a hundred red, blue, and white candles were fastened to the branches. Dolls that looked exactly like real live children—the tree had never seen anything of the sort before—floated among the green branches, and up at the top was fixed a large star of gold tinsel; it was magnificent beyond words!

"Tonight," they all said, "tonight it will be lit up."

"Oh!" thought the tree. "If only it were already night! If only the candles were already lit! And later—what will happen then? Will trees from the forest come and look at me? Will the sparrows peep in at the windows? Shall I grow roots here and keep my decorations winter and summer?"

How little it knew! All those longings had brought on a very bad barkache—and it is just as bad for a tree to have a barkache as it is for us to have a headache.

At last the candles were lighted. What a blaze of splendor! The tree trembled so much in all its branches that one of the candles set fire to a twig—and what a scorching pain that was!

"Oh, dear!" cried the young ladies, and they quickly put out the fire. Now the tree did not even dare to quiver—it was awful! It was so afraid of losing some of its decorations, and felt quite overwhelmed with all that splendor. . . . And now at last the folding doors were flung open and dozens of noisy children came tumbling in as if they were going to upset the whole tree. The older people followed more calmly behind. The little ones stood quite speechless, but only for a minute—then they shrieked again with excitement, danced joyfully round it, and took down one present after another.

"What are they doing?" thought the tree. "What is going to happen?" The candles burnt right down to the branches and were put out as fast as they were burnt; then the children were allowed to plunder the tree. They rushed at it with such force that all the branches creaked; if it had not been fastened to the ceiling by the string and the gold star, it would have toppled over. The children danced round and round with their beautiful toys. No one looked at the tree except the old nurse who was peering about among the branches to see if by any chance a fig or an apple had not been forgotten.

"A story! A story!" demanded the children, pulling a little fat man towards the tree, and he sat down just beneath it. "Here we are in the green wood," he said, "and it will do the tree a lot of good to listen. But I shall only tell one story. Would you like the one about Hey-diddle-diddle, or the one about Humpty-dumpty who fell down the stairs, and yet ascended the throne and married the

Princess?"

"Hey-diddle-diddle," cried some; "Humpty-dumpty," cried others; and there was a great deal of shrieking and shouting. Only the fir tree stood quite silent, and thought, "Am I not to be in this at all? Am I not to take part in anything?" But it had been in the evening's fun. It had played its part.

So the little fat man told about Humpty-dumpty who fell down the stairs and yet ascended the throne and married the Princess. And the children clapped their hands, shouting, "Another! another!" for they wanted the story of Hey-diddle-diddle too, but they had to be content with Humpty-dumpty.

The fir tree stood quite silent and thoughtful—never had the birds in the forest told such a story as that. "Humpty-dumpty fell down the stairs and yet married the Princess. Well! Well! that's the way things happen in the world," thought the fir tree, believing it must all have been true, because such a nice man had told the story. "Well, who knows? I, too, may fall downstairs and win my Princess!" And it looked forward to being decorated again the next day with candles and toys, tinsel and fruit.

"Tomorrow I shall not tremble," it thought. "I shall rejoice in all my splendor. Tomorrow I shall hear the story of Humpty-dumpty again, and perhaps the one about Hey-diddle-diddle too." And it remained quiet and thoughtful all night.

In the morning the man came in with one of the servants.

"Now the festivities are going to begin again," thought the tree. But they dragged it out of the room, up the stairs to the attic, and there they put it in a dark corner where no daylight penetrated. "What does this mean?" thought the tree. "What am I to do in this place? What am I to hear?" And it leant against the wall, lost in deep thought. . . . It had time enough, for days and nights went by, and nobody came up. When at last someone did come, it was only to move some big boxes into the corner. The tree was so well hidden away that one might think it had been quite forgotten.

"It's winter outside now," thought the tree. "The ground is hard and covered with snow; I cannot be planted now, and that is probably why I am to be sheltered here until the springtime. How con-

siderate of them! How kind people are! I only wish it weren't so dark here and so terribly lonely—not even a little hare! After all, it was nice in the forest when the snow covered the ground, and the hare sped by—yes, even when it jumped over me it was fun, but I didn't think so then. This loneliness is perfectly unbearable!"

" 'Eak! 'Eak!" squeaked a little mouse just then, running out on the floor, and followed by another one. They sniffed at the fir tree, slipping in and out among the branches.

"It's frightfully cold," said the two little mice, "otherwise it's very pleasant here. Don't you think so, you old fir tree?"

"I'm not old at all," answered the fir tree. "There are many much older than I."

"Where do you come from?" asked the mice, "and what do you know?"

Weren't they outrageously inquisitive?

"Tell us about the most attractive place on earth; have you ever been there? Have you ever been in the larder, where there are cheeses on the shelves, and hams hang from the ceiling, where you can dance over tallow candles, and slip in thin and come out fat?"

"I don't know that place," replied the tree, "but I know the forest where the sun shines and the birds sing!" And it told all about its youth, and the little mice had never heard anything like it. They listened very attentively and said, "My, what a lot you must have seen! How happy you must have been!"

"I?" said the fir tree, thinking about what it had been saying. "Yes, after all, those days were rather pleasant." Then it told them all about the Christmas Eve when it had been decorated with sweets and candles.

"Oh!" said the little mice. "How happy you've been, you old fir tree!"

"I'm not old at all," said the fir tree. "It was only this winter that I came out of the forest; I'm in the prime of life, and I've only just stopped growing for the time being."

"How beautifully you tell things!" said the little mice; and the next night they brought four other mice to hear the tree tell all about its life, and the more the tree told, the more clearly did it remember everything, and thought, "Those really were quite happy days. But they may return—they may return once more. Humpty-dumpty fell down the stairs and still he won the Princess! Perhaps

I too may marry a Princess!" And the fir thought of a most adorable little birch that grew out in the forest—for to the fir tree that little birch was a beautiful real Princess.

"Who is Humpty-dumpty?" asked the little mice. The fir tree then told them the whole story, for it remembered every word, and the little mice were so delighted that they almost leaped to the very top of the tree. The next night many more mice came, and on Sunday even two rats appeared—but they said the story was not amusing, which made the little mice rather sad, for now they did not think much of it either.

"Do you know only that one story?" asked the rats.

"Only that one," answered the tree. "I heard it on the happiest evening of my life, but I never knew then how happy I was!"

"It's a very boring story. Don't you know any about pork and tallow candles? Any larder stories?"

"No," said the tree.

"Thank you, then we shan't bother you any more," said the rats, and they returned to the bosom of their families.

Finally the little mice kept away too, and now the tree sighed: "After all, it was rather cozy when those nimble little mice sat round listening to what I told them. All that is over too; but I shall remember to enjoy myself when I'm taken out from here!"

But when would that happen?

Well, it happened one morning when people came to tidy up the attic. The boxes were moved. The tree was pulled out from the corner and thrown rather brutally on the floor, but at once one of the men dragged it towards the stairs where it saw daylight once more. "Now life is beginning again," thought the tree. It felt the fresh air and the first sunbeams—and now it was out in the courtyard. All happened so quickly that the tree quite forgot to look at itself, there was so much to see all round. The courtyard was next to a garden where all the flowers were in bloom; the roses hung in great fragrant clusters over the little fence, the lime trees were in full blossom, and the swallows flew high and low, twittering, "Kvee-ve-ve, kvee-ve-ve—my love has come!"—but it was not the fir tree they meant.

"Now I am really going to live!" exclaimed the fir tree, bursting with happiness, and it stretched out all its branches. Alas! they were all withered and yellow—it found itself in a corner amongst weeds and nettles. The tinsel star was still fastened to the top, and sparkled in the bright sunshine.

Some of the merry children who had danced round the tree at Christmas-time, and had taken such a delight in it then, were playing in the courtyard. One of the smallest rushed at it and pulled off the gold star.

"Look what is still hanging on that ugly old Christmas tree!" he said, trampling on the branches that crackled under his feet.

And the tree looked at the beauty and splendor of the flowers in the garden, and then looked at itself, and wished it had remained in that dark corner of the attic. It thought of its fresh green youth in the forest, of the merry Christmas Eve, and of the little mice which had listened with so much pleasure to the story of Humpty-dumpty.

"All over and done with," said the poor tree. "Why didn't I enjoy them while I could? Done with! Done with!"

And the man came and chopped the tree up into small pieces; they made quite a heap. A great blaze flared up under the big copper, and the tree moaned so deeply that each moan was like a faint shot. The children were attracted by the sound, made a ring round the fire, gazed into it and shouted, "Bing! bang!" But at each explosion—which was a deep moan—the tree thought of a beautiful summer's day in the forest, or of a starry winter's night out there; it thought of Christmas Eve and of Humpty-dumpty, the only story it had ever heard and been able to tell . . . and by now the tree was burnt to ashes.

The boys played in the courtyard, and the youngest one wore on his breast the gold star which had decorated the tree on the happiest evening of its life.

Now that was done with, and the tree was done with, and the story is done with! done with! done with! And that's what happens to all stories.

THE TOP AND THE BALL

A TOP and a ball were lying together in a drawer amongst all kinds of other toys. Said the top to the ball, "Don't you think we might as well be sweethearts, since we live in the same drawer?" But the ball, who was made of morocco leather, thought as much of herself as if she were an elegant lady, and did not even deign to answer such a question.

The following day, the little boy who owned the toys took out the top, painted it red and yellow all over, and hammered a brass-headed nail into its very center. So now the top looked very grand as it went spinning round and round.

"Look at me!" said the top to the ball. "What do you say now? Don't you think after all we might be sweethearts? We're just made for each other. You bounce and I dance; we should make the happiest couple in the world."

"Oh, you think so, do you?" said the ball. "You don't seem to realize that my father and mother were a pair of morocco slippers, and that I have a cork inside."

"Quite, but I'm made of solid mahogany," said the top. "The Lord Mayor himself turned me on his own lathe, and he had great fun doing it."

"Hmm! am I to believe that?" said the ball.

"May never a whip touch me again if I'm lying," answered the top.

"You speak very well for yourself," said the ball, "but I'm afraid it's out of the question. I'm as good as half-engaged to a swallow. Every time I bounce up into the air, the swallow puts his head out of his nest and says, 'Sweetie, say you will! Sweetie, say you will!' and now I've said, 'I will!'—just to myself—and that's as good as being half-engaged. But I promise I shall never forget you."

"A lot of good that will do me," said the top. And after that they did not speak to each other any more.

The following day the ball was taken out to play, and the top watched her flying high into the air, just like a bird, so high that she was lost to sight. She came back every time, though, but bounced high up again as soon as she touched the ground; and this, no doubt, was either because of her longing for the swallow—or because of her cork inside! The ninth time, the ball disappeared and did not come down again. The boy looked and looked for her, but she was gone for good.

"Ah!" sighed the top. "I know where she is—she's in the swallow's nest, and married to the swallow."

The more the top thought it over, the more infatuated he became with the ball. Just because he could not get her, his love for her increased; the funny part of it was that she had accepted another. And the top danced round spinning and humming, always thinking of the ball, who in his thoughts became more and more beautiful.

Thus many years went by . . . and now it was nothing but an old love affair.

The top was no longer young! But then one fine day he was painted all over with gold; never in his life had he looked so splendid. He was a golden top now, and he went spinning round and round, humming and humming. This certainly made life worth living! Then suddenly he jumped too high, and, hey presto—vanished!

They looked and looked, searched everywhere, even down in the cellar, but he was not to be found.

And where do you think he was?

He had jumped into the dustbin where all sorts of rubbish was

collected: cabbage-stalks, sweepings, and dirt from the gutter under the roof.

"Humph! a nice place to land in, this is! My fine gilding won't last long here. And what in the world is this riff-raff I have fallen in with?" he murmured, looking askance at a long scraggy cabbage-stalk, and at a strange round thing that looked like an old wrinkled apple—but it was not an apple at all, it was an old ball that had been lying for many years in the gutter, and had been soaked through and through by the rain-water.

"Thank goodness, at last somebody of my own class to talk to!" said the ball, glancing at the golden top. "I'd like you to know that I'm really made of morocco; every stitch is the work of a lady, and I have a cork inside, but no one would ever think so to look at me. Yes, I was just going to marry a swallow, but I landed up in the gutter instead, and that's where I've been the last five years—soaking. It's a long time, believe me, for a young girl."

But the top said nothing. He thought of his old sweetheart, and the more he listened, the more certain he felt that it was she.

At that moment the servant came to empty the dustbin. "Did you ever!" she cried. "Why, here's the golden top!"

So the top was taken back into the house, and was honored and admired by everybody; but nothing more was heard of the ball, and the top never said a word about his old sweetheart; for love, you know, dies when your sweetheart has been soaking for five years in a gutter; in fact you never recognize her when you meet her in a dustbin.

THUMBELINA

ONCE upon a time there was a woman who wanted very much to get herself a little tiny child, but she had not the slightest idea where she could find one. So she went to an old witch and said to her, "I should very much like to have a little child; won't you please tell me where to get one?"

"That's as easy as winking!" said the witch. "Take this barley-corn—it's not a bit like the kind that grows in the farmers' fields, or that the chickens are fed with. Put it in a flower-pot, and you'll see what you'll see."

"Thank you so much," said the woman, and she gave the witch twelve pennies for it; then she went home and planted the barley-corn. Immediately a beautiful great flower came up; it looked exactly like a tulip, but the petals were closed up tightly as if it were still a bud.

"That's a lovely flower!" said the woman, and she kissed the pretty red and yellow petals. But the very moment her lips touched them the flower burst open with a bang. It was a real tulip, but on the green stool in the middle of the flower sat the tiniest little girl you ever saw, the most delicate and graceful one imaginable, and she was not even as big as one's thumb—that's why she was called "Thumbelina."

She was given a highly polished walnut-shell for a cradle, blue violet petals for a mattress, and a rose petal for a quilt. There she slept at night, but in the daytime she played on the table, where the woman had put a plate with a wreath of flowers round it. The stems dipped into the water where a big tulip petal was floating.

When Thumbelina wanted to get from one side of the plate to the other, she used the petal for a boat and rowed herself across, with two white horse-hairs for oars. It was so pretty to see her! She could sing, too, with a tiny silvery voice the like of which had never been heard.

One night, as she lay in her pretty bed, a horrid toad hopped in at the window, for one of the panes was broken. The toad was a nasty big wet one; she hopped right down on to the table where Thumbelina was sleeping under the red rose-petal.

"What a lovely wife for my son!" said the toad, grabbing the walnut-shell in which Thumbelina was sleeping, and she hopped off with her through the window down into the garden.

A big broad stream flowed through it, but near the edge the ground was all marshy and muddy, and here the toad lived with her son. Ugh! he was ugly, and horrid too, just like his mother. "Koax, koax, brekke-ke-kex" was all he could say when he saw the lovely little girl in the walnut-shell.

"Don't talk so loud or you'll wake her," said the old toad. "She might still run away from us, for she is as light as swan's-down. Let's put her out in the stream on one of the broad water-lily leaves. She's so light and little that it will be just like an island for her. She won't be able to escape from there while we're turning the best parlor under the mud into a home for you."

Growing in the stream were masses of water-lilies with broad green leaves that looked as if they were floating on the water. The leaf which was farthest out was also the biggest of all. The old toad swam out to that one, and put the walnut-shell, with Thumbelina, on it.

The poor little mite woke up very early in the morning, and when she saw where she was, she began to cry bitterly, because the big green leaf was surrounded by water, and she could not possibly get back to the shore.

The old toad stayed down in the mud, decorating her room with rushes and yellow water-lilies; she wanted it to look spick and span for her new daughter-in-law. Then she swam out with her ugly son to the leaf where Thumbelina was standing; they had come to fetch her dainty bed, as they wanted to put it up in the bridal-chamber before she came there herself. The old toad curtseyed low before her in the water and said, "Let me introduce my son. He is going to be your husband, and you will have a delightful home in the mud."

"Koax, koax, brekke-ke-kex!" was all the son could say.

Then they took the dainty little bed and swam off with it, but Thumbelina sat all alone upon the green leaf and wept, for she did not want to live with the horrid toad, neither did she want the toad's ugly son for a husband. The little fishes swimming in the water below had seen the toad and had also heard what she said, so they poked their heads out, for they were anxious to see the little girl. As soon as they saw her they thought her perfectly charming, and they felt so very sorry that she was going down to live with the ugly toad. No, that should never happen! So they crowded all round the green stalk which held the leaf she was standing on, and gnawed it through with their teeth; then the leaf went floating down the stream, and away went Thumbelina, far away, where the toad could not reach her.

She sailed past many places, and the little birds in the bushes saw her and sang, "What a charming little girl!" The leaf floated further and further away with her, and thus Thumbelina went on her travels.

A beautiful white butterfly kept flying round her, and at last alighted on the leaf, for it was so fond of Thumbelina; and she was very happy because now the toad could not get at her, and everything was so lovely where she was sailing. The sun shone on the water, making it gleam like gold. She took off her sash, tied one end of it to the butterfly, and fastened the other end of the ribbon to

the leaf; it glided much faster now, and she with it, for you will remember she was standing on the leaf.

Just then a big cockchafer came flying by and caught sight of her. At once he grabbed her by her slender waist with his claws, and flew up with her into a tree, while the green leaf went floating down the stream and the butterfly with it, because he was tied to the leaf and could not get free.

Goodness me! how frightened poor Thumbelina was when the cockchafer flew up into the tree with her, but she was most sorry for the beautiful white butterfly she had tied to the leaf, for if he could not get loose he was bound to starve to death. But what did the cockchafer care? He seated himself with her on the largest green leaf of the tree, gave her sweet honey from the flowers to eat, and told her she was very pretty, though she did not look in the least like a cockchafer. Later on, all the other cockchafers who lived in the tree came to call. They looked at Thumbelina, and the cockchafer-girls turned up their feelers at her and said, "Why, look at her legs! She has only got two—what a pitiful sight! She has got no feelers!" they said. "She goes right in at the waist! How disgusting—she looks like a human being! Did you ever see anything uglier?" said all the lady-cockchafers. And yet Thumbelina was as pretty as a picture! The cockchafer who had carried her off was also of that opinion, but when all the others declared she was ugly, he finally thought so too and would not have her at all; she could go wherever she liked. They flew down from the tree with her, and deposited her on a daisy; here she sat and wept because she was so ugly that the cockchafers would not have her; yet for all that she was the loveliest thing one could imagine, as delicate and tender as the loveliest rose petal.

The whole summer through, poor Thumbelina lived quite alone in the great wood. She wove herself a bed of grass-stems and hung it under a great leaf of wild rhubarb to protect herself from the rain; she took honey from the flowers to eat, and she drank the dew which lay every morning on the leaves. Thus she spent the summer and autumn; but now came winter, the long cold winter. All the birds that had sung so prettily to her flew away, the trees and flowers withered, the big wild rhubarb leaf under which she had lived shriveled up and turned to nothing but a yellow dry stalk; she was dreadfully cold, for her clothes were in rags, and she herself was so tiny and delicate—poor Thumbelina! She would be frozen to death. It began to snow, and every snowflake that fell on her was like a whole shovelful thrown upon us, for we are big, and she was only an inch high. She wrapped herself up in a withered leaf, but that would not warm her, and she shivered with cold.

She had now arrived at the edge of the wood where there was a large cornfield, but the corn had gone long ago; nothing remained but the bare dry stubble sticking out of the frozen ground. It seemed to her as if she were wandering through a great forest. Oh, how she shivered with cold! At last she came to a field-mouse's door. It was nothing but a hole among the stubble. There the field-mouse lived snug and happy; she had a whole room full of corn, and a glorious kitchen with a larder. Poor Thumbelina crept inside the door just like any poor beggar-girl, and asked for a little bit of a barleycorn, as she hadn't had anything to eat for the last two days.

"You poor little mite!" said the field-mouse, for she was really a kind-hearted old creature. "You had better come into my warm room and have dinner with me."

As she had now taken a fancy to Thumbelina, she said, "If you like, you may stay with me through the winter, but you must keep my room nice and clean and tell me stories, for I'm very fond of them." Thumbelina did as the kind-hearted old field-mouse asked, and led a very pleasant life with her.

"We shall have a visitor, you will see," said the field-mouse. "My neighbor calls on me once a week. He is even more comfortably off than I am; he has a suite of large rooms, and wears a most beautiful black velvet coat. If you could get him for a husband, you would be well provided for; but he cannot see a thing. You must tell him all the most beautiful stories you know."

But Thumbelina did not like the idea—nothing would induce her to marry the neighbor, for he was a mole. He came to call in his black velvet coat. He was very rich and very learned, said the field-mouse, his flat was more than twenty times larger than hers, but in spite of his learning he couldn't bear the sun, nor the beautiful flowers; he hadn't anything good to say of them, for he had never seen them. Thumbelina had to sing, and she sang both "Cockchafer, cockchafer, fly away home!" and "Here we go round the mulberry-bush." And the mole fell in love with her because of her pretty voice, but he said nothing, for he was such a deliberate man.

He had recently dug a long passage through the earth from his own house to theirs, and he gave Thumbelina and the field-mouse permission to walk there whenever they liked. But he told them not to be afraid of the dead bird lying in the tunnel. It was a whole bird with beak and feathers, which had probably died quite recently, at the beginning of winter, and was now buried just where he had made his passage.

The mole took a bit of touchwood in his mouth—for that shines like fire in the dark—and preceding them, lighted them through the long dark passage. When they came to the place where the dead bird was lying, the mole put his broad nose against the ceiling and pushed the earth away, making a big hole through which the daylight could enter. In the middle of the floor lay a dead swallow with his pretty wings pressed close to his sides, and his legs and head drawn in under the feathers; the poor bird had no doubt died of cold. Thumbelina felt very sorry for him; she was so fond of all the little birds that had sung and twittered so prettily for her all the summer long, but the mole kicked him with his stumpy legs and said, "He won't be squeaking any more! What a pitiful thing it must be to be born a little bird! Thank God none of my children will turn out to be that. A creature of that sort has nothing but his 'tweet, tweet,' and is bound to starve to death in the winter."

"There speaks a sensible person," said the field-mouse. "What's the use of all this 'tweet, tweet' to the bird when winter comes? He

has to starve and freeze. But I suppose that's considered very grand!"

Thumbelina said nothing, but when the other two turned their backs on the bird, she stooped down, parted the feathers which covered his head, and kissed him upon his closed eyes. "He might have been the one that sang so prettily to me in the summer," she thought. "What a lot of pleasure he gave me, the dear beautiful bird."

The mole now filled up the hole through which the daylight shone in, and he saw the ladies home. But that night Thumbelina could not sleep at all, so she got out of bed and wove a beautiful big blanket of hay, which she carried down and tucked round the dead bird, and she put soft cotton-wool she had found in the field-mouse's room round him, so that he might lie warmly in the cold ground.

"Good-by, you pretty little bird," she said. "Good-by! and thank you for your lovely song this summer, when all the trees were green, and the sun warmed us so nicely!" Then she laid her head against the bird's breast, but it gave her quite a fright, for she fancied she felt something beating inside. It was the bird's heart. He was not dead, but only benumbed, and now that he had been warmed, he had come to life again.

In autumn, you know, all the swallows fly away to warm countries, but if one of them is late in starting, he gets so cold that he falls down as if dead, and lies where he falls, and then the cold snow covers him.

Thumbelina was so frightened that she trembled from head to foot, for the bird was so large, so very large compared with herself who was only an inch high, but she pulled herself together, laid the cotton-wool closer round the poor swallow, and brought a mint-leaf that she had used for a quilt, and laid it over the bird's head.

The next night she stole down to him again—and now he was quite alive, but so weak that he could only open his eyes for a second and look at Thumbelina, who stood there with a bit of touchwood in her hand, for she had no other lantern.

"Thank you, my pretty little child," said the sick swallow. "I have been beautifully warmed. Soon I shall get my strength back, and shall be able to fly again in the warm sunshine."

"Oh," she said, "it's so cold outside, it's snowing and freezing. Stay in your warm bed, and I promise I'll nurse you."

Then she brought the swallow some water in a flower-petal, and he drank, and then told her how he had torn one of his wings on a thorn-bush, and therefore had been unable to fly as quickly as the other swallows when they flew away, far away to the warm countries. At last he had fallen down to the ground, but he could remember nothing more, and did not know at all how he had arrived where he was.

All winter the swallow stayed down there, and Thumbelina looked after him and loved him tenderly. Neither the mole nor the field-mouse was told anything about it, for they did not like the poor miserable swallow.

When spring came, and the sun warmed the ground thoroughly, the swallow said good-by to Thumbelina, who opened the hole which the mole had made in the ceiling. The sun shone gloriously down upon them, and the swallow asked if Thumbelina would not come too. She could sit on his back, and they would fly far away into the green woods. But Thumbelina knew that the old field-mouse would be sorry if she left her like that.

"No, I'm afraid I can't," said Thumbelina.

"Good-by, good-by, you kind pretty girl," said the swallow, flying out into the sunshine. Thumbelina looked after him and tears came into her eyes, for she was so very fond of the poor swallow.

"Tweet, tweet!" sang the bird, and flew off into the green woods.

Thumbelina felt very sad. She was strictly forbidden to go out into the warm sunshine; besides, the corn that had been sown in the field above the field-mouse's house was so tall that it made a thick forest for the poor little girl who was only an inch high.

"You must work at your trousseau this summer," said the field-mouse, for their neighbor, the tiresome mole in the black velvet coat, had proposed to her. "You must have both woolen and linen. You shall be comfortable whether you want to sit up or lie down, when you are Mrs. Mole."

Thumbelina had to spin with a distaff, and the field-mouse hired four spiders to spin and weave day and night.

Every evening the mole called, and he was always talking about the end of the summer, when the sun would not be nearly as hot as it was then, baking the earth as hard as a stone. Yes, when summer was over, his wedding with Thumbelina was to take place; but she was not at all happy, for she did not care one bit for the tiresome mole. Every morning when the sun rose, and every evening when it set, she stole out to the door, and then when the wind blew the ears of corn apart, so that she could see the blue sky, she thought how bright and beautiful it was outside, and wished so much to see her dear swallow again, but he never came back. He was sure to be flying about far away in the beautiful green woods.

When autumn came, Thumbelina had her whole trousseau ready.

"In four weeks you shall be married," the field-mouse told her, but Thumbelina wept and declared that she would not marry the tiresome mole.

"Fiddlesticks!" said the field-mouse, "don't be obstinate, or I'll bite you with my white teeth. What are you talking about? You're getting a splendid husband. The Queen herself hasn't the like of his black velvet coat. His kitchen and cellar are well stocked. You ought to thank your Maker for him."

And now the wedding day had come. The mole had already arrived to fetch Thumbelina; she would have to live with him deep under the earth, and never come out into the warm sunshine again, for he did not like it. The poor little mite felt very miserable; now she had to bid farewell to the glorious sun, which the field-mouse had at least allowed her to look at from the threshold of the door.

"Good-by, good-by, you bright sun," she said, stretching out her arms towards it and going a few steps away from the field-mouse's house, for now the corn had been reaped, and only the dry stubble was left in the fields. "Good-by, good-by," she said again, and threw her tiny arms round a little red flower which was still blooming there. "Give the dear swallow my love if you ever see him again."

"Tweet-tweet, tweet-tweet!" she suddenly heard above her head. She looked up, and there was the swallow, just flying by. He was delighted to see Thumbelina, and she told him how she would hate to have the ugly mole for a husband, and how she would have to live deep down under the ground where the sun never shone. She could not help crying while she was telling him.

"The cold winter is coming now," said the swallow. "I'm flying far away to the warm countries. Will you come with me? You can sit on my back; just tie yourself fast with your sash, and we'll fly far away from the ugly mole and his dark home, far away over the mountains to the warm countries where the sun shines more beautifully than here, and where there is always summer and lovely flowers. Do fly away with me, sweet little Thumbelina, you who saved my life when I lay frozen in the dark earth-cellar."

"Yes, I will come with you!" said Thumbelina, and she seated herself on the bird's back, placed her feet on his outspread wings, and tied her sash to one of the strongest feathers. Then the swallow shot high up into the air, and flew over forests and lakes, high above the great mountains that are always covered with snow, and when Thumbelina felt cold in the bleak air, she crept in under the bird's feathers, and only put her little head out to see all the beauties beneath her.

At last they arrived in the warm countries. The sun shone there much brighter than it does here, and the sky seemed twice as high, and over hedges and ditches there grew the most wonderful green and purple grapes. Lemons and oranges hung in the woods, the air was fragrant with the scent of myrtle and mint, and on the roads the loveliest children were running about playing with the big many-colored butterflies.

But the swallow flew still further away, and the countries grew more and more beautiful. Under majestic green trees, by a blue lake, stood a palace of dazzling white marble built in olden times; vines twined in garlands up the lofty pillars. At the top were many swallows' nests, and one of these was the home of the swallow that had carried Thumbelina.

"Here is my house," said the swallow, "but now you must choose for yourself one of the most beautiful flowers growing down below, then I will put you on it and you will be as happy as happy can be!"

"That will be lovely," she said, and clapped her little hands.

There lay a great white marble column which had fallen to the ground and broken into three pieces, but between the pieces grew beautiful big white flowers. The swallow flew down with Thumbelina and placed her on one of the broad petals; but what a surprise she got! A little man was sitting in the middle of the flower, as white and transparent as if he had been made of glass; he wore the daintiest little gold crown you could imagine on his head, and the most brilliantly clear wings on his shoulders, and he was no bigger than Thumbelina. He was the elf of the flower. In each of the flowers there lived another little man or woman just like himself, but he was the King of them all.

"Isn't he handsome?" whispered Thumbelina to the swallow. The little King got quite frightened at the swallow, which seemed a giant bird to such a tiny creature as himself, but when he saw Thumbelina he was very glad, for she was by far the prettiest little maid he had ever seen. So he took his golden crown off his head, put it upon hers, and asked her what her name was, and whether she would be his wife, for then she would become Queen of all the flowers. What a different kind of husband that would be from the toad's son, or the mole with the black velvet coat! So she said "Yes" to the handsome King; and out of every flower came a tiny little man or woman, as pretty as a picture. Each one brought Thumbelina a present, but the best of all was a pair of beautiful wings from a big white fly. They were fastened to her back, and then she too could flit from flower to flower. Everyone was so happy, and the swallow sat above them in his nest and sang his best for them, though at heart he was sad, for he was so fond of Thumbelina, and would have liked never to be parted from her.

"You shall not be called Thumbelina," said the elf of the flower to her. It's an ugly name, and you are too lovely for that. We shall call you Maia."

"Good-by, good-by," said the swallow, flying away again from the warm countries, far, far away back to Denmark. There it had a little nest above the window of the man who tells such nice fairy tales. To him it sang, "Tweet-tweet! Tweet-tweet!"—and that's how we got the whole story.

NUMSKULL JACK

SOMEWHERE in the country there was an old manor house, and in the old manor house there lived an old squire. He had two sons, and these sons were too brainy by half. They both decided to propose to the Princess, and felt quite equal to the task, as she had publicly announced that she would take for her husband the man who was never at a loss for an answer.

Now these two prepared themselves for a whole week; it was the longest time allowed, but they thought it was plenty, because they had been well drilled and grounded, and that is always useful. One of them knew the whole Latin dictionary by heart, as well as every issue of the local newspaper for the last three years, and he could reel them off backwards or forwards at will. The other one had read up all the statutes of the guilds and knew what every alderman was supposed to know, his idea being that this would enable him to discuss affairs of state. He was also expert at embroidering braces, for he was clever with his fingers.

"I shall win the Princess," each one said, and their father gave each of them a beautiful horse: the brother who knew the dictionary and the newspapers by heart received a coal-black one; the brother who knew all about guilds and who embroidered braces, a milk-white one. Then they smeared their mouths with cod-liver oil to make them more glib.

All the servants were down in the courtyard to see them mount, and at that very moment the third brother appeared—for there were three of them, though nobody ever looked upon this one as a brother because he was less accomplished than the other two, and that was why they called him "Numskull Jack."

"Where are you going, dressed up in your best clothes?" he asked.

"To Court, to talk ourselves into the graces of the Princess. Haven't you heard what every town-crier is proclaiming throughout the country?" And they told him all about it.

"By Jove, I mustn't be out of this!" said Numskull, and his brothers roared with laughter and rode away.

"Father, let me have a horse!" he shouted. "All of a sudden I feel like getting married. If she takes me she takes me, and if she doesn't take me I'll take her just the same!"

"Stuff and nonsense!" said the father. "You shall have no horse from me. Why, you never have a word to say for yourself. But as for your brothers—that's a different matter, they're a couple of bright sparks, if you like!"

"If I can't have a horse," said Numskull, "I shall take the billygoat; it's my own, and it's quite strong enough to carry me." And he seated himself astride the billygoat, dug his heels into its sides, and galloped away down the high-road. Whee-ee! He was off at breakneck speed!

"Hey-ho! Out of my way!" shouted Numskull Jack, and he sang so loud that his voice was heard far and wide.

But the brothers rode quietly on ahead; they never spoke a word, because they were practicing their answers, which had to be very smart and clever.

"Hey-ho!" shouted Numskull. "Out of my way! Look what I've found!" And he showed them a dead crow he had picked up on the road.

"Numskull!" they said. "What are you going to do with that?"

"I'm going to give it to the Princess."

"I should, if I were you!" they said, laughing, and rode on.

"Hey-ho! Out of my way! Look what I've picked up now! You don't find this sort of thing on the road every day." And the

brothers turned round to see what it was. "Numskull!" they said. "It's nothing but an old wooden shoe with the front part missing! And is the Princess to have that too?"

"To be sure!" said Numskull, and the brothers laughed again and were soon far ahead.

"Hey-ho! Out of my way!" he shouted. "It's getting better and better. Hey-ho! This is gorgeous!"

"What have you found this time?" asked the brothers.

"Oh!" said Numskull Jack, "I really can't tell you. Won't the Princess be pleased?"

"Bah!" said the brothers, "it's mud out of the ditch."

"That's just what it is, and the finest quality too, it slips right through your fingers." And he filled his pockets with the mud.

But the brothers rode on fast and furious, arriving a full hour ahead of him at the city gate where each suitor was at once given a number. They were placed in rows of six, and so closely packed together that they couldn't move their arms, which was lucky as otherwise each one would have knifed the man in front of him, simply because he happened to be there.

All the other inhabitants of the country were crowding round the Palace, pressing close to the windows to see the Princess receive her suitors.

The minute he entered the hall, every suitor became tongue-tied.

"No good," said the Princess. "Scoot!"

Now came the turn of the brother who used to know the dictionary by heart, but he had clean forgotten it while waiting in line. The floor creaked, and the ceiling was covered with looking-glass so he saw himself standing on his head. At each window there stood three clerks and an Alderman; they took down every word that was spoken, to have it ready for the newspaper and sold for a halfpenny at the street corner.

It was a terrible ordeal, and apart from that, the stove had been so stoked up that the pipe was red-hot.

"It's dreadfully hot in here," said the first brother.

"That's because my father is roasting cockerels today," said the Princess.

Blahhhhh!—there he stood—he certainly hadn't expected a remark like that. Not a single word could he say, though he wanted to say something very smart. Blahhhhh!

"No good," said the Princess. "Scoot!" And he had to.

And now for the second brother.

"It's awfully hot in here," he said.

"Yes, we're roasting cockerels today," said the Princess.

"I be-beg-be-beg you—" he said, and all the clerks wrote, "I be-beg-be-beg—"

"No good," said the Princess. "Scoot!"

And now for Numskull Jack.

He rode right into the hall on his billygoat.

"It's terrifically hot in here," he said.

"That's because I'm roasting cockerels," said the Princess.

"Isn't that a bit of luck!" said Numskull. "Then I suppose I can get a crow roasted?"

"Easily!" said the Princess. "But have you anything to roast it in? I've got neither pot nor pan."

"But I have," he said. "Here's a cooking-pot with a brass handle." And he held out the wooden shoe and put the crow in it.

"That's enough for a whole meal," said the Princess, "but where do we get the dripping from?"

"I've got it in my pocket," said Numskull Jack. "I've got enough and to spare." And he poured some of the mud out of his pocket.

"Splendid!" said the Princess. "You can answer back; you've got something to say for yourself, and you're the one I'm going to marry! But do you realize that every word we've said and are saying is being written down, and will be published in tomorrow's newspaper? You see there are three clerks and an old Alderman standing at each window; the Alderman is the worst, for he doesn't understand anything." She just said this to frighten him, but all the clerks suddenly whinnied with delight, and shook a blot of ink on to the floor.

"I'm sure those are the Quality," said Numskull. "Then the Alderman must have the best I've got." So he emptied his pockets and flung the mud in the Alderman's face.

"Well done!" said the Princess. "I should never have thought of that! But I shall learn in time."

Then Numskull Jack became King. He won a wife of his own, a crown of his own, and a throne of his own: and we've got all this straight from the Alderman's newspaper—not a very reliable one.

THE WILD SWANS

FAR, far away, in a land to which the swallows fly while we have winter, there once lived a King who had eleven sons and one daughter, Elise. The eleven brothers—Princes they were, of course—went to school with stars on their breasts and swords at their sides. They wrote upon golden slates with diamond pencils, and knew their lessons just as well by heart as if they were reading them from the book; one could tell at once that they were Princes. Their sister, Elise, sat on a little glass footstool, and looked at a picture book which had cost half the kingdom. These children had such a happy time, but it did not last long.

Their father, who was King of the whole country, married a wicked Queen who was not at all nice to his poor children. They felt this on the very first day. While the wedding festivities were going on in the Palace, the children played at receiving visitors; but instead of getting all the cakes and baked apples they could eat, as they used to, she only gave them sand in a teacup, and said they could pretend it was something nice.

The following week she sent little Elise into the country to be looked after by some farmers; and it was not long before the wicked Queen had succeeded in making the King believe such terrible things about the poor Princes that he ceased to have any affection for them.

"Fly out into the world and provide for yourselves," said the wicked Queen. "Fly away in the shape of big voiceless birds!" But she could not do all the harm she wanted to, for the Princes turned into eleven beautiful white swans. With a strange cry they flew out of the Palace windows, circling over the park and the woods.

It was still early morning when they passed the place where their sister Elise lay asleep in the farmer's house. They hovered over the roof, turned and twisted their long necks, and flapped their wings, but nobody heard or saw them. They had to fly on, high up under the clouds, far, far out into the wide world, and once there they flew into a great dark forest which stretched away to the seashore.

Poor little Elise was standing in the farmer's house, playing with a green leaf, the only toy she had. She pricked a hole in the leaf and looked through it up at the sun, and it seemed to her that she saw the bright eyes of her brothers. Whenever the warm sunbeams shone on her cheeks, it reminded her of their kisses.

One day passed just like another. When the wind swept through the rose bushes outside the house, it whispered to the roses, "Could anyone be prettier than you?" And the roses nodded their heads and answered, "Yes, Elise!" And on Sundays, when the old woman sat in the doorway, reading her hymn-book, the wind turned the leaves and said to the book, "Could anyone be more saintly than you?" "Yes, Elise!" said the hymn-book: and what the roses and the hymn-book said was the honest truth.

At the age of fifteen she was supposed to return home, but when the Queen saw how beautiful the Princess was, she grew angry and full of hatred towards her. She would gladly have turned her into a wild swan like her brothers, but she was afraid to do so at once, for the King wanted to see his daughter.

Early one morning the Queen went into the great bath, which was built of marble and adorned with soft cushions and the most beautiful rugs one could imagine. She took three toads, kissed them, and said to the first, "Sit on Elise's head when she gets into the water, so that she may become as sluggish as you! Sit on her forehead," she said to the second, "so that she may become as ugly as you, and that her father may not know her. Rest upon her heart," she whispered to the third, "so that she may be cursed with an evil mind and tormented."

Then the Queen put the toads into the clear water, which at once took on a greenish tinge, called Elise, undressed her, and bade her go into the water. As Elise plunged in, the first toad clung to her hair, the second to her forehead, and the third to her bosom, but she did not seem to notice it; as soon as she rose, three red poppies were seen floating on the water. If the creatures had not been poisonous, and had not been kissed by the witch, they would have been changed into red roses; yet they became flowers merely from resting on Elise's head and heart. She was too good and too innocent for witchcraft to have any power over her.

When the wicked Queen saw that, she rubbed her with walnut-juice so that she looked dark brown, smeared her beautiful face with an evil-smelling ointment, and let her lovely hair get all tangled. No one would have known the beautiful Elise.

When her father saw her, he was quite horrified, and said she was not his daughter: no one recognized her except the watch-dog and the swallows, but they were miserable creatures whose opinion did not count.

Poor Elise burst out crying and thought of her eleven brothers who had disappeared. With a heavy heart she stole out of the Palace, and wandered the whole day over fields and moors as far as the great forest. She had no idea where to go, but felt very sorrowful, and longed for her brothers who had probably been driven out into the wide world like herself, and she was determined to find them. She had only been a short time in the forest when night fell; having lost track of every path, she lay down on the soft moss, said her evening prayers and rested her head against a tree-stump. All was still, the air was very mild, and in the grass and moss were more than a hundred glow-worms shining like green fire. When she gently touched one of the branches above her head, the shining insects fell down upon her like a shower of shooting stars.

All night long she dreamt of her brothers. Once more they were playing together as they did when they were children, writing with diamond pencils on golden slates, and looking at the wonderful picture-book which had cost half a kingdom. But they no longer made strokes and pothooks as they used to; no, they wrote down all that they had seen and done, and all their boldest exploits. In the picture-book everything was alive; the birds sang, and the people walked out of the book and talked to Elise and her brothers, but when she turned the page, they immediately skipped back again so as not to cause confusion in the pictures.

When she awoke, the sun was already high; she could not see it clearly, for the lofty trees spread their tangled branches above her, and the rays shimmered like glittering, glimmering gauze. There was a delicious fragrance of grass in the air, and the birds almost perched on her shoulders. She heard the splashing of water from numerous springs all flowing into a pond with the most beautiful sandy bottom one could imagine. True, it was surrounded by thick bushes, but in one place the deer had trampled them down and trodden a wide path along which Elise could get to the water. It was so transparent that had not the breeze swayed the branches and bushes, she would have thought they were painted on the bottom of the pond, because every leaf was clearly reflected, whether the sun shone upon it or whether it lay in shadow.

As soon as she saw her own face, she got quite a shock, it was so brown and ugly; but when she wetted her little hand and rubbed her eyes and forehead, the white skin appeared again. Then she laid aside all her clothes and went into the fresh water. A more beautiful King's daughter than Elise could not have been found in all the world.

When she had dressed herself again and plaited her long hair, she went to the bubbling spring and drank from the hollow of her hand. Then she wandered deeper into the forest without knowing where she was going. She thought of her brothers, and she thought of the good God who would certainly not forsake her. He made the crab-apples grow to feed the hungry, and He showed her a tree with the boughs bending under the weight of its fruit. Here she took her midday meal, and having propped up the heavy boughs, went into the darkest part of the forest. It was so quiet there that she could hear her own footsteps, hear every withered little leaf that crackled under her feet. Not a single bird was to be seen, not a ray of sunlight could penetrate through the tangled branches and leaves. The tall tree trunks stood so close together that when she looked straight before her it seemed as though she were imprisoned by a high fence of timber formed by the great trees. Oh, here was such a solitude as she had never known.

The night grew very dark, not a single glow-worm now gleamed in the moss, and with a heavy heart she lay down to sleep. Then it seemed to her that the branches above her head parted, and that Our Lord, surrounded by little angels, looked down upon her. When she awoke in the morning she did not know if she had dreamt it, or if it had really been true.

She had only walked a few steps when she met an old woman with a basket full of berries. The woman gave her some of them, and Elise asked if she had not seen eleven Princes riding through the forest.

"No," said the old woman, "but yesterday I saw eleven swans, with golden crowns on their heads, swimming down the stream close by."

She led Elise a little farther on, to the edge of a high bank at the foot of which was a winding stream. The trees on either side stretched their long leafy branches towards each other; where the distance was too great to let them meet, they had torn their roots out of the ground and bent over the water with their branches intertwined. Elise said good-by to the old woman, and followed the

stream until it reached the great open shore.

The whole glorious sea lay spread out before the young girl's eyes; not a sail was in sight, not a single boat was to be seen. How could she get any further? On the beach she looked at the millions of pebbles which the water had worn quite smooth. Glass, iron, stones, all that had been washed up, had been rounded by the water which was even softer than her own delicate hands.

"It rolls on unweariedly, and so, little by little, the rough becomes smooth. I will be just as tireless! Thank you for your lesson, you clear rolling waves! My heart tells me that one day you will carry me to my dear brothers."

Among the washed-up sea-wrack, Elise found eleven white swan's feathers, which she tied into a sheaf; drops of water were on them, but whether dew or tears, no one could tell. It was very lonely by the shore, but she did not mind it, for the sea was ever changing; in fact it changed more often in a few hours than the fresh-water lakes did in a whole year. When a big black cloud spread across the sky, it seemed as if the sea wanted to say, "I too can look black." Then the wind rose and the waves shook their white manes; but when the wind slept and the clouds turned red, the sea was like the petal of a rose; sometimes it was green, sometimes white; but however calm it might be there was always a slight motion at the shore. The water rose and fell softly like the breast of a sleeping child.

When the sun was about to set, Elise saw eleven wild swans, with golden crowns on their heads, flying towards the shore; they floated along, one behind the other, looking like a long white ribbon. She climbed up the steep bank and hid behind a bush. The swans alighted near her and flapped their great white wings. As soon as the sun had disappeared beneath the water, the swans' plumage vanished, and there stood eleven handsome Princes, Elise's brothers. She uttered a loud cry, for although they were greatly altered, she knew them instinctively, sprang into their arms, and called them by their names.

The Princes were overjoyed when they saw their little sister who had grown so tall and fair. They laughed and cried, and soon realized how wicked their stepmother had been to them all.

"We brothers," said the eldest, "fly about as wild swans as long as the sun is in the sky, but when it has set we return to our human shape. That is why at sunset we must always look for solid ground, for as human beings we should crash to death, if we were then flying high up among the clouds. We do not live here. A land just as beautiful as this lies beyond the sea, but far away; we must cross the mighty ocean to reach it, and there is no island on the way, where we could pass the night; in the middle of the ocean though, one single little rock rises above the water. It is just big enough to hold us when we rest huddled closely together. If the sea is rough, the spray splashes far above us, yet we thank God for the resting-place. There we pass the night in our human forms; but were it not for this rock, we could never visit our own dear land, for our flight takes two of the longest days. Only once a year are we allowed to visit our father's home, and then we dare only stay eleven days. When we fly over the big forest we can see the Palace in which we were born and in which our father lives, and we see the tall tower of the church where our mother lies buried. Here we fancy that the tall trees and bushes are related to us; here the wild horses gallop over the plains, as they used to do in our childhood; here the charcoal-burner sings the old songs to which we danced as children, here is our own land, the place to which we are drawn—and here we have found you, our dear little sister. We may stay for two more days, and then we must again fly over the sea to a country that is beautiful, but is not our own. How can we carry you away? We have neither ship nor boat."

"How can I possibly set you free?" asked the sister. And they went on talking far into the night, sleeping only for a few hours. Elise was wakened by the sound of swans' wings rustling above her.

The brothers were once more transformed and flew round in great circles, finally disappearing; but one of them, the youngest, stayed behind, and laid its head against her bosom, while she stroked its white wings. They remained together all day; then towards evening the others returned, and when the sun had set they appeared again in their human forms.

"Tomorrow we shall fly away, and we dare not come back for a whole year, but we cannot leave you like this. Have you got the courage to come with us? As my arm is strong enough to carry you through the forest, surely all our wings together would be strong enough to carry you over the sea."

"Yes, take me with you," said Elise.

They spent the whole of that night making a net with the flexible bark of the willow, and tough rushes, and it was large and strong. Elise lay down on the net, and then when the sun rose the brothers were changed into wild swans again; they seized the net with their beaks and flew high up towards the clouds with their dear sister, who was still asleep. The sunbeams fell upon her face, and one of the swans flew overhead, to shade her with its broad wings.

They were far from land when she awoke. She thought she was still dreaming, for it seemed so strange to be carried through the air, high up above the sea. By her side lay a branch with beautiful ripe berries, and a bundle of sweet-tasting roots. The youngest brother had gathered them and put them there for her; she smiled gratefully at him, for she knew he was the one flying above her head, shading her with his wings.

They flew so high up that the first ship they saw appeared like a white seagull floating on the water. A great cloud, as big as a mountain, came up behind them, and Elise saw her own shadow and the shadow of the eleven swans thrown against it; a gigantic vision in flight. It was a more beautiful picture than any she had ever seen, but as the sun rose higher the cloud gradually dwindled away, and the floating shadow-picture disappeared.

The whole day the swans flew on like arrows whizzing through the air, yet they moved more slowly than usual, for they had their sister to carry. A storm came up as evening drew near. Elise was terrified to see the sun sinking, for the solitary rock was not yet visible. It seemed to her that the swans plied their wings more quickly than before. Alas! it was her fault that they could not fly fast enough; after sunset they would become human beings once more, and crash down into the sea and drown. From the very bottom of her heart she prayed to God, but still she could see no rock. A black cloud-bank came up, gusts of wind foretold a storm. The clouds formed one huge threatening wave rolling forward like a mass of lead. Flash after flash of lightning streaked the sky.

The sun touched the edge of the sea, and Elise's heart trembled; suddenly the swans plunged downwards so swiftly that she thought they were falling—but again they glided on. The sun was half hidden below the water, and not until then did she catch a glimpse of the little rock below; it looked no bigger than the head of a seal sticking out of the water. The sun sank very quickly; it was only like a star now, and at this very moment her foot touched the solid ground, then the sun died out like a last spark of burning paper. She saw her brothers standing round her arm in arm—but there was only just room enough for them and her. The waves beat against the rock and drenched them with a shower like rain. The heavens were lighted up by a constant blaze of fire, and the thunder rolled and rumbled, but the brothers and their sister held each other by the hand and sang a hymn, which gave them comfort and courage.

At dawn the air was clear and calm, and as soon as the sun rose, the swans flew away from the islet with Elise. The sea was still rough, and from the height at which they were flying, the white foam on the dark green sea looked like millions of swans floating upon the water.

When the sun rose higher, Elise saw before her, half-floating in the air, a mountainous country with shining glaciers on the rocky peaks; and in the middle rose a palace stretching for miles and miles, with rows of daring colonnades built one above the other. Palm trees swayed below, and gorgeous flowers grew there as large as mill-wheels. She asked if this was the land to which she was supposed to be going, but the swans shook their heads, for what she beheld was the beautiful ever-changing cloud-palace of Fata Morgana. They dared bring no mortal inside its walls. As Elise gazed at it, mountain, trees, and Palace suddenly crumbled away, and in their place stood twenty noble churches, all alike, with lofty spires and pointed windows. She fancied she heard the sound of an organ, but it was the sea she heard. When she was quite near the churches they seemed to change into a fleet of ships sailing beneath her, but when she looked down it was only the sea mist scudding over the water. A constantly shifting scene kept passing before her eyes, till finally she saw the real land for which she was bound. There arose before her beautiful blue mountains with cedar woods, towns, and palaces. Long before the sun went down, she was sitting on the mountainside in front of a large cavern overgrown with delicate green creeping plants that looked like embroidered hangings.

"Now let's see what you'll dream of here tonight," said the youngest brother, showing her where she was to sleep.

"I wish I could dream how to set you free," she said, and her mind was entirely filled with this thought. She prayed fervently to God for His help, and even in her sleep continued her prayer. Then it seemed to her as if she flew high up through the air to the cloud-palace of Fata Morgana, and that the fairy, beautiful and glittering, came out to greet her, and yet she looked exactly like the old woman who had given her the berries in the forest and told her of the swans with golden crowns.

"Your brothers can be set free," she said, "but have you enough courage and endurance? It is true that the sea is softer than your delicate hands, and yet it changes the shape of sharp stones, but it does not feel the pain your fingers will feel. The sea has no heart, and does not suffer the fear and anguish you will have to endure. Do you see the stinging nettle in my hand? This kind grows plentifully round the cavern in which you sleep. Only these and the ones that grow on the graves in the churchyard can be used, you must remember that! They are the ones you must gather, though they will blister your skin. Crush the nettles with your feet and you will have flax. That flax you must spin and knit into eleven tunics with long sleeves; throw them over the eleven wild swans and the spell will be broken. But remember this; from the moment you begin this work until it is finished, though it should take years, you are not to speak! The first word you utter will pierce the hearts of your brothers like a deadly dagger. Their lives hang on your tongue. Mark these things well!"

As she spoke, she touched Elise's hand with the nettles; they burnt her like a fire and wakened her. It was broad daylight, and close to the place where she had slept lay a nettle like the one she had seen in her dream. She fell on her knees, thanked God, and left the cavern to begin her task.

With her delicate hands she seized the horrible nettles—they scorched like flames; great blisters appeared on her hands and arms, but she would endure them willingly if by so doing she could succeed in freeing her dear brothers; with her bare feet she crushed every nettle and then spun the green flax.

At sun-down the brothers came back, and were alarmed to find her so silent. They thought it was some new sorcery of their wicked stepmother's, but when they saw her hands they understood that her efforts were for their sake.

The youngest brother wept, and where his tears fell Elise felt no more pain, and the burning blisters disappeared.

She worked the whole night long, for she could not rest until she had freed her beloved brothers. All the next day while the swans were absent she sat alone, but never had the time flown so quickly. One tunic was already finished and she set to work on the second.

Then hunting horns rang out from the mountains, and she trembled with fear. As the sound came nearer she heard the baying of hounds. Terrified, she ran into the cavern, and tying the nettles she had gathered and crushed into a bundle, she sat down upon it.

At that moment a big hound came bounding out of the thicket, and behind him came another, and yet another. They bayed loudly, ran back into the thicket, and came out again. Only a few minutes passed before the huntsmen stood outside the cavern, and the handsomest of them all was the King of the country. He came towards Elise; never had he seen a fairer maid.

"How did you come here, you beautiful maiden?" he asked.

Elise shook her head, not daring to speak—the freedom and the lives of her brothers were at stake. She hid her hands under her apron so that the King might not see what she was suffering.

"Come with me," he said. "You must not remain here. If you are as good as you are beautiful, I will dress you in silks and velvets, place a golden crown upon your head, and you shall have your home in my richest palace." Then he lifted her on to his horse, but she wept and wrung her hands. The King said, "I only want to make you happy! One day you will thank me for this." And he galloped off among the mountains, holding her before him on his horse, while the huntsmen sped after them.

At sunset the King's magnificent city with its spires and domes lay before them, and the King led her into the Palace where great fountains were playing in the lofty marble halls, and where the walls and ceilings were adorned with paintings; but she had no eyes for any of it. She could only weep and grieve. Listlessly she allowed the women to dress her in royal robes, to weave pearls through her hair, and to put soft gloves on her blistered hands.

Standing there in all this glory, she was so dazzlingly beautiful that the entire court bowed even deeper than before, and the King chose her for his bride, though the Archbishop shook his head and whispered that the beautiful forest maid was probably a witch as she had blinded their eyes and beguiled the King's heart.

But the King paid no attention to this. He ordered the musicians to play, the costliest dishes to be brought forth, and the loveliest maidens to dance round her. She was led through perfumed gardens into gorgeous halls, but not a smile came to her lips nor to her eyes, from which the sorrow could not be driven out. Then the King opened the door of a little chamber close by, where she was to sleep. It was adorned with costly green hangings, and looked exactly like the cavern in which he had found her. On the floor lay the bundle of flax she had spun from the nettles, and from the ceiling hung the tunic she had completed. One of the huntsmen had brought them with him as curiosities.

"Here you may dream you are back in your old home," said the King. "Here is the work you were doing there. Now in the midst of all your splendor, you can amuse yourself by thinking of the old days."

When Elise saw all these things so dear to her heart, a smile played about her lips, and the blood rushed back into her cheeks. She thought of her brothers' freedom, and kissed the King's hand. He pressed her to his heart, and ordered the church bells to peal for the marriage festival. The lovely dumb girl from the forest was to be Queen of the land!

Then the Archbishop whispered evil words in the King's ear, but they did not penetrate into his heart. He insisted upon the marriage. The Archbishop himself had to place the crown upon her head, and out of spite he pressed the narrow circlet so tightly that it hurt her —but a heavier ring encircled her heart; her grief for her brothers kept her from feeling the physical pain. She was pledged not to speak a single word, for one single word would mean death to her brothers, but her eyes were filled with love for the good and handsome King who was doing all in his power to please her. Day after day her heart went out to him. Oh, if she could but confide in him and tell him of her sufferings! But dumb she must remain, and in silence finish her task. Therefore at night she stole from his side, quietly entered the little chamber decorated like the cavern, and there knitted one tunic after another; but when she began the seventh she found there was not enough flax to finish it.

She knew that the nettles she required grew in the churchyard, but she must gather them herself. How was she to get there?

"Oh, what is the pain in my fingers compared with the anguish of my heart!" she thought. "I must risk it. The good Lord will not desert me!" With fear in her heart, as if she were committing a crime, one moonlight night she stole into the garden, through the long alleys and through the empty streets to the churchyard. There she saw a group of lamias sitting in a circle on one of the largest gravestones. These hideous witches took off their rags as if to bathe, but began clawing the newly made graves with their long bony fingers, then they snatched up the corpses, and devoured the flesh. Elise had to pass close by them, while they fastened their evil eyes upon her, but she said her prayers, gathered the stinging nettles, and carried them back to the Palace.

Only one person had seen her—the Archbishop. He was awake while everyone else slept. After all, he was right in what he thought. Everything was not as it should be with the Queen. She was a witch, and that was how she had beguiled the King and all the people.

In the confessional he told the King what he had seen and what he feared, and as he spoke these cruel words, the carved images of the saints in the cathedral shook their heads, as if to say, "It is not true, Elise is innocent." The Archbishop, however, interpreted this differently; he said they were bearing witness against her, and that they shook their heads at her sinfulness. Then two heavy tears rolled down the King's cheeks, and he returned home with doubt in his heart. He pretended to be asleep all night, but no quiet sleep came to his eyes. He noticed that Elise got up every night, and each time

he followed her quietly and saw that she disappeared into her private room. Every day his face became more gloomy. Elise noticed this and did not understand the reason, yet it troubled her and added to what she already suffered in her heart for her brothers. Her hot tears flowed down upon her royal robes of purple velvet, looking like glittering diamonds, and everyone who saw the splendor of her costly garments would have liked to be Queen.

Meanwhile she had almost finished her task; only one tunic remained to be completed, but she had no more flax, and not one single nettle. Once more, just this once, she must go to the churchyard and gather a few handfuls. She thought with horror of the lonely journey and the terrifying lamias, but her will was as unshakable as her trust in God.

She went on her quest, and the King and the Archbishop followed her. They saw her disappear through the iron gates into the churchyard, and when they were near enough, they, like Elise, saw the lamias sitting on the gravestones. The King turned away, for he imagined she was amongst them—she whose head, that very evening, had been resting against his breast.

"The people must judge her," he said. And the people said she must die by fire.

She was led away from the magnificent royal halls to a dark damp dungeon, where the wind whistled through the barred window. They gave her the bundle of nettles she had gathered, in place of silk and velvet, to lay her head upon. The coarse, burning tunics she had knitted were to be her covering—and they could have given her nothing that she cherished more. She started her work again, and prayed to her Father in Heaven. Outside the street urchins were singing slanderous songs about her, and not a soul comforted her with a kind word.

Towards evening she heard the whirring of swans' wings close to the window; it was the youngest of the brothers who had found his sister. She sobbed aloud for joy, though she knew that the coming night was perhaps the last she had to live; however, her work was almost done, and her brothers had arrived.

The Archbishop came, as he had promised the King to spend the last night with her, but she shook her head, and with looks and gestures begged him to leave her. This was the last night she had to complete her work, or all would have been in vain—all the suffering, the tears, and the sleepless nights. Speaking bitter words, the Archbishop withdrew, but poor Elise knew that she was innocent, and went on with her work.

The little mice ran about on the floor and dragged the nettles to her feet in order to help her, if ever so little. The thrush sat on the grating near and sang the whole night through as merrily as could be, to give her courage.

It was still a little before daybreak, about an hour before sunrise, when the eleven brothers, standing at the Palace gate, demanded to be taken before the King. This could not be done, they were told; it was still night, the King was asleep and should not be disturbed. As they begged and threatened, the guard turned out, and even the King himself came and asked what the disturbance meant. At that moment the sun came up and the brothers disappeared, but eleven wild swans were seen flying over the Palace.

The whole population came streaming out of the town gates, for they all wanted to see the witch burnt. A wretched old horse drew the cart in which Elise sat. They had dressed her in a garment of coarse sackcloth; her beautiful long hair hung loose about her fair head; in her deathly white face her lips moved slightly as her fingers twisted the green flax. Even on the way to her death she did not interrupt the work she had begun. The ten tunics lay at her feet and she was finishing the eleventh.

The mob jeered, "Look at the mumbling witch! She's not holding a hymn-book in her hand, no—it's her ugly sorcery, that's what she's holding. Take it away from her! Tear it into a thousand pieces!"

Just as they all rushed at her to destroy her work, eleven white swans swept down and perched round her on the cart, flapping their great wings.

The crowd drew back in terror.

"That is a sign from heaven! Perhaps she is innocent!" many whispered, but they did not dare to say it aloud.

The executioner seized her by the hand, but she quickly threw the eleven tunics over the swans, and eleven handsome Princes stood there—but the youngest had a swan's wing in place of one arm, for Elise had not been able to finish the second sleeve of his tunic.

"Now I dare speak!" she said. "I am innocent."

And the people who saw what had happened, bowed down to her as before a saint, but the strain, the anxiety, and the suffering had exhausted her, and she sank as if lifeless into the arms of her brothers.

"Yes, innocent she is," said the eldest brother, and he told them all that had happened. As he spoke, a perfume as of a million roses scented the air, for every faggot at the stake had taken root and put forth branches, and a great fragrant bush covered with red roses appeared. At the very top a single flower of dazzling whiteness shone like a star. The King picked it and laid it on Elise's breast, and she awoke with peace and happiness in her heart.

And all the church bells rang out joyfully of their own accord, and great flocks of birds appeared. A bridal procession, the like of which no King had ever seen before, returned to the Palace.

BOUND
HUNTTING
WITHDRAWN